SMOKE

D. B. BORTON

BOOMERANG BOOKS

To Carol Blum, for her friendship and her artistic passion

ACKNOWLEDGMENT

The author wishes to thank Stefania Bertolini Puckett for her editorial assistance with the Italian chapters.

MACDUFF
What's the disease he means?
MALCOLM
'Tis called the evil.
Macbeth, Act IV, Scene iii

PROLOGUE I

Thunder and lightning. The rain fell harder now. It washed the smoke from the air and brought a clean, metallic scent, but it made the two figures harder to see at a distance. The shorter of the two figures staggered under the weight of the crate they carried between them, but ducked its head and stumbled on. When they reached the trash bin, the taller one braced against the box to improve its grip. The heavy lid was already open, gleaming in the floodlight, and after some awkward jostling, the two heaved the crate over the side of the bin. The sound made when the crate hit bottom wasn't audible over the ambient sound of the rain, but perhaps the contents of the bin had cushioned its fall, and it had made no sound at all. The sounds of footsteps—wet sandals against pavement—were drowned out by the rain.

The taller figure pulled itself up and over the side of the container, and disappeared inside. The shorter figure turned back toward the building and froze. The watcher, backlit against the doorway, shrank back, and so didn't see the figure rap on the side of the bin or hear the words that passed between the two. The watcher, who knew the building well, fled down the maze of corridors and slipped inside a cabinet. But the building settled into silence.

In the morning, the only person found there was a single drowsy guard.

PROLOGUE II

SAN MINIATO, TUSCANY, LATE SPRING, 2015

The old man drowsed in the shade cast by the grape arbor, his soft snores harmonizing with the buzzing of bees overhead. His stork's legs extended in front of him, crossed at the ankles over sandals. His knobby knees showed below his khaki shorts, white chest hair above his open collar. What hair he had left on his head was the same white, but barely visible beneath the cap she made him wear. His mottled hands draped over the chair arms, and sometimes his fingers twitched until Giulia wondered what they were doing in his dreams. She had her suspicions.

This was how he spent most of his days now, and Giulia regarded him with concern. Several times lately, he had called her Vittoria, though Vittoria had been gone eight years. He was slipping, and she felt something ought to be done about it. She ought to do something about it.

That slick rascal of a second cousin would never have wormed his way into the old man's confidence in the old days. Giulia felt responsible for the cousin because she had let down her guard—that was how she saw it. He had come while she was out doing her marketing, or he would never have made it past the front garden. By the time she had arrived

3

home, he and the cousin had been chatting away like old friends—a fait accompli, as the French say. And truthfully, she ought to feel grateful that someone from the old man's family had finally taken an interest. Certainly, the old man enjoyed his company. And certainly, the cousin was all easy amiability—thoughtful, generous, polite, charming. But before his mind had begun to slip away, the old man had been notoriously close-mouthed. He had never talked about the past, except to rare visitors. To most of his neighbors, he had materialized in San Miniato as if newly formed, casting no shadow. Of course, there was talk. All the townsfolk believed that he was some kind of criminal, though the specific kind had never been agreed upon. Giulia believed they were right. Yet he had always treated her with the utmost kindness and courtesy, and so earned her loyalty and affection and aroused her protective instincts. That was why the cousin, with his affable questions about the past, made her uneasy.

"Leave it alone, Giulia," her husband told her. "He's an old crook, and his friends are bound to be old crooks as well. Don't get involved. You'll stir up trouble for yourself."

Still, Giulia could not shake the feeling that something should be done about the old man. And that she was the one to do it, because who else was there?

She decided to write a letter. There was one person, an American lady, who had visited several times since Giulia had come to the Villa Offuscata. He had talked to her in English about the old days, and they had laughed together until Giulia had decided that perhaps they had once been lovers. It was hard to believe, when one looked at him now, that he had once been handsome, but everyone said that it was so. And Giulia knew of a certain photograph, tucked away in a drawer, that bore witness to the youthful good looks of the two of them—Signor Giorgio and the American lady.

Giulia would look in the little black address book in the top desk drawer and sit down and write a letter. She would tell the American lady *about his condition, and about the cousin, and she would urge the lady to get in touch with his family.*

Of course, the cousin, when he reappeared, might be angry with her, but she wasn't worried about that. She thought that if anybody could do something for Signor Giorgio, it would be the nice American lady, with whom he appeared to have shared so much of his past.

1

The first witch had a bad cold. Her voice was thick.

"When shall we three meet again? In thunder, lightning, or in—in—in—."

The witch sneezed. The sneeze dislodged her witch's hat and it plummeted to the floor, nearly spearing Claude, the tubby gray longhair who was impersonating the witches' familiar. The hat didn't have far to go, since the witch was seated. Claude slumbered on.

Like a magician producing a vanished handkerchief, the first witch pulled from her cardigan sleeve a crumpled tissue. She applied it to her nose and blew vigorously. She readjusted her glasses, stuffed the wad in her sleeve again, and accepted her hat from the third witch, who had retrieved it where it lay next to the snoring familiar. With a sigh and an upward glance of trepidation, she set the hat on her head again. This was dress rehearsal, after all, and dress rehearsal meant hats.

She began again. "When shall we three meet again? In thunder, lightning, or in rain?"

The second witch was distracted by the passing of the Bingo cards. A perky young aide in a bright flowered polyester pantsuit swished down the hall carrying the distinctive box. I suspected that the second witch had a gambling addiction. Anybody involved in a nursing home production of Shakespeare ought to be addicted to gambling. What were the odds that the entire cast and crew would survive until opening night? The second witch screwed her head around to look at the clock on the wall behind her, and when it turned back, her hat listed to one side like a Vaudevillian sot.

The first witch, who had kept her eyes on the page in front of her, assumed that the second witch had not heard the cue, so she repeated her lines, louder this time, just as the second witch spoke hers.

"When shall we three meet again, in thunder, lightning, or in rain?" said the first witch.

"When the hurly-burly's done, when the battle's lost and won," said the second witch. Her voice was a little breathy, and I wondered whether I should wheel the oxygen tank closer.

The third witch, who was in fact hard of hearing, stared at them, disconcerted. Had her cue been given or not? She decided that it had, so looking down at the page, she said in a rush, "Fair is foul, and foul is fair. Hover through the fog and filthy air."

At this point, I was supposed to wave around a bedpan full of dry ice, but I knew the timing was off. Anyway, I didn't have the dry ice yet, just the bedpan. And Guy, the sound effects man, was in physical therapy, so there wasn't much point. But I felt the director's eyes on me, so from where I was sitting, I waved the bedpan. I would save my strength for the performance.

The first witch and second witch looked at each other. "Not yet, Addie," said the second witch, and reached over to pat the hand of the third witch. "We're on the 'set of sun' business."

The third witch frowned, still confused, but found her line and read it. "That will be ere the set of sun." Her tone was tentative, but when she looked up again, the second witch gave her a thumbs-up.

"Where the place?" asked the first witch, shrugging her shoulders and showing us her palms—a daring move, since it had the effect of moving her script out of her sightline and causing her hat to wobble.

The second witch was tugging her hat back in place, and again took a few seconds to answer. "Upon the heath." She pronounced the last word so that it rhymed with "death."

"That's 'heath,' Theo," the first witch corrected her gently.

But the second witch had already realized her mistake, and corrected herself. "Heath. Well, I'm sorry, but I don't see why it doesn't rhyme with 'death' and 'Macbeth.' And anyway, isn't that where heather grows? Why do they call it 'heather' if it grows on the heath?"

The third witch always kept a romance novel stashed under her walker seat, and they often featured covers depicting the locale under discussion, so she knew all about heaths. She said, "That's a very good point," and nodded. This time the brim of the witch's hat did strike Claude on the rump when it fell, but he just stirred and rolled over. He was well padded. "There to meet with Macbeth," she added, bending over with a grunt to pick up her hat. The move dislodged the walker propped against her chair, and it clattered to the floor. Claude opened one eye.

"I come, Graymalkin!" cried the first witch, and she rose from her wheelchair, bracing herself with one hand on the chair arm, and pumped the other fist in the air.

Happily, Graymalkin was not a speaking role. The actor playing it yawned, stretched, and closed his eyes again.

"Paddock calls," said the second witch, and she gripped her cane as if intending to rise. We all knew that the first witch was the only one of the three capable of anything resembling a swift exit, and that was only because she could really burn rubber in that wheelchair when she wanted to. The second witch was constrained not only by her cane but also by her portable oxygen tank.

After a beat, the third witch looked down and found her place. "Anon," she said.

Then the three witches grinned at each other. This was the part they liked best.

Together, they chanted, "Fair is foul and foul is fair, hover through the fog and filthy air."

Then they all turned to me. I waved the bedpan around again, just to show what a good sport I was, and wondered how I got myself into these situations. Worse, if Tom Nakagawa didn't return immediately from his ring-toss session in the therapy room, I'd soon be playing Duncan, King of Scotland and pre-eminent murder victim.

"Bravi!" a voice boomed in my ear, accompanied by a two-handed version of thunderous applause. "Oh, that was perfectly lovely, ladies. And I think we made the right decision to rehearse with the hats, don't you? By tomorrow, if you practice wearing them, you'll have them mastered."

This was the play's director and its biggest fan, Julius Radcliffe-Jones, a.k.a. Jasper Riddle Jones. He was Jasper on his driver's license, but I didn't blame him for changing it. Besides, I had my own catalog of aliases, so who was I to squawk? The moustache and full head of wavy hair were real, though helped to their current color by a small unlabeled bottle on the shelf above his sink.

How do I know this? I'm a sneak—a professional sneak, as it happens, so I'm pretty good at it. Radcliffe-Jones also had a bottle of something stronger than hair dye secreted in the pocket of a jacket that hung in his closet, but I wasn't about to rat him out. I had a similar bottle myself.

His enthusiasm for Shakespeare was genuine enough. And even though I resented the way he'd jollied me into participating in this dramatic extravaganza, his enthusiasm was infectious. The play had created some little excitement at The Elms Relaxation and Recuperation Center and excitement was in short supply around here. He'd said it would distract us from our pain, and he'd been right about that. The players loved him. And however he behaved when he had real actors and crew members to work with, around here he was everybody's biggest fan—the unshakeable optimist. Under the circumstances, optimism was hard to sustain. The effort to sustain it probably distracted him from his own prognosis.

So I welcomed Julius Radcliffe-Jones in all his tweedy good cheer, and hoped that his name, his hair, his bright blue contact lenses, and his British accent constituted the whole of his phoniness, and if not, that I wouldn't have to deal with the rest.

We weren't doing the play in its entirety, thank God. Even Julius wasn't that ambitious. There weren't enough actors on the short-term care wing, even if they were supplemented by the few permanent residents who were still capable of reading, let alone reading Shakespeare. Besides, Shakespeare's shortest tragedy was still too long for our intended audience, who might be captive but couldn't be relied upon to stay awake for five acts between *Days of Our Lives* and dinner, never mind the Elizabethan English.

"My hat keeps slipping down and covering my eyes and ears," the third witch was saying to Julius, who sat in an orange plastic chair behind me, legal pad at the ready, taking notes. This was Ada Baker, a short, pleasantly plump African-American woman of indeterminate age in a flowered muumuu who spoke a few decibels louder than her sidekicks so that she could hear herself. Addie wore orthopedic shoes that probably weighed half as much as she did. Her short curly hair showed off the skills of the Elms beauticians, whom she visited regularly. "I'm so afraid I'll miss my cue."

"Addie, you've got to remember to put your hearing aids in," said the first witch, Dottie Rivers, from her wheelchair as she dabbed at her nose. She spoke in a loud voice with exaggerated articulation. Dottie wore a plain white blouse under her thin, old-fashioned cardigan, a navy skirt, and pink terrycloth bedroom slippers. She had pinned her cloud of white hair under her witches' hat, but numerous dislodgings of the hat had caused the cloud to hang lower until now it curtained her neck like a fogbank.

"I keep telling you, don't worry," said the second witch, Theodora Underwood. "We won't let you miss your cue." Theo wore an elegant gray pantsuit accented with red piping, reading glasses tethered to her neck by a slim red cord, and red high-top sneakers. Her hair, a thick, unruly mass that she sometimes pulled back in a ponytail or bun, showed red and gray as well. She turned to Julius. "Julius, are you sure you don't want us to try some Scottish accents? It would be more authentic."

"Theo, I take your point," Julius said. "I really do. But I fear that your audience will have enough trouble understanding the Shakespearean English without unusual accents."

"I couldn't possibly do a Scottish accent," Dottie said, blowing her nose again for emphasis. "But if I don't get rid of this cold, they won't understand me anyway." She was a thin, pale woman with a long, thin nose now red and swollen from repeated blowing.

Theo was the tallest of the women, but we were all shorter than we used to be. Even in her wheelchair, Dottie's hunched shoulders hinted at osteoporosis, and just looking at her made me straighten up and pull my shoulders back. Ada was the only one wearing a wedding ring.

"Positive thinking, darling, positive thinking!" Julius said. "I understood every syllable, but then, I know the play."

"The hats are hard to keep on," I pointed out.

"Yes, ye-e-es," Julius said, forefinger to his lips and a deep frown furrowing his brow. "You're right, Marge, of course, you're right. We'll have to think of something there. But a chin strap would be too—too—."

"Inauthentic," I said.

"Quite," Julius said. "Perhaps all we need is a bit more practice."

He rubbed his hands together energetically as if demonstrating his willingness to pitch in and do his fair share of the practicing, though in point of fact he wasn't wearing a pointy hat. "Shall we run through it one more time?"

Theo's head swiveled to look at the clock again. Julius also raised his eyes to the clock. At this point, Helen, one of the physical therapists, advanced on the group and pointed the finger of doom at me. "Marge Smith, you're up," she said.

"Ah, well, perhaps not," Julius said. "I see it's time for Bingo. Well, I wish you all luck, and I shall see you at dinner. Why don't you wear the hats for the rest of the day to get used to them?"

"Come on, Claudie," Theo said to the inert pile of fur at her feet. "Bingo!"

Claude cracked an eye, saw the bustle around him, rolled to his feet, yawned and stretched.

They abandoned me to my fate.

There was a lot of that going around.

When I'd broken my leg, I'd planned to recuperate at home, surrounded by the comforts of home. My bosses had other plans.

Didi had gazed at me earnestly over an enormous bouquet of flowers and said, "We found a great place for you, M.J.—beautiful grounds, gourmet meals, excellent nursing care, and the best physical therapy around. Really, we've had excellent reports." He let a blond lock fall over his forehead as he ducked his head and smiled up at me, a ploy he'd been using all his life to get his way. "They even have a cat in residence."

"I have a great place already," I said. "It has all that and two cats in residence."

"Too many stairs," his father said, frowning. Emile, founder of both Levesque Security and Quixote, Ltd., had been admiring the view from my tenth-floor hospital window. "And too many temptations."

Both men were impeccably dressed, as always. Emile wore a

gray suit that could have been dyed to match the precise gray in his eyes and his sideburns, while Didi wore a brown one that contained so many gradations of the color that you knew it was expensive. Beneath the cloying scent of hothouse flowers, I could detect both men's signature scents, subtly masculine yet distinctive —Emile's with a hint of pipe tobacco mixed with his cologne while Didi's ran more to leather and horses. Otherwise, Didi, in his late forties, was a boyish image of his father. Gray eyes, wavy dark hair, strong jawlines, and trim, athletic builds still turned women's heads. "French men are sooo sexy," they'd sigh.

I looked at Emile. "Temptations to do what?" I said. "Just what is it you think I'll be tempted to do with this cast on my leg?" I rapped it with my knuckles. "Take rumba lessons? Set up a limbo bar across the doorway to the bathroom?"

"If I know you," Emile said, his native tongue still audible in his accent and intonation, "you'll be weeding the garden on your first day home. You'll be hanging from the gutter on your second. What you won't be doing is your physical therapy exercises." He crossed his arms and gave me a stern look.

I knew he'd come along to play the bad cop. Absent from the delegation was Didi's wife Bernie, who had probably refused to take any part in their bullying.

"You're not as young as you used to be, M.J.," Didi pleaded. "If you don't do your exercises and take care of yourself, you could be down for the count."

I started to point out that physical therapists make house calls, then stopped. I folded my own arms across the sheet and studied them.

I said, "There's something else, isn't there?"

"Well," Emile said, "since you ask—."

So here I was, fresh from a star turn as bedpan waver, stumping along on my crutches to the torture chamber. My leg hurt like hell where it didn't itch and I was paying an arm and a leg to have someone make it hurt even more—or rather, Quixote was paying. I was supposed to be "keeping an eye on things" at the Home, which meant keeping an eye on the people, but who or why I didn't know because they wouldn't tell me. That could mean that the whole bloody mission was just a ploy to get me here for my own good, but I didn't actually think so.

It was driving me crazy. Who was I supposed to be watching? Mr. Nakagawa, a retired deputy chief at the FCC, was over at the ring toss. Mrs. Winchell, a counsel to the director of the Bureau of Consumer Protection, was throwing a ball to Mr. Banerjee, a cultural attaché with the Indian Embassy, and he was throwing it back. Mr. Sanchez, who had just negotiated a major trade agreement with Mexico, was stacking cups on high shelves in the occupational therapy section, using some kind of a gripper device with an extension. Ms. Amy, a lobbyist for the National Corn Growers Association, was using a shorter gripper stick to put socks on, take them off, then put them on again.

I sighed. I knew my turn with the sock stick was coming. I looked over at Congressman Ballou, who was draped over the Swiss ball, a grimace contorting his face, and resolved to blow the joint before they tried that on me.

I lay down on the table and resigned myself to my fate —for now.

Not for the first time, the providential appearance of Jonas Lafitte saved me. Since I had my eyes closed against the pain, I heard his voice before I saw him.

"Smitty, Smitty, Smitty," it said. "I knew that bike would do you in. I tried to tell them it was a mistake to give a machine that powerful to a speed demon like you, but they wouldn't listen."

I opened my eyes and looked into his. They were entirely too humorous for the occasion.

"It was just a Scrambler, for god's sake, not a Streetfighter. And the accident wasn't my fault," I said. I closed my eyes again but that recalled an image of my beautiful blood-red Duc lying mangled on the sidewalk, so I opened them again.

"Of course, it wasn't," he said.

"Damn tourist driving a minivan and checking the map on his cell phone was about to take me out," I said. "I didn't have any choice."

His eyes traveled down my leg to my cast. He'd seen me in a burqa, a kimono, a jelabiya, a sari, jeans, cargo pants, a bodysuit, a wet suit, a hazmat suit, several police and guard uniforms, a chef's apron, a nurse's uniform, and a nun's habit but never in cut-offs. My visible leg looked like a map of the Mississippi watershed but reassuringly muscular. He nodded at the cast. "First time?"

"Yes," I said. Setting aside the bullet wounds, my injuries up to now had been relatively light. In all my colorful career, the only broken bones I'd ever suffered had been arms and wrists and ribs and collarbones—one of each. To lose a leg, even temporarily, to a tourist on Dupont Circle was beyond aggravating.

His eyes moved up to my hair, which was mostly gray and short but longer than it should have been.

"Getting shaggy on top," he observed. Lafitte always noticed things like that—one of the attributes that endeared him to women.

"I'm afraid to go near the beauty shop," I confessed. "I'm afraid I'll end up with a purple perm. Anyway, you're shaggy yourself."

He ran a hand through his hair. "Yes, but it's part of my look."

The therapist was still pulling on my leg. "Miss Margie," she said, "is this your son, your nephew, or your boyfriend?"

Lafitte winked at her. "Someone who wants to get her alone," he said. "She could be done with this, right?" He had dark blond hair, always a bit messy, blue eyes, a day's worth of beard stubble, and the kind of rugged good looks women go for. He always looked fresh from the shower after a fun-filled day of herding cattle or racing dirt bikes or rock climbing. His well-worn jeans fit him like a second skin and his white tee shirt showed off his muscles under his bad-boy bomber jacket. When he winked, he got his way with every woman except me.

So between the two of them they pulled me upright and onto my crutches, and Lafitte and I retired to the courtyard with the smokers and loungers. In the old days, this former group would have included Lafitte and me, but nowadays there were no smokers among the agents at Quixote. Smoking was a dangerous addiction to take into the field, where the scrape of a match or the glow of a cigarette end or the faintest whiff of tobacco could betray your presence. We still didn't know how we'd lost Considine, but it was after his death that the non-smoking rule was instigated. In solidarity, Emile had given up everything but the occasional pipe, even though he had retired from the field by that point.

Lafitte looked around the courtyard, opened his jacket, removed a packet from an oversized inner pocket, unzipped it and brought out two plastic champagne glasses and a small bottle of Moët & Chandon. That explained the bomber jacket in July.

"We're celebrating?" I said.

"Smitty, when I'm with you, I'm always celebrating," he said. He unwound the wire, covered the cork with a handkerchief, and coughed loudly to cover the pop. He assembled the glasses, poured and toasted me. Then he winked and said, "I left something more to your liking in your room, but you have to find it."

I grinned at him. Champagne wasn't my beverage of choice, but it would do in a pinch. I raised my glass to him.

"All those warnings about mixing painkillers and booze," he said, "I think it's crap. What do you think?"

"All crap," I agreed. I shifted in the chair to find a comfortable position, and winced. "Besides, I think I got the placebo."

"Ah. In that case, drink up," he said.

I looked across the patio to where a mother and daughter sat. It was a pleasant summer day in the low 80s, but the wheelchair-bound older woman was bundled up in a sweatsuit, blanket, socks, and slippers. She appeared to be sleeping, her head tipped forward, her chin resting on her chest. She was probably older than I was, but I have a bad habit of assuming that, with less reason, as the years go by, for doing so.

"There are worse ways to go," I said.

He followed my gaze. "True," he said. "Here's to dying with our boots on."

I clinked plastic with him, and the base fell off.

We eyed it as it rolled and came to rest next to his foot.

"It would probably be therapeutic if you picked that up yourself," he said. He looked up at me, grinned, and said, "Permit me." He bent to retrieve the base.

"Has Bruiser been around?" he asked.

Bruce "Bruiser" Varga is my personal trainer. You can't continue on active duty as a Quixote agent unless you're in top physical condition. Two weeks ago, I had been.

"Once," I said. "Then he left for an extended vacation to visit family in the old country."

He grimaced. "Tough luck," he said.

"Do you know why I'm here?" I asked, once he got the glass reassembled.

"Because you broke your leg?" he said.

I shook my head. "Not good enough," I said. "They've got something up their sleeves."

"Don't know," he said. "Just got back."

"From Syria?"

"Algeria. Syria was last week."

"Go all right?"

He nodded. "Well enough."

"You're no help."

He gave me an injured look. "Smitty," he said, "who else would bring you a bottle of Bombay Sapphire, a bottle of Moët, five pounds of Belgian chocolates, and a dozen donuts from Migue's?"

I smiled. "Nobody but you, Lafitte," I said.

"Damn straight," he said.

I drained my glass, and for the first time in a long while, felt no pain.

2

I had a lot of information about my fellow inmates at The Elms, thanks to my laptop. It helped that we were in the D.C. area—just inside the Beltway, in fact—and most of the people who could afford to convalesce here were officials or retired officials of one government or another, or lobbyists trying to influence officials of one government or another. The only ones I couldn't get a line on, in fact, were the witches. They had left almost no footprints on the Web, which was something of a feat. I should know; I'd managed it myself. Ada was the only one of them who had a *Facebook* page, but it was blank and I suspected she'd joined so that she could follow kids and grandkids. I could find addresses and phone numbers, but that didn't tell me much.

So after dinner, when everybody else in the place was either watching *Jeopardy!* or snoozing in front of *Jeopardy!* I took my box of chocolates and went to the day room in search of them. I'd noticed before that they bucked the televisual trend.

They were sitting at one of the long tables, wearing their witches' hats. Someone had dragged a couple of floor lamps over to give them more light. Dottie was laboring over a paint-by-numbers painting of three Scotties with bows. Since most of the colors were neutral shades—variations of gray, black, white, and brown—it looked unbearably tedious to me, but she was almost finished. Theo, who was sporting a witch's hat that completely covered her hair and appeared to be balancing atop her ears, was crocheting something, and Ada was playing solitaire.

"Don't come too close, Marge," Dottie said, fending me off with a wave of the hand. "I don't want to give you my cold. Sit over there."

Theo and Ada sat facing each other, with a seat between them and Dottie.

"Where's Claude?" I said.

"Around," Theo said with a vague wave of her hand.

"Claude likes *Jeopardy!*" Ada said, frowning down at her cards. "He's obsessed with that Vanna White."

I sat down next to Theo and propped my crutches against the table. I set the box of chocolates on the table. "Have one," I said.

"Ooh," Ada said. "Do you mean that good-looking young man brought you champagne *and* chocolates?"

"He's a keeper," Theo said, and set down her crocheting to lean over and select a chocolate from the box. She handed it to Dottie.

I craned my neck to see Dottie's painting. "That's quite a project," I said.

"It's turned out well, hasn't it?" Theo said. The oxygen tank was nowhere in sight, and I worried about that.

Dottie held up her painting for me to see. Then she turned it back and looked at it over her reading glasses.

I supposed it had, if you liked that kind of thing, so I said, "It's very nice."

"I'm no artist," Dottie said, admiring her work, "but I love the way it looks like one thing, and then turns into something else altogether. Don't you?" She smiled at me.

"Pretty remarkable," I agreed.

She beamed at me. "I'm glad you like it. I'm going to give it to you when I'm done."

"Oh," I said, "I couldn't accept it! After all your hard work—."

She waved her brush. "Don't be silly!" she said. "It's just a little souvenir of our brief encounter." She sneezed, caught her hat before it hit the painting, blew her nose. Into her tissue, she said, "I'll just start another one tomorrow. I have plenty more at home." She set the hat on the table. "Well, perhaps not tomorrow."

"Tomorrow is our premiere," Ada remarked.

"Opening afternoon," Theo said.

"Too bad it's not opening night," Dottie said, and they sighed in unison.

Ada's heartfelt sigh dislodged her hat and it landed in the middle of her card layout. "Oh, damn!" she said. "I'm sure I would've gone out that time."

The performance had been scheduled for the afternoon of Friday, July 3rd, because many families would have the day off. The noise and bustle of visitors would disrupt the soap opera routine in any case, and the director had decided to boost our audience and show off the residents' dramatic talents by planning a matinee performance of the Scottish play. If nobody croaked or landed in the Emergency Room, we'd repeat it on Saturday and Sunday afternoons.

"Then there will be the cast party, and so on," Ada said.

"They say that you get an adrenaline rush when you act in front of an audience," Theo said, "and it's hard to come down after that. Of course, I'm not an actor, so I don't really know, but that's what they say."

I took the opportunity she'd offered me. "What did you used to do, Theo?" I said. "I mean, did you used to have a job?" She didn't wear a wedding ring, but I didn't make any assumptions. I didn't wear one, and any guesses about my life were likely to fall wide of the mark.

"I worked in a jewelry store," she said, "and later in an auction house."

"Was this in D.C.?" I said.

"The jewelry store was in Dubuque," she said. "The auction house was in San Francisco. But I followed a client here when he wanted his collections appraised. And then I did some appraising for other clients. I'm practically retired, but if something comes along, I might take it on. It's really just for fun."

"You must have a really interesting set of skills," I said.

"You'd be surprised," she said. She held up her crochet work, which just looked like a long cylindrical bag to me, and eyed it critically, tilting her head up to find it through her reading glasses.

"She once told me that my grandmother's pearls were fake," Ada said. "Isn't that something?" I noticed that she didn't have any trouble hearing, and guessed that her hearing aids were in place, though I couldn't see them.

I turned to her. "And what did you do?" I said. "Did you have a job?"

"My father was an electrician," she said. "He had his own company, and after I married an electrician, he joined the company, so I always worked for the family business. My son has it now."

"Addie's a seamstress, too," Dottie said. "She can make anything. She's amazing!"

"Oh—," Ada said, and looked down. But she didn't contradict Dottie.

"And you?" I asked Dottie. "What did you do?"

"Oh, I was just a secretary," she said. "Nothing very exciting."

"Me, too," I said. "Who did you work for?"

"I worked for an art publisher," she said. "It was a small house. They don't even exist anymore."

"How about you, Marge?" Theo asked. "Who did you work for?"

"A family-owned consulting and operations management company," I said.

"What did they consult on?" Theo asked. "What kinds of operations?"

"Oh, security, mostly," I said.

Sometimes I said more. My nephews and their families had always thought that I was a private secretary to Emile Levesque, who did some kind of consulting. If pressed for a specialty, sometimes I said "security," and sometimes I said "extrications." They never heard about the bullet wounds. As for the broken bones, they thought I was a klutz. When I said "extrications," most people heard "extractions" and assumed that we were in the oil and gas business. By design, Quixote, Ltd., was not a company with a high profile.

"I'll bet you were good at it," Dottie said.

"How are you feeling?" I said to Dottie. "You must be miserable."

"I've felt better," she admitted.

"Well, hell," Theo said, "there's nothing like doing time in a joint that's named for an extinct species to make you feel expendable."

"True," I said. "If they wanted to inspire thoughts of longevity, they should have called it 'The Kudzu.'"

"Or 'Dandelion House,'" Ada offered.

"Or 'Crabgrass Haven,'" Theo said.

We grinned at each other.

"Though technically," Dottie said, "it's only the Dutch elms that have died out in this country. There are healthier varieties."

"What are you in for?" I asked Dottie. My ideas on their various conditions were vague.

She grimaced. "The usual. Broken hip. So clichéd."

"You?" I said to Theo.

"Hip replacement," she said. "With luck, I won't be back with Dottie's problem. Once my lungs are clear, I can ditch the oxygen tank. I should have a few more miles on me."

Before I could ask, Ada said, "Heart valve replacement," and tapped her chest. "Pretty routine these days. Doesn't even hurt that much anymore. My husband says we'll go dancing in another two weeks."

"No dancing for you, though," Theo said, nodding at the crutches. "How'd you do it?"

"Traffic accident," I said.

Ada reacted with sympathy. "What happened?" she said.

"I was on a motorcycle, and nearly got sideswiped by a minivan, so I maneuvered to get out of his way and crashed," I said.

Ada made a sympathetic "Oh!" sound, but Theo said, "What kind of bike?"

"Ducati Scrambler." An old lady's bike, really, so I felt abashed, but still I had loved it and couldn't bring myself to upgrade it to three people who would never have occasion to confirm my story.

"Red or yellow?" Dottie asked.

"Red."

"What happened to it?" Theo asked.

"It didn't survive the crash," I said, embarrassed to be so choked up.

"Oh," said Dottie and Theo, and now they looked as sympathetic as Ada.

"Could have been worse," I said, and it could have been. Didi had outfitted the bike with Crashbar Engine Guards and Crash Bobbins, so at least I hadn't suffered third-degree burns while I was trying to extricate my broken leg from the tangle of hot metal. And I'd been wearing a full-face helmet, so I'd come away with my brains and beauty more or less intact.

"How long you in for?" Theo asked.

"I hope to be out next week," I said.

"Don't we all?" Dottie said. Everybody sighed. Since Ada had left her hat on the table, her solitaire layout survived.

"Actually," Theo said, "I have a fantasy that on Sunday morning, when it's really dead around here, Dr. Know-It-All shows up and says, 'Your limo is waiting to take you home, Ms. Underwood.' And I walk out the door. Period. No packing, no nurse's instructions, and no oxygen tank."

We all confessed to similar fantasies, except that mine involved Lafitte with an extra motorcycle helmet.

"Say, who was that good-looking man you were drinking champagne with in the courtyard today, Marge?" Ada said. "Your son?"

I shook my head. "Just a co-worker," I said.

"How come none of my coworkers ever looks like that?" Dottie said.

"Or nurses, either," Theo said. "If that smiley-faced guy on the night shift tells me one more time to 'have a blessed day,' I'm liable to clock him with my cane."

"Oh, I hate that one," Dottie said. "So goddamned cheerful all the time!"

"Did you guys know each other before you got here?" I asked. "You did, right?"

"Oh, hell, yes," Theo said. "I've known Ada since—well, I don't know since when, but a long time."

"Since that party at the Egyptian Embassy that time," Ada said. "You told me you needed some electrical work, remember?"

"God, that was ages ago, Addie," Theo said. "I can't remember what I had for dinner two hours ago."

"And how did you meet Dottie?" I asked the other two.

They looked at each other as if trying to remember.

"And how did you all end up here at the same time?" I added.

"That one's easy," Theo said. "Addie and I both needed surgery, and I said, 'I will if you will.'"

"And I said, 'I will if you will,'" Ada agreed.

"We think Dottie was just jealous," Theo said. "She fell off that stepladder so that she wouldn't miss out on all the fun."

"Oh, Theo, I just had a thought about your fantasy," Ada said.

"You need to change your fantasy to Monday instead of Sunday. The limo can't come for you until after our final performance of *Macbeth*."

We all stared at her.

"What?" Ada said.

We looked at each other, uncomfortable.

"You're not supposed to say the name, Addie," Dottie said. "Don't you remember?"

Ada clapped her hand to her mouth. "Oh!" she said. "I forgot! I meant 'the Scottish play.'"

But we knew that once the name had been spoken, it couldn't be taken back. Nobody wanted to say what we were all thinking: bad luck.

Dottie broke the silence. "Look!" she said. "It's finished!"

She held up the completed painting of three Scottie dogs. It bore a familial resemblance to the bottom lines on my optometrist's eye chart.

But the others praised it, and I agreed that it was very nice.

As soon as it was dry, it was mine to keep. That was enough bad luck to hold me for a while.

3

I thanked my lucky stars that all of my friends and relations were safely miles away on the day of the big production. My best friend Miki was on assignment in Singapore, but since I'd regaled her via e-mail with accounts of our rehearsals, she sent a dozen roses, with a card that said, "Break an arm!" and a postscript: "Probably in bad taste to say 'Knock 'em dead.'" I e-mailed her my thanks, but wrote, "Probably overkill for a props mistress."

As far as my family was concerned, luck didn't have anything to do with their absence. I loved my brother and his boys, but since I had no intention of confiding the true nature of my work for the Levesques, short visits from long distances were preferable. My sister-in-law had offered to come and look after me while my leg healed, but I assured her that since I was going to a nursing home, there was no need. I suppose I had Didi and Emile to thank for that. On the other hand, I also had them to thank for setting me up as a props wrangler and special effects supervisor for a geriatric production of the Scottish play.

Okay, maybe I envied some of the inmates their visitors. Tom Nakagawa sat in the day room holding hands with his wife. I glimpsed Ada taking a slow walk with her husband around the lake in the company of three grandkids. Two of Sandy Banerjee's grand-daughters were racing wheelchairs in the hall. Gloria Winchell was playing double solitaire in the day room with her twin sister. Jim Sanchez was also in the day room, sitting on the couch flanked by grandkids and watching cartoons. Julius was making the rounds with his longtime partner Bill, a dapper, slightly built man with more hair on his upper lip than on his head. Even Beth Amy had visitors, who could have been grown children, and they too were taking a walk around the lake, but even at this distance I could see Beth's distinctive crooked-elbow posture, which told me she was talking on a cell phone.

Not everybody was happy. Dottie sat with two people at the lunchtime cookout on the patio—presumably her niece and the niece's boyfriend. When I saw her, she rolled her eyes at me. The niece was middle-aged and overweight, dressed in a flowered sundress too short for her age and body type. A purple clip-on bow overpowered her short, wavy hair, and sweat was melting her make-up. The boyfriend could have been ten years her junior. At first glance, I agreed with Dottie's assessment of him: he was slick. He wasn't especially good-looking, but you could see that he thought he was, and attitude often carries the day with women. He kept a smile plastered on his face, but there was something sharky about it.

I wondered where the nephew was. I'd seen him before, and remained unimpressed. If the boyfriend looked determinedly cheerful, the nephew had the look of a malcontent. Even when he wasn't actively frowning, you felt that a frown was just around the corner. He had brown hair cut close to his head, and a soul patch just distinguishable from the stubble that constituted his unshaven look. Although Lafitte always looked as though he'd been too busy scaling cliffs to think about shaving, the nephew looked as though he'd given it a lot of thought while gazing at himself in a mirror.

As I was considering this contrast, I registered that someone was standing at my elbow.

"Marjorie?" he was saying. "Marjorie? I don't mean to break in on your reverie."

This was Dr. Gao, who constituted the second string of The Elms's attending physicians. He looked too young to have finished college, let alone medical school. My body parts were twice his age —so old school and low tech that I didn't see how he could hope to repair them. Hell, I wore sneakers older than he was. But if I doubted his skills, I gave him points for trying.

"Oh, hello," I said. I didn't bother to correct my name.

"All alone?" he said, looking around. He was dressed in khakis and an Izod shirt and carrying a tray. His stethoscope was nowhere in sight. "Me, too. Mind if I join you?"

A voice over my shoulder said, "Great! We'd love it."

I looked up to see Lafitte sliding a well laden tray onto the table.

"Here you go, Smitty," he said. "Bon appetit!" He gave me a broad smile.

"What are you doing here?" I said. "You were just here yesterday."

"Yes, and that's when I found out about the big performance!" He offered his hand to Dr. Gao. "Jonas Lafitte. Pleased to meet you."

Lafitte always climbed into a chair as if he were mounting a horse. He waved a finger at me. "Ah, now, Smitty," he said, "you should've told me. You shouldn't be so modest. Props mistress! That's a lot of responsibility."

Under this speech, Dr. Gao delivered his name. Now he said, "Yes, we're all looking forward to the play."

"Yes, we are," Lafitte said, impervious to my scowl. "I hope you're not too nervous to eat."

"How'd you find out?" I said. I picked up the hamburger he'd set in front of me. I wanted to know how many of the staff were on his payroll.

"Helen, your physical therapist, told me," he said.

He was still smiling when we ran into Julius on the way to the empty room he'd commandeered to serve as our green room.

"Oh, Marge, there you are," he said, as if I'd been M.I.A. "I just found out that Art Ballou threw his back out on the Swiss ball, and they've given him Percocet, so he's too drugged to play his part. Wherever will I find another Banquo on such short notice?" It went without saying that we'd barely found enough inmates sufficiently healthy to fill the cast and crew, so there weren't any understudies.

I balanced on my crutches and grabbed Lafitte by his sleeve. "My friend here will do it," I said. "He'd be glad to."

Lafitte stopped smiling.

Julius beamed at him. "Oh, that's marvelous!" he said. "We'd be so grateful."

"But I don't know the part," Lafitte objected.

"It's easy," I said. "All you have to do is read the script. You know the play, right?"

He squinted and stared off into the middle distance. "Three witches tell a bloke he'll be king of Scotland, so he offs the bird who already has the job, with the encouragement of his wife. Afterward, he's sorry and she's barmy—sees blood everywhere or something."

"That's the one," I said.

"What a relief!" Julius said. "Follow me, and I'll get you your script and costume."

"Costume?" Lafitte said, looking at me.

"You get a swell cape," I said. I didn't tell him it was borrowed from the beauty salon, and had prancing pink poodles all over it.

In the event, he got into the part, as I knew he would. It helped that Jim Sanchez, who was playing the lead, was our best actor. And the witches were dazzling, in their own way, although Dottie looked worse than she had the day before, flushed and a little feverish. Her hand trembled when she drew out the pilot's thumb, and I wasn't sure whether she was doing it for effect or not. Lafitte, meanwhile, as the most mobile member of the cast, was swanning around our small staging area at the back of the day room, swishing his cape with gusto. Claude sat upright, watching him, and I thought any minute Claude would attack the fluttering plastic and then maybe we would see a little honest-to-god blood.

I was watching through a gap in a curtain that the maintenance guys had rigged up. I could see Dottie's nephew and niece in the second row. The niece was smiling at her boyfriend. The nephew was paying more attention than I would have expected. Julius's partner Bill sat behind them, smiling broadly.

On cue, I waved around the bedpan full of dry ice and blew the clouds through the gap to cover the witches' exit, which took a while. Guy, the sound effects man, beat a drum with one hand while rattling his sheet of tin with the other—a feat as impressive as anything happening on stage. The boyfriend clapped and whistled when the witches left the stage. I noticed that Dottie was patting down her face with a tissue, though we didn't have the kind of stage lights that make acting such a sweaty business. But then I turned back to see how Mrs. Winchell was getting on with Lady Macbeth's soliloquy and I forgot about Dottie.

Next I had to prepare the visionary dagger. Julius had really wanted a flaming dagger, just as he'd wanted a real smoke machine, but he couldn't persuade the warden to disconnect the smoke detectors for the duration of the performance, so he had to settle for a pocket of dry ice on the back of the dagger and phosphorescent paint on the front, which wasn't visible in the sunlit room. It was just as well, I thought; the flame-retardant gloves I would have had to wear would have spoiled the effect.

I wasn't prepared to be tackled from behind by Dottie, who must have launched herself off her wheelchair and struck me with such force that we crashed through the curtain, upsetting my props bin. My armed head rolled toward the audience. My bloody baby doll goosed Claude and propelled him onto Macbeth's shoulder.

"No, not the knife," Dottie said. "No knives, remember?"

Her eyes were wild, her pupils dilated, and her flushed face was slick with sweat. Her hands were hot on my wrist and I dropped the dagger.

"It's not a real dagger, Dottie," I said soothingly. "It's just a prop."

"We do it right. We don't need knives," she said, her voice fading to a whisper. Then she looked around the room at the audience, squinting against the light. Out of the corner of my eye I saw Dr. Gao and two nurses rushing the stage. Dottie's three family members stood on the edge of the circle of horrified observers, but I couldn't tell if she could see them or not. "And now the vultures are gathering," Dottie whispered. "But they won't get what isn't theirs." I realized that I was holding her hand when she squeezed it. "Smoke," she breathed. "Good work."

As the nurses pulled her off of me, she collapsed completely. "So hot," she sighed. "And—and—what's happening to me? I can't—."

Dr. Gao was taking her pulse, and a nurse opened a kit and set it on the floor next to him. He shone a light in her face but she closed her eyes and turned away. The hand she raised to block the light was trembling.

I was dimly aware of the murmur of voices outside our small circle. I felt a hand on my shoulder and Lafitte's voice said, "You all right, Smitty?"

I nodded as Dr. Gao selected a filled syringe, tested it, and injected Dottie with its contents. Dr. Gao laid her limp hand, no longer trembling, across her chest.

She was dead by the time the EMTs arrived.

And I was left to wonder how she knew that name: Smoke.

4

Monday morning I was called into the office on short notice. Apparently, Emile and Didi had forgotten to worry about my bum leg just as they had withdrawn their objections to my return home after Dottie had died. Of course, I hadn't been the only patient to decamp, but not everyone blamed the nursing home for the sudden death of a frail elderly woman who had tempted fate with her thespian antics.

We were meeting in a fourth-floor conference room, which usually signaled a job for Levesque Security rather than Quixote. That puzzled me, because most of my work involved the latter, especially now that I was semi-retired from the field. I couldn't imagine what kind of job they thought I would better qualified to do than their regular operatives, especially in my hobbled state. Did they need a gimpy Gray Panther for a stakeout?

Between the physical therapy and all of the things I'd been doing that I wasn't supposed to be doing, my leg hurt like hell, but I popped some pills and gritted my teeth. Marco Antonio drove me in his cab, and insisted on going upstairs with me. But he and his wife Fina, my housekeeper, had taken good care of me without babying me, so I didn't squawk.

I was late because I still hadn't accepted my tortoise pace, and hadn't left enough time. Marco Antonio was saner than the average D.C. cabbie and wouldn't be rushed.

"They'll wait for you," he said. "They need you or they wouldn't be dragging you down there in a leg cast."

So when I entered the conference room, the clients were already seated at the table and well supplied with coffee and pastry. We stared at each other.

"Ah, M.J.," Emile said. "I believe you already know Ms. Underwood and Mrs. Baker."

I nodded at the witches, propped my crutches against the table, and sat down across from them in a chair left vacant between Emile and Didi. Theo wore a stylish dusky red pantsuit and Ada wore a seersucker suit. I didn't see Theo's oxygen tank, but the handle of her cane was visible propped against the conference table. The sun streamed in through the banks of windows along two walls, glinted off Ada's rings, and lent an air of normalcy to the scene. Didi's competent but silent assistant Astur was already pouring me coffee.

Ada looked from Emile to me and said, "You mean, you're Mr. Levesque's secretary?"

"Not exactly," I said. "I used to be." It was so long ago that I barely remembered it. Certainly my typing and dictation skills had deteriorated over time. But I still had a steno pad, as handy for doodling as for taking notes, and I took it out now.

Theo eyed me. "So what were you doing at The Elms?" she said.

"The same thing you were doing, Ms. Underwood," Emile said. "Recuperating." He leaned back in his chair. He did everything gracefully, as if he were born to do it better than the average human, and that applied to sitting and standing.

Didi added, "But we sent her to The Elms because Mrs. Rivers had contacted us about doing some work for her before she broke her hip. We didn't really know what the situation was, only that she wanted to upgrade her security system, and she seemed anxious to move quickly on it. Then she fell and ended up in the nursing home. We had no particular reason to believe that she was in danger, just one of my father's infamous hunches. So we sent M.J., who had so providentially broken her leg." He smiled at me.

"I could have done a better job of protecting Dottie," I said sourly, "if I'd known I was protecting her."

"Oh, you weren't really protecting her, M.J.," Emile said. "Just keeping an eye on things. As Didi said, we didn't think that Mrs. Rivers was in any personal danger, only that you might be able to find out what was troubling her."

"Yes," Didi said, "and we always trust you to be looking out for suspicious characters."

My eyes wandered to the two remaining witches, who looked away from me.

"Well, I suppose if such a character showed up at the table during Bingo and asked to borrow a key to the vault, I might have known something was up," I said.

Theo and Ada looked at each other.

"So you knew about the vault?" Theo said.

"What vault?" I said.

"Perhaps we should begin at the beginning," Didi said, spreading his hands. "Mrs. Rivers spoke to me at some length—perhaps thirty minutes—the day before she had her accident." He held up a hand as if he expected to be interrupted. "And before you ask, as far as we can tell from our investigations, which we conducted the day after Mrs. Rivers was hospitalized, it *was* an accident. She fell off a step ladder in her kitchen, and we found no evidence that anything had been tampered with."

"As you know, ladies," Emile put in, "at our age, we can experience a spontaneous break, and that may have been what caused

Mrs. Rivers's fall in the first place. Of course, the autopsy may reveal an underlying cause as yet unknown to us."

"Unlikely," Theo said. "When old farts like us land in the hospital, they run every expensive test they can think of, once they get their mitts on us. Hard to believe she'd have an undiagnosed anything."

Emile bowed to acknowledge this remark. "I'm inclined to agree with you, Ms. Underwood. I only mention the possibility."

"Frankly, Mr. Levesque," Ada said, "We're more interested in who caused her death than in who caused her fall."

"And we want to know who cleaned out the vault," Theo said.

"What vault?" I said.

"As far as the death is concerned," Emile said, "we won't know the official cause until the autopsy results are in, but from what M.J. has told us, they don't seem likely to be all that helpful. M.J. said that she thought Mrs. Rivers was poisoned, and she strongly recommended to the attending physician a toxicology screen for alkaloids." He turned to me. "Isn't that right?"

I nodded. "She had the symptoms," I said. "Dilated pupils, hypersensitivity to light, tremors, confusion, hallucination—there was more going on than a heart attack."

Tears filled Ada's eyes and she looked down. I felt sorry for her, but we had to be able to talk about these things if we wanted to find out what had really happened and why.

"When Dr. Gao backed me up, they called in a homicide detective, guy named Medlock, Walter Medlock," I said. "I assume he talked to all of us." The others nodded. "Seemed bright enough."

Theo said, "Gao is worried that everyone will think he injected her with atropine by mistake, either out of incompetence or negligence."

I shook my head. "Her symptoms were already severe before he injected her," I said. "So even if he made a mistake, which I doubt, he probably didn't cause her death."

"Agreed," Theo said.

"The coroner couldn't rule out poisoning," Didi said, "so he did order a toxicology screen, but we won't have the results for another two weeks. In the meantime, perhaps we should assume that we're dealing with a murder."

"And if it was some kind of alkaloid," I said, "it had to have been administered to her not long before she died."

"How long?" Theo asked.

I shrugged. I'd looked into this question, of course, but forensic toxicology was no more exact than human biology could make it. "Probably half an hour at most," I said.

Theo paled. "I ate lunch with them," she said. "I didn't see anything. I'm sure I'd remember something, wouldn't I?"

"You hadn't joined them when I saw them," I pointed out. "It wouldn't take long. And afterward, you never looked away? You never turned your head to see if Julius looked nervous, for example, or where the congressman was?"

Theo looked crestfallen. "All right, okay, you're right. I probably did."

"So you're saying that it had to be either the niece or the boyfriend," Ada said.

"I wouldn't go quite that far," I said. "What happened to the nephew, Theo? He'd be my favorite candidate, but I didn't see him at lunch."

"His stomach was bothering him," she said. "He didn't want to eat. He went off to make a phone call, and I didn't see him again until curtain time."

"Oh, too bad!" Ada said. "I don't like him, either. Oh, wait!" She raised a finger. "Maybe that makes him more suspicious because he'd already poisoned something and he didn't want to eat it himself. But it would have to be something that only Dottie ate, in that case." Clearly, romance wasn't the only genre Ada read, and she had the imagination of an avid reader. I recognized it, because I had it myself.

"Well, the time frame makes him less likely," I said, "but it doesn't rule him out altogether. Did she go right from lunch to the day room for the performance?"

"She went to her room to get her hat," Theo said.

"So she could have eaten something then," I said. I thought of the chocolates Lafitte had brought me. "Candy? Alcohol? A drink to steady her nerves, maybe?"

Theo shrugged. "Those are all possibilities, Marge," she said.

"Even more likely, it seems to me," I said, "would be her medicines—heart medicine, blood thinner, pain meds, maybe sleeping pills—."

"Cold medicine," Theo put in.

"Right," I agreed. "If I were plotting to kill Dottie, that's what I would have done. You couldn't predict when she'd use it, but that might improve your alibi."

"Remind me never to piss you off, Marge," Theo said.

"I do think that the police went through her room and bagged some things to take away with them," Ada said, "so perhaps they took all of her medicines as well."

"Probably," Emile agreed. "They would need to check to make sure that she didn't have an adverse reaction to something she was taking."

"Forgive me if this is an indelicate question," Didi said, "but I believe that Mrs. Rivers was moderately wealthy? Or perhaps more than moderately wealthy? We haven't been able to confirm all of her holdings."

I felt my eyebrows lift in surprise. If Didi's wife Bernie, our top computer wizard, couldn't confirm all of Dottie's holdings, and knew that she couldn't, that meant she'd found traces of accounts she couldn't access, and if Bernie couldn't access them, then they were extremely well secured. I thought again of the witches' obscurity on the Web, and wondered.

"She was moderately wealthy," Theo said evenly.

"*Cui bono?*" Ada said. "That's what you're going to ask, isn't it?"

"We could probably speculate all afternoon, based on our scant data, but perhaps we should move on," Emile said, with a dismissive wave of his hand. "Murder is a police matter, and they are really very good at dealing with it. You are not hiring us to find a murderer, although it is obviously in our best interests, and yours, to be aware of the murderer's existence and look out for him or her. What concerns us are the missing contents of the vault."

"What vault?" I said.

"It's really a safe room," Ada said to me.

"You should know, M.J, that Ms. Underwood is Mrs. Rivers's executor," Didi said to me.

"You can imagine how that went over," Theo said to me.

"Dottie made a new will," Ada told me in a voice full of capitals and italics, "just last week."

"They're going to challenge it in court, of course, the nephew and niece," Theo said.

"You might be called to testify, Marge," Ada put in, "that she wasn't off her rocker."

"I don't know the details myself," Theo continued, "but I do know that Dottie left them less in the new will than the old one. She didn't trust the boyfriend—or the nephew, either, for that matter."

I raised my voice. "What vault?" I said.

After a beat of silence, Theo said, "Dottie was something of an art collector, Marge."

I thought of my paint-by-number Scotties, and said the first thing that came to mind. "You're kidding."

"I'm not," Theo said. Then perhaps she remembered the Scotties, too, because she added, "She had eclectic tastes, but she owned some rather valuable pieces, as it turned out."

"Quite valuable," Ada agreed. "We knew that she liked to buy paintings, but we had no idea—." Here she looked at Didi. "Well, the extent and worth of her collection."

"Which she kept in a safe room," I said.

"Exactly," Theo said. "At least, the most valuable works. And she had some nice antiques as well, and silver. But she was starting to worry lately about security, and that's why she contacted Mr. Levesque." She nodded at him. "She'd had the best possible security when it was first installed, but that was thirty years ago or more. She thought she could improve on it."

"Did she have any specific cause to be concerned?" I asked.

"I don't really know," Theo said. "She just said, 'Oh, I should have upgraded a long time ago.' I think breaking her hip made her realize just how vulnerable she was. That may have been it."

"Or she could have read in the paper about a burglary in her neighborhood," Ada said. "That happens to me. I read about a local crime and go around checking all my door locks."

I refrained from pointing out that there was a world of difference between checking your door locks and engaging a high-tech, top-flight specialty firm like Levesque Security.

"But then Sunday—." Ada turned to Theo to continue the story.

"Well, yes, as you know, she didn't have a chance to act on her plan before she broke her hip," Theo said. "Sunday was our first opportunity to go to Dottie's house. I asked Ada to come along. Dottie's desk with all her papers was in the first-floor office, and we just wanted to get a sense of what was there. I didn't think we could manage the stairs and didn't see any reason to try. I couldn't have gotten into the safe room at that point because I didn't have the combination. I wasn't even sure where the room was. And I wouldn't have found it, if the burglars hadn't tracked so much dirt on the carpet in the office and left the closet door open. The door to the safe room was in one of the closet walls. We think it was behind an empty file cabinet we found upended outside the closet door. They hadn't bothered with the combination lock, they just cut a hole in the door. There was an odor of some kind of fuel, like gasoline or kerosene. The safe room was empty—cleaned out."

"Sounds like the door would have been well concealed," I said.

Theo started to say something, then changed her mind. "Probably," she said. "Anyway, you could tell from the hangers on the wall inside the room that there had been paintings. There could have been other things, too—I just don't know. There weren't any cabinets or display cases or tables for jewelry boxes or anything like that."

I made a note on my pad, then looked up. "How many paintings? How big? How long would it take to move them out?"

Theo and Ada looked at each other. "Fifteen paintings, as far as we know," Theo said.

"Some small, but some quite big," Ada said, and spread her arms wide to demonstrate. "We have a list that includes measurements. We never saw them."

"If you had a van parked in the garage and didn't care what condition you got them out in," Theo said, "I'd say that it would take one person more than an hour, if he rushed, and if he had a system for moving large objects. But of course, he wouldn't want to damage them, and maneuvering them out of the closet would have been tricky. More than one person could do it faster, of course. But a couple of the paintings were more than five feet tall. And of course, we don't know how heavy the frames would have been, if they were framed."

I felt my scalp prickle.

"If you were prepared with some crates, it could be a matter of just slipping them into their separate compartments, once you got them to the van," I observed. I could feel Emile's eyes on me. "Do we know whether it was one person or more than one?"

"We don't know," Didi said. "The footprints all look the same to me."

"What did the police say?" I asked.

"We didn't call the police," Theo said. "We called Mr. Levesque right away and asked for his advice. We have reason to want to avoid publicity, not least of which is the harassment we're likely to get from the heirs."

If that wasn't the least reason, I wondered about the others. "You're hoping that we'll get the paintings back for you?" I said. "Do we have any idea who took them?"

They both shook their heads.

"We don't even know whether the heirs knew about them or not," Theo said.

"We didn't even know about them," Ada said. "We only found out when Dottie's lawyer gave Theo a copy of the will on Saturday. And it doesn't say anything about paintings, only 'the contents of the safe room, as itemized on the list to be found in my safe deposit box.'" Ada raised her hands and curled her fingers to make air quotes. "When we saw the empty room, we assumed it was paintings, but we didn't know for sure until we opened the safe deposit box with the lawyer this morning."

"If the heirs knew about the paintings," Theo said, "they probably assumed that they'd inherit them, so no reason to steal them."

"Unless one of them didn't want to share with the others," I said.

"But who else could have known about them if we didn't?" Ada said. "I don't know if we were her closest friends, but we were pretty close."

I shrugged. "Many big collectors follow the sales," I said. "They usually know who's bought what, and for how much."

I noticed that they weren't making eye contact with each other. They were staring at me, and trying hard not to blink. Ada fingered some papers before her on the conference table.

"The legitimate sales, I mean," I said.

"Yes," Theo said, "I guess that's true."

"We don't know when they were taken, I suppose," I said. "They could have been taken any time after Dottie was hospitalized, though it would have made sense to take advantage of all the noise and commotion on the Fourth. That's what I would have done."

"We do know when they were taken," Theo said. "And you're right—they were taken on the night of the Fourth."

"We have a video from a security camera," Ada said.

Astur, the silent assistant, got up and pushed the buttons that dimmed the lights and dropped the shades. The screen was already lowered, so I assumed that I was the only one who hadn't yet seen the video.

The image betrayed the camera's age: it was grainy, unfocused. At first we were looking at darkness, then a light came on and showed the interior of a storage closet. I suspected that the color was unreliable. The time stamp was clear enough, though: Saturday, July 4th, at 10:07 P.M. A figure moved into view, its back to the camera as it wrestled with a tall file cabinet, which disappeared out of frame with the figure. The figure returned, turned toward the camera, and raised a face wearing a ski mask. It lifted a black-gloved hand holding a dark cloth and then the image went black.

Didi was shaking his head. "Whoever advised her to install a camera like that should be sued," he said. "Why not just hang a hammer from it and a sign that says, 'In case of burglary, break camera'?"

"Better lit than you might expect, though," Theo observed.

"Run it again, please, Astur," I said.

As the burglar raised his hand, I said, "Stop!" I leaned forward, as if closing the distance between myself and the image could improve its quality. "He's got a tattoo."

"Where?" Didi said doubtfully.

"Between the glove and the sleeve," I said. "See it?"

"I see something," Didi said, "but—."

Emile got up and went closer. "It could be a tattoo," he said.

"I just see dark spots," Didi said. "Could be anything."

"Give it to Bernie," I said. "See what she can do with it."

"Sure," Didi said, "I can do that."

"Have you been over the scene?" I asked him.

He shook his head. "We want you to see it first."

"Is there a housekeeper?" I asked the two women.

"There's a housekeeper who comes once a week," Theo said. "She's never been inside the safe room, or so she claims—didn't even know it was there."

"It is a tape, I assume." I directed this question at Astur. "Not a digital recording?"

She nodded. "An antique," she said. "VHS."

Like me, I thought. "Better than nothing," I said. I refrained from pointing out that it had still performed its function, right up to the end. Something to aim for.

"So do we have a list of paintings?" I said. "Or would that make it too easy?"

Wordlessly, Theo handed me a paper.

I scanned the list. Picasso's *Painter and Model* and *Fenêtre ouverte sur le rue de Penthièvre*. A Monet *Environ de Giverny*. Gaughin's *Nature morte á estampe Japonaise*. Roualt, Vuillard, Degas, Hopper, Miró. Emile hadn't warned me, and I silently cursed him. I willed my face to maintain the impassivity that I so carefully cultivated.

It wasn't easy.

I knew these paintings.

I'd stolen most of them myself.

5

"How much do they know?" I said to Emile when they'd gone. Cursing him out loud would be a waste of breath, so I didn't bother.

"Honestly, M.J., I don't know," he said.

"I'd say we were being set up," I said, "except that Dottie really died, right in front of me, and it wasn't fake. She might have just been in the way, but I'd swear that they were—well, gob-smacked—when she died."

"Bernie's doing the background check on them," Didi said. "But it's not easy, I know that."

"I know it, too," I said. "I tried myself. As far as the Web knows, Ada is a grandmother who worked for an electrician all her life and Theo lives in an apartment in Georgetown and doesn't have a life. Dottie lived an anonymous life in suburban Maryland."

"What do you make of the list?" Emile said, nodding at the paper in my hand.

"What do I make of it?" I said, exasperated. "Eight of these titles match the forgeries we have in storage. I think either Dottie was bamboozled into buying a bunch of forgeries, which is

46

certainly a possibility if her tastes ran to paint-by-number Scottie dogs—."

"Or?" Emile prompted.

"Or Dottie had the real paintings all along," I said. "The paintings we went to so much trouble to steal, only to find out that more than half of them were forgeries. I told you at the time that I had a bad feeling about the Tehran business, and I've got a worse feeling now."

I was talking mostly to Emile now, since Didi had been just a kid at the time—not even a teenager.

"Are the Iranians behind this?" I said. "They never announced the thefts. Maybe, after all these years, they've tracked down their paintings. There was that flap over the Picasso when the Swiss requested it a few years back and got turned down. The Iranians were probably embarrassed to admit that they didn't have it. Maybe they stepped up their efforts to find their missing paintings."

"But how?" Emile said. "And who made the original switch? And when? That's what I asked at the time, M.J., and I still want to know. I refuse to believe that a museum with the international stature of the Tehran Museum of Contemporary Art never owned the original paintings. Queen Farah paid top dollar for the expertise she needed to build one of the best collections of modern art in the world. Hundreds of experts from all over the world went to Tehran to see it. Some of them were bound to have had the expertise to spot the forgeries—even good ones—before the revolutionary government sent the whole collection to the basement." Most of this was for Didi's benefit, since Emile and I had been over this ground many times.

"Without a chemistry lab and special equipment?" I said. "I'm not so sure. Even your experts said they were extraordinarily good. And they were using carbon-14 analysis." I held my palms out. "But yes, Emile, on the whole I agree with you. Somebody else took advantage of the chaos in the city at the time of the revolution to make the switch. As we know, you could get just about anything with a well-placed bribe. But I'd sure as hell like to know who besides us had the expertise to get a fucking five-foot Picasso out of the building."

Emile sighed. "At least they didn't take the Ernst, as far as we know. I've always regretted that one, but in the end, we had to make choices and it was just too big."

"We got the Miró," I said, "and it was genuine."

"We should have taken the Pollock, too," Emile said. "It would have been genuine as well—too hard to counterfeit. But also too big."

"If we had," I said, smiling, "we would have averted an Iranian internal crisis."

Didi exchanged a look with Astur, who shrugged. "What crisis?" he asked.

"The painting, *Mural on Red Ground,* was loaned to the Japanese for an exhibition," I said, "in a rare show of generosity by the Iranian government. When it arrived back in Iran, the customs people seized it and held it hostage over some unpaid debt they claimed the Culture Ministry owed them. I guess the two agencies worked it out, because I read that the painting's now back at the museum."

Didi waved his hands. "Okay, okay," he said. "The history is very interesting, and possibly useful. But Ms. Underwood and Mrs. Baker are our clients, and they've hired us to recover the paintings, so that's our first job. We can worry about what happens to them when and if we get them back."

"But Didi," I said, "what if they're back in Tehran? Are we planning to steal them back?"

"Well," Emile said, "they are not likely to be back in Tehran so soon. They will not be easy to transport out of the country."

"I disagree," I said. "They could ship them out in a container of carpets bound for Saudi Arabia."

Emile frowned. "Carpets? From the U.S. to the Middle East?"

"A Wal-Mart container?" I said. "Okay, scrap that. A container of electronics. Something that might be sensitive enough to require climate control, assuming they care about preservation."

"Well," Emile said, "if we find out that the Iranians have them, we will need to reassess. But let's remember that there are fifteen paintings on the list, and only eight of them match our forgeries. I'll have someone trace the other seven titles to see if they were also in the Tehran collection. Or if they've been reported stolen from other venues."

I leaned forward. "And speaking of real paintings, are they safe?"

"Yes," Emile said. "After Didi spoke to Ms. Underwood this morning, I went to check. Everything is still there—the forgeries as well as the originals."

Didi straightened his papers and stood up.

"I know that we're not investigating the murder," I said, "but it could be related. Has anyone run background checks on the family members?"

"No," Didi said, "but you can ask Bernie to do it, if you like."

When he reached the door, I said, "It wouldn't hurt to check up on the Pahlavis, either. The queen still lives around here, doesn't she? Because she has a son and grandchildren in the area? I'm betting she's still got a bundle in a Swiss bank, and could bankroll a caper like this one without putting a dent in her flatbread budget."

"Tell Bernie," Didi said, and went out, shadowed by Astur.

Emile was also standing. "Can I help you with your crutches, M.J.?" he asked.

"Emile, she called me 'Smoke,'" I said.

He sat back down. "Who did?"

"Dottie, when she was dying," I said. "She called me 'Smoke' and squeezed my hand."

"Are you sure you heard it correctly?" he said.

"No," I said. "She was whispering. And she must have been practically blind at that point, so I'd like to think that it was some reference to the way the room looked to her. That would be easier to believe if she hadn't squeezed my hand. And she said, 'No knives. We don't need knives.'" The lowest of art thieves will cut a painting out of its frame, and Emile and I both knew that.

"You think she knew who you were," he said. "But how? You think she recognized you?"

I looked out through the tinted windows. I could see the sunlit spire of the Washington Monument in the distance and a jet trail even farther, white against the blue sky.

"When we returned from Tehran in 1979," I said, "I told you that I thought I'd seen someone watching us from a doorway of the museum. Brian didn't see them, and when we got away clean, I thought maybe it wasn't important. Maybe the watcher was just a menial worker, like a cleaner, and didn't want to get involved. It was just another piece of luck, like finding the guard sound asleep at his post. But once we found out that eight of our twelve paintings were phonies, it bothered me all over again. What if the person who was watching us was the same person who stole the real paintings and substituted the forgeries? What if she—or he—was laughing at us the whole time?" I grimaced. "Not that I would have blamed them. I would have found it pretty funny myself to watch a couple of mugs working hard to steal what I'd already stolen. On the other hand, maybe we queered their game, so it wasn't very funny after all. Their plan was to get away clean before anybody even knew that the paintings had been stolen. Who knows how long it would have taken the Iranians to notice the substitutions, with the whole collection locked up in the basement?"

"But M.J.," Emile objected. "The substitutions could have happened at any time."

We'd had this argument before, but the stakes were higher now. "Any time after the revolution, when the collection was moved to the basement," I said. "Surely it would have been too risky before then—to sneak into a gallery exhibiting one of the world's most famous collections, remove a painting from its frame, and put another in its place? I wouldn't have done it."

"Still, that leaves plenty of time," Emile said. "The revolution started in 1978 with violent demonstrations. The country was in turmoil all that year, before Khomeini returned from exile in February of '79. Surely the collections had already been moved to the basement by that time for safekeeping. I read later that they were threatened by Islamic radicals, and that during the worst of the demonstrations, people made a human chain around the museum to protect it."

I'd always admired Emile's command of historical detail and his faculty for remembering dates. "You could be right."

"We were too slow to react," he said, shaking his head. "I've always regretted that."

"You've got lots of company in that boat," I said. "But remember, that was in the days before the Internet, and before CNN. You couldn't have known much about what was going on there. The American media just wasn't that interested."

"It was my business to know," he said. "I dropped the ball."

I didn't have an answer for that.

After a moment of silence, he said, "She or he? This person you saw. You're sure you couldn't tell?"

"I couldn't tell," I said. "It was just a shadow against the light of the doorway, and then it was gone."

"But still, M.J.—to know your name," he said.

"Thirty-five years seems like a long time," I sighed. "But it was after the jobs in Pakistan and Cambodia in '77 that someone first gave me that name. What if this person guessed who I was?"

"This person might just as well have thought that Brian was Smoke," Emile said. "It was a name for an invisible agent—someone nobody ever saw."

"Yes, of course," I said. "But Brian has been dead for fifteen years, and the invisible agent has continued to be connected to certain—certain unexplainable events. And if the watcher saw my face, it wouldn't be impossible to conclude that I was Smoke."

"You're saying the watcher was Dorothy Rivers?" Emile said.

"I don't see how that could be," I said. I considered, visualized Dottie in her witch's hat, then bent over her Scotties. "No, not possible."

Emile smiled at me then. "Now, M.J.," he said, shaking his head. "What is our motto at Quixote?"

I gave him a rueful smile. "Anything's possible," I said.

6

By then it was lunchtime, so I found Bernie teaching her yoga class in the sixth-floor gym. When she'd first proposed the idea, Didi had been skeptical, but he never said no to her. The class had proven to be a big hit, and when Bernie found out that some people were skipping lunch to attend, or worse, in Bernie's eyes, bolting fast food at their desks afterward, she'd started serving a healthy lunch after the class.

I'd attended the class often myself, and I knew it wasn't for wimps. Some of our buffest employees attended, and there was just something about watching two hulks walking shoulder to shoulder down the hall with their yoga matts tucked under their arms that made me smile.

I couldn't tell who was in the room now, though, because they were in the downward facing dog position, and all I could see was a sea of derrieres. Some overachievers were going for the dancer pose, and as I watched, one of the bulkiest of these wobbled and crashed. The floor shook, but nobody reacted.

It was Spike Doroshevich. Cheek against his mat, he spotted me and mimed a scream of pain. I wiped an imaginary tear from my eye.

I stayed for lunch, and left with a new set of graffiti on my cast. I was anxious to get on with the investigation, but the yoga class and lunch buffet were a rite that couldn't be canceled except for the direst of reasons, so I had forced myself to chill out. I had to put up with a lot of compliments on my appearance that were based solely on the fact that I was wearing a dress—not, I might add, a designer dress but an abandoned shirtwaist from a case thirty years ago when I had impersonated a banker's secretary. Completing my look was a single Saucony running shoe.

After the fourth "nice dress" comment, one of the women present turned on the complimenter and said, "What is it with you guys? You never tell M.J. she looks nice when she's wearing pants, even though she does."

"I'm used to seeing her in pants," the offender objected. "I never see her in a dress. I forget she's a woman most of the time."

"That'll be the day," said another woman.

"Nice gym shorts, Stash," said a third woman to a man standing next to her.

"Same back at ya, Marker," he said.

Afterward, I stumped along to Bernie's office while she slowed her pace to match mine. We were accompanied by Archie, a lovable mutt who was one of the most enthusiastic participants in Bernie's yoga class—and just about everything else. Bernie was Haitian—thin, trim, and beautiful, with beaded black braids that clicked when she moved. She moved quickly, as a rule, with long, graceful strides, but when she was in front of a computer screen, there was a Zenlike stillness about her.

Her opening topic was my health, which was not of much interest to me.

"Seriously, M.J.," she said, "I'm going to give you some stretches for your good leg and some toe exercises for the bad one. I hope you're exercising the good one or the muscles will atrophy. It's too bad Bruce is out of town." She'd lost much of her Haitian accent to four years at Cambridge and four years of graduate work at Harvard. That was where she'd met Didi.

"The thing is," I said, annoyed to open my mouth and find I was out of breath. "The thing is, if we don't move fast on the Rivers business, the paintings will leave the area and then they'll be harder to trace."

She held the door of her office for me, and waited for me to catch up and pass through it. She had a corner office off the computer command center on the fifth floor. Light poured in, only partially blocked by a collection of plants, hanging and otherwise.

"If they're not gone already," she said. "Yes, I know."

"Do you think they're gone already?" I asked.

"No way to know." She wheeled a chair over for me. "Depends how far they were going, I suppose. Where would you like to start?"

"Let's start with the video," I said. "That's our best clue so far."

She ran the video and we watched it on the monitor. Archie put his blond head in my lap and I scratched behind his ears, but when he offered me his belly, I shook my head. No belly rubs until the cast came off. I couldn't bend over that far.

I showed Bernie the place where I'd spotted the tattoo, and she began working to enhance the image, first by digitizing it and then by running it through various filters. I didn't have high hopes about the results, but as usual, she exceeded them.

"That's the best I can do," she said at last.

We stared at two curved lines and three small diamonds.

"Write down what it reminds you of, and I will, too," she said. "Write down anything that comes to mind. Then I'll rotate it and we'll do it again. When we're finished, we'll compare notes."

This was one of Bernie's tactics, and I'd found it useful in the past. Once somebody starts theorizing, it tends to close off the options for those listening, until they can't see anything other than what the first speaker saw.

When we began, I was fairly certain that we were looking at part of a face, a kind of caricature. But when she'd turned it 180 degrees, I lost my certainty, because now I saw waves and the prow of a boat, with three seabirds suspended above the prow. When she returned to the first image, which really did look like a face, I reported my guesses.

"I see both possibilities," she said when I'd finished. "But I think it's Persian calligraphy." She turned the image 180 degrees again.

"You're right!" I said, because now that she'd said it, that's exactly what it looked like. "Can you read it?"

"No," she said. "Can you?"

I shook my head. "My crash course in Farsi was a long time ago," I said. I'd had many occasions since to use Arabic, but although Farsi uses the same writing system, that system only supplies the short consonants and long vowels, relying on the reader to supply the rest of the sounds.

"My Farsi is too rusty as well," Bernie said.

"Do we know anyone who can?" I said.

"Probably," she said. "But let's try something else first." She typed "Persian tattoos" into the search box and hit Enter. "Maybe we'll get lucky and discover that our perp isn't very original."

She clicked on one of the many Persian tattoo sites and began scrolling down the list of sample phrases. Since Arabic is cursive, and calligraphers all have different styles, it seemed hopeless to me. I saw several examples with three seabirds as Bernie blew past them.

She went back to the list and clicked on another site. Then she stopped.

"There it is," she said, and pointed.

The site illustrated the same phrase in several different calligraphic styles. In one example, the three seabirds were clustered together, while in another, they were separated, two on one side and one on the other. It turned out that there were two additional seabirds we hadn't been able to see, hidden by the thief's sleeve. In one example, they trailed the ship and in the other floated alongside.

I read the caption aloud. "Do not fear."

Bernie and I grinned at each other. "We'll see," she said.

"That was too easy," I said. "Now all we have to do is find an Iranian with that tattoo, which is apparently popular."

"Or a non-Iranian," she said.

"It occurred to me that the Iranian government might be trying to get the paintings back," I said. "But in the first place, how would they know where to look? I didn't know, and Emile didn't know. Of course, it could have been an inside job all along, and someone finally copped to it, under duress or not. That would make sense, since most art heists are inside jobs. But even supposing someone told them where to look, it doesn't seem like the most opportune moment to try burglary, with Kerry negotiating a nuclear deal with them in Switzerland. Why wouldn't the Iranians simply raise the issue at the negotiating table, and demand their paintings back?"

"Because they've never admitted the theft?" Bernie offered. "They didn't want the embarrassment, or the international criticism. I doubt that even the Ayatollah wanted to be accused of lax guardianship of some of the world greatest art treasures, whether he'd admit it or not. Nobody wants to look that inept. But why are you assuming that Dottie's paintings were genuine?"

"I'm not, really." I sighed. "They were probably all forgeries. Still, the fact that most of the paintings on Dottie's list came from that one collection looks suspicious, especially because the thefts were never made public, and as far as I know, aren't generally suspected. I'm trying to imagine a scenario in which a shady dealer would approach Dottie and say, 'Keep this under your hat, but some of the best pieces in the Tehran collection were stolen at the time of the revolution, and I happen to have them for sale.' I just can't. Unless he was related to the guard or someone in the Culture Ministry—which could include a lot of people, I admit—the theft story would be a coincidence, and a pretty amazing one at that. The paintings on the list included eight that I know were stolen. Others that weren't stolen, as far as I know, weren't there—the Pollock, for example, and the Warhol series of Maos."

"Okay, so what next?" Bernie said, her hands poised on the keyboard. "Shall I search the NCIC for an Iranian with a 'Do Not Fear' tattoo?"

I never ask her how she manages to have access to restricted databases like the National Crime Information Center. Once she's on the Web, Bernie is a mouse, able to crawl through the smallest openings and move freely wherever she wants to go.

"Sure," I said. I sat back and checked my watch. "But I have to go. I have a meeting with the clients at the Rivers house in an hour."

Bernie turned toward me and laid a hand on my arm. "I'm sorry for your loss, M.J.," she said. "I really am. It must have been terrible for you."

This was such a Bernie gesture. It had never occurred to Emile and Didi that Dottie might have been someone I'd liked and cared about. But it did to Bernie, and I loved her for it.

"Dottie had a lot of spirit," I said. "I liked her. She might have been a bad painter, but she made a great witch." I couldn't think of anything else to say. I felt an unfamiliar stinging sensation at the backs of my eyes and fumbled for my crutches.

Bernie watched me, sympathy written all over her face. "Let me know if you need anything else," she said. "And I'm not just talking about computer searches."

On my way out, I encountered one of my least favorite people, Matt Hicks, a sandy-haired bodybuilder with a permanent smirk on his puss. He held the door open for me.

"Hey, M.J., I heard you totaled your hog," he said. "Tough luck. I hear they got these airbag suits now. You should check it out."

"I hear they can graft muscle tissue from your biceps onto your brain now," I said. "You should check it out."

His grin just grew wider. "Nice dress," he said. "Didn't know you owned any."

I considered whacking him on the shin with my crutch as I hobbled past, but decided that would be undignified.

By the time I got downstairs, Marco Antonio was waiting for me out front. I clambered in and he stashed my crutches.

"Where to?" he said.

"Prince George's County," I said, and I gave him Dottie's address in Bowie.

When Marco Antonio had retired from the Postal Service at the age of 62 last year, he'd had plenty of options. He was good at making things and fixing things, including cars, and could have started his own business if he'd wanted. What he'd wanted was to drive a cab. He worked when he wanted to, and enjoyed the contact with people. He wasn't a big talker, but a good listener, and found his fares to be consistently entertaining. When he tired of them, he found a place to park and read a book. Uber was encroaching on his business, but he didn't seem to mind.

We headed out in companionable silence while I turned things over in my mind. Who had known about Dottie's paintings? The obvious answer was: the person who sold them to her. The alternative, that she had stolen them herself, still seemed implausible to me, though, as Emile had pointed out, possible. That meant that the person who had sold them to her was trying to get them back, or that someone—an underling, say, or the actual thief—knew about the sale or had found a record of the transaction. But I was still trying to wrap my head around the fundamental contradictions in Dottie's nature as I knew about them: she was a paint-by-numbers enthusiast with a secret stash of some of the world's most valuable paintings. It didn't add up. Of course, there are collectors who enjoy the thrill of possessing secret treasures, but Dottie just didn't seem the type. Surely she wouldn't have named Theo her executor if they hadn't been close friends. The obvious conclusion was that Theo was lying when she claimed to know nothing about the paintings. I pictured her in her witch's hat, grinning maniacally over her hemlock root and goat's gall, and decided that was a strong possibility.

7

Dottie's house was a two-story brick in very suburban, very upscale Bowie, Maryland. It was set back from the street and partially screened by trees. A long driveway led to an attached garage, and you could see more of the second story rising behind the garage. As we approached, we passed an odd-looking man studying a map in a blue Ford Fusion.

Marco Antonio pulled into the driveway and parked next to another car, a white Honda CRV. I opened the door and he came around to hand me my crutches.

"You don't have to wait," I said as I hoisted myself to my feet.

"That's okay," he said. "I got a book."

I turned back to protest but he'd already settled his reading glasses on his nose and was opening his book. I knew from experience that he'd lose himself in his reading and look up in surprise when I returned, whenever that was.

"It's eighty-six degrees outside," I said. "At least come into the house."

He looked around in surprise as if he'd already gone elsewhere. "I'll sit on the porch," he said, and followed me up the walk.

"Nice place," I commented, when Ada opened the door to me. I nodded up the street. "You guys know you're being staked out?"

She glanced at the Fusion. "He's hard to miss," she said, "Theo says it's like Mr. Hyde at the Grand Ol' Opry."

"Nephew or boyfriend?" I said.

"Boyfriend, we think," she said. "We're pretending we don't know he's there."

I was pulling on cotton gloves. As I swung my leg over the threshold, I took another look at her. "Hey!" I said. "You ditched the walker." She was leaning on a three-footed cane.

She nodded. "I talked my doctor into letting me use a cane instead," she said. "It's been almost three weeks, after all, and there's nothing wrong with my hip or leg. Theo's in the office."

"I'd better investigate the bathroom first," I said.

Ada made a face. "That's one of the things I hate most about being old," she said. "I can't go anywhere without investigating the bathroom."

The house had the musty smell of unoccupied places. Above it on the wall was a home security system control box. One look told me all I needed to know about the effectiveness of Dottie's security measures. A quick glance around told me that Dottie's tastes had been, as Theo reported, eclectic, but if you looked at the whole picture rather than focusing on the Victorian highboy flanked by the Chinese lacquered chest against contemporary wallpaper, it all worked. What wouldn't have worked was a smattering of paint-by-number Scotties on the wall, and I didn't see any, or anything in that category.

Ada pointed me to a small bathroom off the entry hall. When I emerged, I followed their voices down the hall. Outside the office I stopped to admire a charcoal sketch. It showed a young dancer petting a cat, and was unsigned.

"Toulouse-Lautrec?" I said.

"Don't ask me," Ada said. "I don't know anything about art."

"That would be my guess," Theo said from a nearby doorway.

I turned to her. "Genuine?"

She shrugged and turned away. "I know just enough to guess the artist," she said. "I'm no expert."

She led the way into an office, which I would have called a library, since the walls were lined with shelves, and the shelves were lined with books. I caught my breath as I realized how many of them were art books. Theo stopped next to the desk, a mammoth, sturdy, utilitarian, wood affair whose surface was covered with papers.

Following my eyes, Theo said, "It's mostly her mail. She was out of town for three weeks, and fell two days after she got home."

That meant she'd called Levesque Security and talked to Didi in the middle of unpacking and maybe checking phone mail and e-mail messages. I wondered what had put the wind up her.

I had stopped inside the door to let my eyes wander the room. There were windows on two walls. Through one I could see the expanse of front lawn I'd already met. Because I was standing, I could see through the other over an exuberant bush another stretch of lawn and then a driveway and neighboring house, neither close nor far.

"How did they get in?" I said. "Doesn't she have a monitoring service?"

Theo nodded. "They loided the front door lock, walked in, opened the control box, and disconnected the phone and power lines. It was easy."

I nodded, hiding my surprise at Theo's use of the term "loided." Lots of people have heard of using celluloid on locks, of course, and lots of people have probably heard the slang term. It just sounded odd coming from her. "Could have been easier," I said. "They could have cut a hole in the window next to the door, reached through and unlocked it." That's what I would have done. With the right tools, it wouldn't have made much noise.

Theo spread her arms in exasperation. "I'd been after Dottie for years to upgrade her security system. And I didn't even know about the secret art gallery, I was just thinking about the Toulouse-Lautrec, if that's what it is, and a few other pieces of art, as well as her jewelry."

"She always put it off," Ada agreed, "until lately."

I turned my attention to the dirt on the carpet.

"So you're not a secretary," Ada said.

"What are you—like, an investigator of some kind?" Theo said.

"Not really," I said. I looked up at them. "What are you?"

"What do you mean?" Ada said.

I shrugged as well as I could shrug with crutches jammed under both shoulders. "I think you know more than you let on, that's all," I said. I wasn't ready yet to discuss the Tehran business with them.

"You think *we* stole Dottie's paintings?" Ada looked more bewildered than offended.

I laughed. "No, Addie," I said. "If I thought that, I'd be seriously underestimating your intelligence. If you'd stolen the paintings, you'd hire a much less competent firm than Levesque Security to attempt to recover them. I think they're really gone and I think you want them back."

I extracted a digital camera from my pocket and snapped a few pictures of the desk, working my way around it awkwardly. Lots of bills, catalogs, advertisements, and pleas for donations, but I spotted some foreign stamps among the piles that bore further investigation.

I felt small prickles of anxiety in the room behind me.

"Why do you want pictures of her desk?" Theo asked.

"No reason," I said. "Part of the crime scene. We might find out they took something from it."

I opened a file drawer in the desk, trying my best to appear only casually interested. "What didn't they steal, when they had the opportunity?" I said. "Good to know that, too." The files were labeled in a neat hand, but I couldn't read the labels without bending over or sitting at the desk, and I couldn't do either without making a production out of it. I'd have to come back to them. I opened the drawers on the other side for a quick look, and then the center drawer. I got lucky. Lying casually among the date-books, checkbooks, pens, and pencils, in the back of the drawer, were several small, familiar green and blue books—U.S. passports.

"I don't think they took anything else," Theo said. I could feel her eyes on my hand as I lifted the passports and flipped through them. "They were pretty focused on the safe room."

"But they didn't go right to it," I said, and pointed. "Which means they didn't know where it was."

As they turned their eyes to the dirty trail of footprints to the desk, I pocketed the passports.

"They must have searched the desk. They looked in other rooms, too," I said. "Or rather, he did."

"You think they're all the same size—the footprints," Theo said.

"Don't you?" I said.

"Yes," she said, "I do."

"Aren't you going to measure them," Addie said, "and collect dirt in an evidence bag?"

"And use your magnifying glass and tape measure?" Theo added, though her mouth was twitching.

"Not my top priority," I said. I snapped a few photographs of the carpet. "By the way," I added, not looking up, "you mentioned that the nephew and niece expected to inherit the paintings, but nobody asked if they were right." Now I did look up. "Assuming we find them, who gets them?"

"It's the strangest thing," Ada said.

"They go to the Iranian government," Theo said.

"Ah," I said.

Nobody else spoke for a minute. Then Theo grinned and said,

"Marge, I have a feeling you're going to be a whole lot of fun to hang out with."

Someone's watch beeped and we all three patted our pockets in search of pills.

I made my way to the closet, where I stood before the gaping hole in the steel door to the safe room. As Theo had reported, the burglar had simply used an acetylene torch on it. The opening was a little shorter than I was and rather narrow. The thief had been impatient—or short.

"Not much room," I observed.

"A clue!" Ada said, with apparent delight.

"Can you get through it with your crutches?" Theo said. "Want to borrow my cane?"

I traded her crutches for cane, ducked, and slipped sideways through the opening. Picasso would have gone sideways as well, I reflected. Theo handed my crutches through, and I got them into position and turned to survey the safe room. I felt a bit like an Egyptian archeologist breaking through to a burial chamber, only to find that it had long since been stripped of its treasures.

A motion sensor had apparently triggered the lights. What I was looking at were four blank walls, painted off-white and decorated with empty picture hooks. The room was long and narrow, perhaps because the house wrapped around it to make it undetectable from the outside. That meant it was not an especially good room for viewing, especially of two five-foot Picassos, only for storing. I made a slow circuit of the room, counting the places where the paintings had hung, identifiable because the walls had faded around them. I could tell where the Picassos had hung from the size of the darker rectangles on the wall. Eleven faded rectangles. Damn.

I did it again. Eleven. Four fewer than the inventory contained. Had four of them stood against the wall? Been stacked on the floor?

"What do you know about the four paintings on the inventory

that don't have corresponding spaces on the wall?" I asked. "Are they hung elsewhere in the house?"

"Not a thing," Ada said. She wasn't surprised; they were expecting the question. They had made their own count.

"We didn't know about the room, and we didn't know about the inventory before Dottie died," Theo said. "I suppose she could have them upstairs somewhere. We haven't seen anything down here that looks like a match."

"Or maybe she sold them since she made the inventory," Ada said.

That possibility was certainly plausible, since the inventory page had showed signs of age—some yellowing and brittleness. A black market sale of any of the paintings from the Tehran collection could have kept Dottie in paint-by-numbers Scotties for a lifetime.

In the silence that followed, I heard the air conditioning kick in, and looked around until I spotted a single register in the floor to my right, just the other side of the closet wall. Then I looked around for a thermostat and hygrometer, but I didn't see any. I made a third slow circuit of the room to look, even though the room was so bare that I didn't expect to find anything. I didn't.

"What are you looking for?" Ada asked.

"Thermostat," I said. "Humidistat."

"We didn't find either," Theo said.

"So we're thinking what?" I said. "That Dottie didn't know enough to install climate control equipment? Or that she ran out of money after she built this room and never got around to finishing it? The walls haven't been painted recently. Do we think she never came in here?"

"Your guess is as good as mine," Theo said.

"I doubt that," I said. "What did you conclude?"

"She wasn't stupid," Ada said, "so she must've known."

"The control panel might be elsewhere," Theo said. "It's not in the closet, as far as we can tell, but it wouldn't have to be, would it? The system could be wireless. As long as the sensors are somewhere in the room—and they could be tiny—the controls could be anywhere."

I grinned at her. "I like that theory, Theo," I said. "I really do. My only problem with it is the age of that camera out there and the age of the door itself. Hard to believe she'd upgrade her climate control after the wireless revolution and neglect to upgrade everything else."

"I know," Theo admitted placidly. "It doesn't make sense."

"Yoo-hoo!" someone shouted in the distance. "Yoo-hoo!"

8

We all started. Ada hot-footed it to the exit, as much as she was capable of doing, and we followed her out to see who it was. I closed the closet door behind us.

A woman appeared in the door to the office. She had strawberry blond hair and a dark tan and freckles, under a sun visor. She wore a knit shirt, a short printed skirt that looked like a tennis skirt, tennis shoes, and peds with pom-poms protruding at the heels.

"Oh, phew, I'm glad it's not burglars," she said with a friendly smile. She gave her forehead an exaggerated swipe with the back of her hand. "I'm Judy from next door. I saw the cars and thought I ought to investigate. The taxi's just sitting there, and so I thought maybe you were Dottie's relatives. Listen, I am so sorry for your loss, I really am. Dottie was one of my favorite people. Maybe a little eccentric, but who isn't?"

We introduced ourselves as friends of Dottie's, and Theo identified herself as Dottie's executor.

"So you're the executor?" she said to Theo. "Well, I expect Dottie did that because she knew that Steve and Monica would fight like dogs over a bone. And they will, too—you wait and see. I don't envy you your job."

"Do you have a key to the house?" I asked her.

"No," she said, "I never did. I told Steve that the other day."

"Steve was here?" I said. "When was that?"

"Oh, let's see, I guess it was Saturday," Judy said, looking thoughtful. "He wanted to get into the house. I told him that the name of the security company was in a decal by the front door, so he should probably call them and explain the situation and ask them to let him in. I did think it was odd that he didn't have the keys from Dottie's purse, but maybe Monica had that, I don't know."

Nobody was going to mention the homicide investigation to Judy, so we didn't interrupt.

"I thought she might want me to have a key, you know, so I could check on things while she was gone—especially after she had that leak in the basement, and they practically had to dig up the whole backyard," Judy said. "And you know one time when our other neighbors, the Haddads, were out of town, their roof leaked and they didn't know a thing about it until they came home and found everything soaking wet. So now I have a key for their house, and the Baumgardners', because I feed their cat Trixie when they're away.

"Anyway, I offered to keep a key for Dottie, but she said no. And I wasn't going to press her, you know. I took one of my keys over and told her I wanted her to keep it, but she said she didn't want the responsibility." Judy spread her ringed fingers in a gesture of repudiation, perhaps in imitation of the recalcitrant Dottie. "She told me that I could leave it under her doormat if I wanted to, since no burglar would ever guess that it was a key to the house next door."

I saw Ada glance at Theo, pressing her lips together to suppress laughter, and I looked away before I caught the contagion.

Judy continued, oblivious. "Well, I guess she had a point about that. But I always thought it would've been a good idea if I kept a key for her, and especially after she fell and ended up in the hospital. I went over there to see her and asked if she didn't need her plants watered or anything, but she said she didn't have any plants. I guess I knew that because she'd just been out of town for a few weeks. I went to see her in the nursing home, too, and I felt so sorry for her, with that bad cold on top of everything else. But still, I was shocked when she died. I said to my husband, 'That woman did not look like she was at death's door.' And he said you just never know, and that's right, you don't."

She turned her attention to the desk, and before any of us could get a word in edgewise, she continued. "And now, would you look at that mess. I would have come over here and tidied things up for her. I wouldn't have minded a bit!" She began straightening things into piles.

Theo looked at Ada and Ada said, "Oh, just leave it Judy, really! We have to go through it all anyway."

"Oh, I know, I'm just obsessive," Judy said, and gave us an apologetic smile. "I drive my husband crazy." She stopped straightening, but clearly not without regret, then took a resolute step away from the desk.

While she was waging battle with her impulses, I said, "You said you thought we might be burglars. Do you have a burglary problem in this neighborhood?"

"Oh, I was just kidding!" she said. "I didn't really think you were burglars."

"Maybe we should sit down in the living room," Ada said. "My hip is hurting, and Marge looks so uncomfortable I'm getting sympathy pains in my shoulders."

So we moved to the living room and sat down. The furniture was colorful and comfortable, a mixture of styles. I spotted two small paintings that warranted further investigation on the wall next to the fireplace, but even at a distance I could tell they weren't paintings of dogs. Were they masterpieces of modern art? I doubted it.

"I know you didn't really think we were burglars," I said to Judy, who was momentarily silenced by the novelty of the situation. "But I'm asking because we think somebody might have tried to break in while Dottie was away."

Her eyes widened. "No!" she said. "Really? I haven't heard about anything like that around here for a while. I saw all that dirt on the carpet. Are you telling me somebody got into this house?" She looked up, her whole face creased with anxiety.

"No, they didn't get in," I said. "We think the dirt must have been from a carpet installer Dottie had come in to measure for new carpet."

"Well," Judy said indignantly, "I sure wouldn't buy carpet from a company that would track that kind of dirt all over the place. But why do you think somebody tried to break in?"

"Footprints around the outside of the house," I said. "Handprints on some of the windows, things like that."

"My goodness!" Judy said, and pressed her own palms to her chest.

"We're wondering about the Fourth of July. It's a big night for burglary," I said, making it up as I went along. Now that I'd seen the neighborhood, my theory about the Fourth was evolving. "Were you home on the Fourth?"

"No, we weren't," she said. "We took the kids downtown to see the big show on the mall. They're really getting too old for it, but we like to keep up the family tradition. And now you're saying that you think—."

"It's just a theory," I said. "Do you know if any of your neighbors were around that night?"

"Well," she said, eager to play the role of expert, "the Jensens are out of town. That's the house on the other side. But the Barlows —they're kind of across the street and a little down—they always have a big family cookout and set off fireworks and all. The Baum-gardners—they're across the street in the other direction—I think they go to their daughter's house. I don't know about the Haddads —that's my other neighbors, I told you about them—but seems like she might've told me they went into the city. On the other side of the Jensens, that house is for sale, so nobody's living there. They moved to Florida for his business. I told my husband I sure hope they sell that house soon, because I don't like having an empty house in the neighborhood. It attracts the kind of people you're talking about. Maybe I'd better call the police and have them check it out."

"I'm sure the realtor keeps a close eye on it," Theo said.

"I guess so," Judy said. "Lord, I hope so!"

A clock bonged the hour, startling us all, and launched Judy off the couch.

"Look at the time!" she said. "I'm late to pick up the boys." She turned an earnest face on Theo. "I'm so glad to have met you all, and I'm sure I'll see you again. Oh!" She raised her hands. "Of course, I'll see you at the funeral. Do you know when that will be?"

"We don't know yet," Ada said, and I could see that Theo was happy to let her field this one. In fact, the two of them worked together like lifelong teammates who wordlessly triaged all incoming communication according to the expertise of each. Theo would have mentioned the autopsy, cast a pall on the conversation, and raised the prospect of a murder investigation, all of which would have delayed Judy's departure. "But we're hoping this weekend."

"Well," Judy said, "you be sure and let me know if you need anything at all. I'm right next door." She had gained the hall, looked toward the door, and turned back. "By the way, which one of you belongs to that handsome gentleman on the front porch?"

I had struggled to my feet. "I do," I said. "He gave me a ride."

She glanced at my left hand and smiled. "Well," she said, "if I

73

wasn't married—. I do think Latin men age beautifully, don't you think so? And he likes to read. That's a wonderful quality in a man. But he's married?"

"Very," I said. "To a woman who likes to read."

When Ada had closed the door on Judy, Theo asked, "As long as we're here, do you want to see the upstairs?"

I looked up the carpeted stairway and grimaced. "I guess I should," I said.

"He didn't go up there," Ada pointed out.

She was right; the carpet on the stairs was pristine.

Of course, there was no handrail on the cast side and I didn't think either of the other two should try to support me, so Ada went out and interrupted Marco Antonio's conversation with Judy and he came in to help me. But after all that, there wasn't much to see upstairs, just three bedrooms, two bathrooms, and a small room evidently used as an artist's studio. On an easel was an unfinished paint-by-numbers seascape, and the air was redolent with the heady odor of oil paint and turpentine. In addition to a large window that overlooked the back yard, there was a skylight that flooded the room with light.

Theo went to a circular switch of some kind on a nearby wall. "Watch this," she said.

As she turned it, the room grew dimmer, and then brighter again. But it wasn't an ordinary dimmer.

"It controls a reflective panel up there," Theo said, looking up at the skylight. "You can turn it to catch the sun. Isn't it clever?"

I looked up as well, impressed. All that trouble to illuminate all those tiny lines and numbers that went to make up a Scottie dog.

The room had a capacious set of cabinets, which I investigated. I expected them to be piled with paint-by-numbers clowns and still lifes and Parisian street scenes. Instead, I found containers of linseed oil and turpentine, trays of brushes and palette knives, several palettes and palette pads, small bins filled with tubes of oil paints, sorted by color, a bin of rags—some well-used and paint-smeared—and several cases packed with more art supplies. I also found two unopened paint-by-numbers kits. Clearly, Dottie had taken her hobby seriously.

In Dottie's bedroom, I said, "Did she own expensive jewelry?"

"Yes, she had some beautiful pieces," Theo said, "though she rarely wore them."

"Did she keep them here at home?" I asked. "If so, we should have a look, just to be sure they're still here."

"Oh, Theo, Marge is right," Ada said. "Once the house was open, the thief could have come back for the jewelry when he was wearing cleaner shoes."

I was impressed how quickly she'd anticipated the criminal mind. I nodded. "The thief could have been hired to steal the paintings," I agreed. "But he could have returned as a free lance."

"Or he might still intend to," Ada said. "We'd better put the jewelry in her safe deposit box."

Theo went into the bathroom. I followed and stood at the door, leaning against the jamb to take some weight off a crutch. She opened the cabinet under the sink.

"This will take some doing," she said. "I can get down, but I may not be able to get back up without help."

Marco Antonio helped her into a kneeling position. She reached in and then handed me an old Kotex box. I dug under the top layer of pads and saw a tissue-wrapped bundle.

"Ingenious," I said.

"Not that effective against women burglars," Theo said, "but most burglars aren't, and most men won't touch a box of sanitary pads, not even if they know that the owner is too old to need them."

She had dug a pocket knife out of her back pocket and opened it. She removed a can of cleanser and a container of toilet bowl cleaner from the cabinet and set them on the floor. Then she leaned in, and we heard scraping sounds and the dull thud of wood falling on wood.

She handed me a black leather jewelry case and I took it into the bedroom to lay everything out on the bed.

I'm not a big fan of jewelry, but it took my breath away.

I associate expensive jewelry with gaudiness and flash, the impulse to wear it with a desire to arouse envy. But Dottie's pieces weren't like that. There were emeralds, rubies, sapphires, and diamonds, but never in such numbers that they detracted from the exquisitely designed settings.

"Oh, I remember this one," Ada said. She picked up a brooch of graceful lilies, each set with a single pearl at the end of its pistil. "I always liked it." Her voice had thickened, and tears glistened in the corners of her eyes.

But I had been drawn to something else—a gold chain with a pendant. The pendant was a bird, set with diamonds and yellow stones.

"That was her favorite," Theo said, nodding at it.

I could see why. "What are the yellow stones?"

"Sapphires," Theo said.

"I didn't know they came in yellow," I said. I set the necklace on the bed. "I wonder, though, whether she would have made a good target for an experienced jewel thief."

Ada said, "Yes, these pieces are so unique that they could never be resold. The stones would have to be removed and the settings melted down." She sighed. "That would be a terrible shame."

Theo was examining what appeared to be an emerald ring in a contemporary abstract design. "The stones are worth a lot, though," she said. "They're almost perfect, every one of them. Dottie knew her gemstones."

I photographed the lot, paying particular attention to the little bird. Then I turned to Theo. "Tell me she left them to you, or her church, or her local humane society," I said. "Anybody but her relatives."

Theo smiled. "To Addie and me and three other friends. The goldfinch goes back to the person who gave it to her."

While they packed everything up again, Marco Antonio helped me down the stairs. I knew that I had a little time because Theo would be only marginally faster coming down the stairs than I had been. I had Marco Antonio stand guard at the office door while I took out the passports and flipped through them. None was current, but I wasn't looking for a current one.

The earliest one was for "Dorothy Anne Rivers," but later she became "Dorothy A. Rivers Jemison" before returning to "Dorothy Anne Rivers" for the rest of her travels, which were, surprisingly to me, extensive.

Even more surprising: Dottie had traveled to Iran four times in 1977, the year that the Tehran Museum of Contemporary Art had opened, and 1978. She had never stayed for less than a week. Her last visit had been in December of 1978, less than two months before the shah left the country and Ayatollah Khomeini returned from exile. She had worked for an art publisher, she'd told me. Had the publisher negotiated a deal with the Tehran museum to feature its collection in a book? That could explain Dottie's frequent visits and long stays.

Then, in mid-February of 1979, the month of the ayatollah's return, there it was: a stamp from the Turkish government. Maybe she'd made a last clandestine visit to discuss the book project. Or maybe she had traveled to Turkey in conjunction with the theft of eight paintings from the museum, perhaps to negotiate with the thief or the thief's agent—a dealer, say—and arrange for the paintings' safe transit out of Turkey. It was a purchase she could have arranged during a previous visit.

Or maybe she was the thief. If she'd wanted to get into Iran in those turbulent days, she would have had to choose between

Turkey and Saudi Arabia as the closest friendly nations to Tehran. Saudi dress for women offered concealment but restricted mobility. She chose Turkey. It's what I would have done.

In fact, it's what I had done. I had a similar stamp in my passport from March of 1979 to prove it.

The second stamp on the same page was for March 17th, 1979. Dottie had left Turkey two days after I'd stolen twelve paintings from the Tehran museum.

Marcus Antonio cleared his throat and I slipped the passports back into the drawer and ran a hand through the mail on the desk.

As they entered the room, I said, "When do the heirs meet with the attorney to read the will? Or should I say 'family members'?"

Theo grimaced. "Wednesday," she said. "Can't wait to get that over with, though the aftermath is likely to be worse. They do inherit something, just not as much as they're expecting."

"I'm sure they don't know what Dottie was worth," Ada said.

"I'm sure they don't," Theo agreed. "But they have suspicions inflated by expectations, which means they might come close."

"Dottie had been married?" I said. "Everyone calls her 'Mrs. Rivers.'" This probably sounded like a non sequitur, but it wasn't. I was trying to figure out where a secretary for an art publisher got the dough for a house in Prince George's County, an art collection, and a jewelry case full of dazzlers, not to mention frequent foreign travel.

"She was married for a few years in her early thirties," Theo said. "I don't think he's even in the picture anymore, thank god. We don't have to track him down."

With her usual perceptiveness, which bordered alarmingly on mind-reading, Ada remarked, "You know, Marge, Dottie was very smart about investment. She inherited some money from her parents, and she managed it brilliantly. I always went to her for investment advice."

Theo agreed. "She really understood stocks and bonds and all that jazz. She gave great advice."

"And she lived modestly, really," Ada said. "She spent money on travel, because she liked to go places, but that's about it."

Except, I thought, for a collection of the world's most valuable paintings.

But then, maybe she hadn't paid for those.

9

We were tooling down New Hampshire when a particularly obnoxious sound cut into my thoughts. A Harley pulled in front of us. I saw another in the rearview mirror as I turned my head to the right, where a third Harley was keeping pace. They all wore black full-face helmets.

The rider to my right pointed at me. Then he cupped his hand to his ear, and pointed at me again.

I slid down my window.

"Turn your damn phone on, M.J.," he said. I recognized the voice of Harley John, which meant that the other two were Harley Dave and Harley Dan. "Didi wants to talk to you."

I fished my phone out of my pocket and turned it on. I was an old dog resistant to new tricks, but I'd finally trained myself to keep my phone charged and turned on while I was in the field. I still resented it, because half the time I was traveling through the back of beyond with hundreds of miles of scrub or desert or hills between me and the nearest cell phone tower. But it was equipped with a GPS tracker that would send a signal whether the phone was turned on or not, as long as it was charged. I did not turn it on when I was home in the District.

I had five messages from Didi, so rather than listen to all of them, I called him. The Harley Trio roared off.

"Oh, good," Didi said, "they found you. Listen, we want to give you a progress report and hear what you saw at the house, but Bernie says you'll be tired and want to go home, so we're coming to you and bringing dinner."

"I think Fina's making something," I said.

"She's making gazpacho," he said, reminding me yet again that I should never underestimate his intelligence-gathering capabilities. Or more likely, Bernie's intelligence-gathering capabilities. "We're bringing things to go with."

"Okay," I said.

"Bernie says we should give you time to recover," he said, "so we'll be there at seven."

Until he said that, I hadn't realized how tired I was. In spite of my age, I hadn't fully adjusted to living in the body of an old lady, but my injury was forcing me to face my limitations. I went home and crashed, and Bernie woke me up just after seven when everyone had arrived and the food was on the table. Stella and Audrey, my two cats, were nowhere in sight, and I suspected they'd gone downstairs to keep an eye on the dogs.

"You missed your physical therapy today, didn't you?" Bernie said shortly afterward. "We can't let that happen tomorrow."

I was sitting in an armchair in the living room with my leg propped up on a hassock. Bernie was inserting a pillow under my ankle to elevate my foot. Audrey, the black shorthair, was perched on the back of the chair, giving the fish eye to the oblivious Archie and Maisie. I suspected that Stella, the brown tabby, was busy plotting her assault on the food table.

My living room, like the rest of my house, was comfortable and utilitarian, not stylish. The walls were off-white, and the furniture, mostly beiges and browns, said that the person who lived here had no interest in home decoration, and little time for furniture shopping. The colors had been chosen because they were easy to match and would stand up to muddy paws and hairballs.

"I wouldn't say I 'missed' it," I said.

Didi stood by with one of those footed trays I associated with breakfast in bed in old romantic comedies set among the upper crust. He fitted it over my lap.

"Bernie's right," Emile said. "We can't afford to have you on the injured reserve list for long."

After I'd taken a few bites, Bernie passed me a mug shot. "We think this is our man," she said.

She'd identified him not through the NCIC, but through some of her local contacts.

"His name is Farjad Ghaznavi," she said. "The tattoo is described in his jacket. He's some kind of distant cousin to the Pahlavis. His specialty is burglary, but he's never gone after anything like this before. Big-screen HDTVs are more his line."

"So you think he's working for the Pahlavis?" I said. "Somebody told him what to steal because he didn't take the Toulouse-Lautrec that was hanging on the wall even though he passed it more than a dozen times."

"Probably," she said.

"But a guy like that—," Emile said. "He could be working for the highest bidder." Emile's look was elegant casual, as was Didi's. I was willing to bet that their clothes would survive the encounter with the gazpacho, while mine, already rumpled from the impromptu nap, wouldn't.

"Sure," Bernie said. She wore a pale green pantsuit made from a fabric that flowed like water when she moved. "Open mind and all that. However, as it happens, another Pahlavi cousin is visiting from Fort Worth, Texas, where he owns a drilling business and gives lavishly to the arts. He also owns a hundred-acre ranch."

She passed me another printout, a newspaper group shot of smiling arts patrons decked out for a gala.

"How'd you find that out?" I said. "And when?" Involuntarily, I glanced up at the clock. I'd left Bernie at 1:30, six hours ago. But I'd talked to Didi at 5:30, and they must have already known all this.

"Jonas and Spike went dog-walking," Didi said, using another Quixote expression. Archie and his sister Maisie were pets, but they were highly trained working dogs, too, and they had seven counterparts who lived part-time at a kennel at the Levesque building and part-time in a kennel in the Levesque warehouse complex. These dogs were so skilled, in fact, that two of them, Doc and Grumpy, boasted passports more decorated than mine.

"Because of the tattoo, I put Lafitte on Queen Farah's house and Doroshevich on the son's," Didi continued, "not long after you left, before we I.D.ed the burglar. It seemed like a smart thing to do."

"We got lucky, let's face it," Bernie said. "Jonas sent me a photo a little after four. The passenger was Farah Pahlavi and the driver was the cousin, Sami Rouhani. All luck. If he hadn't been driving, we wouldn't have gotten such a good shot of him."

"We put Childers on Ghaznavi," Emile said. "He's still living at his LKA. And we sent Sanchez to help Lafitte out with the cousin."

"The paintings could be long gone," I said.

"We should know in a few days," Didi said. "If nothing happens, we'll give it up and try something else."

"But in the meantime, we can't afford to put all our eggs in one basket," Emile cautioned, ever the voice of reason. "The burglar could have nothing to do with the Pahlavis."

My own report seemed anticlimactic after theirs, except for the confirmation that Dottie had traveled to Iran in 1977 and 1978 and to Turkey in the winter of 1979.

"I'm still finding it hard to believe that she could have had anything to do with the thefts," I said.

"But why?" Emile said. "You and I both know, M.J., that it would be a mistake to judge the past of old people like us by their present."

"It's those damned Scotties," I said. "I can't get past them. Dottie seems now like a bundle of contradictions. Anyway, it's really too bad she didn't call us in earlier. Archie could have got past that security system with one paw tied behind his back."

Archie heard his name, looked up, and gave his goofiest grin. But I still thought he could have outsmarted what passed for security at Dottie's house.

"You're just reluctant to give up your pet theory," Emile said.

I looked at him in surprise. "What's my pet theory?"

"You don't remember?" he said. "You thought at the time it was Birdman."

"Oh, that," I said. "No, I always thought it had to be an inside job—someone with access to the paintings in order to copy them. I thought it was the museum staff. But if it was an outside job, I thought it had to be Birdman. You said it wasn't his style."

"Well, it wasn't," Emile said. "He'd never been known to cover up his thefts by leaving forgeries in their places. Besides, he was primarily a jewel thief, not an art thief. The art he stole was always collateral damage."

"You're probably right," I said, and then smiled. "But it had that certain something about it, didn't it? The flashiness of it. I mean, the total secrecy—that was what was flashy about it. By the time anybody figured it out, they wouldn't even know when it had been done. And on that scale?" I shook my head. "I don't like to think about what happened to the guard afterward."

"You're getting soft in your old age," Emile said, as he fed a piece of bread to Maisie.

"Did you find out any more about the two women, M.J.?" Bernie said. "I haven't had time to work on them, or on Dottie's family connections, with everything else going on."

"Not really," I said, "but there's something shady about them."

"Why do you say that?" Emile said.

"They're not surprised by the things they ought to be surprised by, given their background," I said. "It's not just that they follow my explanations, they're two jumps ahead of me. When I said that Dottie's jewels might make a poor target for a jewel thief, it was Ada who explained why."

"You think they're crooked?" Didi said.

"Well, they could be government agents," I said. "But if they were, why would they need us?"

"Everybody needs us," Didi said.

"Yes, but not everybody knows it," I said. "Especially government agents."

The conversation turned to other things. By nine o'clock, I was struggling to keep my eyes open, and Bernie was preparing the boys for departure, when Didi's cell phone rang.

"Childers," he said, and answered it. "All right," he said into the phone after listening for a few minutes. "Stay on him."

He hung up and pressed a few more buttons. "Where are you?" he said into the phone. Then he said, "Childers is tracking Ghaznavi. They appear to be headed to Baltimore." He listened, then said, "Yes, probably. We're right behind you." He put his phone back in his pocket.

My eyes now fully open, I said, "Baltimore? They're moving the paintings by ship?"

"We can only hope so," he said. "I'll call Lafitte from the car in case it's a decoy—or nothing at all, of course."

I struggled to my feet. "Let's go," I said.

They all looked at me.

"M.J., you're exhausted," Bernie said.

"Not as exhausted as I was five minutes ago," I said.

"She can sleep in the car," Didi said. "Let's go."

"M.J, can I borrow your car?" Bernie asked. She would go back to the command center, where she had the resources to support the operation.

I picked up the key from the kitchen counter and tossed it to her. Then we were out the door.

"Don't let her take any risks with her bad leg," Bernie said to our backs as she headed for the garage.

Didi waved a hand in acknowledgment, but I doubt he even registered the comment.

Like mine, all Levesque Security and Quixote phones are equipped with a GPS that can be monitored from the control center or from another Quixote phone, as long as that phone isn't blocked. It was a useful security precaution, especially for Quixote, in case the extricators needed to be extricated. Didi would now use Childers's phone to track him. His mind was already on the road.

"You know the problem with luck," Emile said, as the Jaguar woke up and began purring.

I propped my throbbing leg on the back seat and made an effort to keep the pain out of my voice.

"Yeah, yeah," I said. "It always runs out."

10

I woke up. The car wasn't moving. It was bathed in a weird purple light, as if an alien spaceship hovered overhead.

"Are we there?" I said. I pulled myself upright and checked my watch, though I hardly needed to look to know that I was overdue for my pain meds.

I now realized that my foot was in someone's lap—Rafael Sanchez's. He grinned at me. "Nice nap?" he said.

Didi and Emile were gone.

"What's up?" I said. I fished my pill box out of my pocket and popped a couple. I could smell sea air under an acrid petrochemical overlay and a rich bouquet of other odors—tar, hot metal, automotive paint, mold, industrial cleaning fluid. We were in a deserted lot lit by dazzling halogen lights. We were parked next to a small cinderblock building, some kind of office. To our left was another lot filled with row upon row of small white SUVs, and to our right a mausoleum constructed of brightly colored shipping containers. I could hear the sounds of a freeway coming from that direction, but the stacked containers blocked the view. There were other sounds, too—the clank and hum of machinery, the scrape of gears being shifted, occasional shouts. The Port of Baltimore never sleeps.

"No thanks," Rafael said. "I just ate. But hey, thanks for offering. Nice dress, by the way." He turned to point out the window. "They went thataway—Didi and Emile. Our targets are working in a warehouse maybe three blocks away."

I felt dismay grip my chest as I looked in the direction he was pointing. Three blocks might as well be three miles in my present condition. I would have to stay put.

"Doing what?" I said.

"Not sure," Rafael said. "We're hoping to get somebody close enough to find out."

"Ghaznavi and Rouhani are both there?" I asked. "Otherwise, you wouldn't be here."

"Yep," he said.

Didi and Emile reappeared and got into the car.

"We'd better move it before the cops find us," Didi said. "I saw a better place to park not far from here."

We all knew that if the cops found four people sitting in a Jaguar at the port late at night, they'd pick us all up and take the car apart looking for drugs.

"Did you see anything?" I asked.

"We couldn't get close enough," Emile said. "They have two armed men standing guard outside. And the windows are covered."

"What we could really use is a climber," Didi said.

We all contemplated my bum leg in silence.

Didi said, "As it is, our only chance would be to wait for the doors to open, throw a smoke bomb, and yell 'fire!'"

"And we'd have to take out the guards in order to do that," Emile said, "and go in wearing gas masks."

Didi looked at him. "It wasn't a serious suggestion," he said.

"One never knows," said his father.

Given the clients' desire for secrecy, they both knew that we

88

couldn't afford to call attention to ourselves with a dramatic rescue operation.

"You'd have to get too close to use a taser," I said. "But a tranquilizer dart would do it. You could get both guards down before they knew what hit them."

The two men looked at each other.

"Well?" Emile said.

"What do you mean, 'well'?" Didi said. "You were supposed to pack the tranquilizer darts."

"No, you were supposed to pack the tranquilizer darts," Emile said.

"Never mind," I said.

Didi started the car and drove a short distance on a winding path to a crumbling warehouse with old fashioned garage doors on tracks. One had already been raised, and he slid the Jaguar inside.

"Let's hope this structure survives the night," Emile said.

We rolled down the windows but the car quickly grew stifling. Outside there had been a breeze coming in off the ocean, but in here the air could have been trapped and heated for decades. I felt sweat pooling on my scalp and running down the back of my neck. I hated like hell to be missing all the action, but I knew that a gimpy old lady on crutches would be a magnet for unwelcome attention. All those gonzo types willing to sacrifice the success of an operation to their own adrenaline addictions would never have lasted at Quixote. The mission came first.

But now I had another problem.

"I'm going for a walk," I announced.

The two heads in the front swiveled to look at me. Two voices chorused, "I'll go with you."

"No," I said firmly. "Some things a girl's gotta do alone."

"But how will you—?" Didi began.

"Never mind," I said. "I'll manage."

"Do you have your phone?" Didi asked. "Call us if you need help."

"No," Emile said. "Call me now so that I can hear if you run into any trouble."

That was a reasonable enough request, so I complied.

Outside the warehouse I filled my lungs with cooler air. I spotted a dark alleyway across an expanse of concrete and made for it, but I had to keep my eyes on the ground to avoid tripping over what appeared to be the entrails of some gargantuan electronic beast. One wall of the alley was formed by stacks of large blue shipping containers, while the other was the cinderblock wall of yet another warehouse. The alley was dark, closed in as it was by the looming containers, but once my eyes adjusted I could just make out the place where it dead-ended in a brick wall. I headed for the corner. The fetid odor suggested that I hadn't been the first to come here for this purpose. I leaned one crutch against a wall, and used the other crutch and the wall to lower myself, thankful once again for the muscle tone in my good leg. I resolved to begin exercising it again the next day.

I struggled to my feet again, retrieved my second crutch and got it positioned under my arm without knocking it to the ground and having to pick it up. Good. I headed for the open end of the alley.

A hand clamped down on my ankle. I lost my grip on the crutch on that side and toppled over onto the body attached to the hand. I descended into a miasma of alcohol and funk.

I heard a grunt, and then a raspy voice. "You can't come in here," it said. "This is private property. This place—it all belongs to me. Don't be thinkin' you can—. I got a knife!"

With my free hand, I felt up his arm to find his chin, then gripped his throat and pressed on his carotid arteries. As soon as his grip on my wrist loosened, I pressed my hand over his mouth, but he was fighting me and he was wiry. I had no choice; I couldn't afford the commotion. I found his carotid again and applied pressure, and he went limp.

Emile was there to pick me up.

"Okay, M.J.?" he said.

"Sure," I said. I looked around and shivered. "People must live in these containers."

"Judging from the odor," Emile said, "I doubt he'll remember you when he wakes up."

I wondered if the old guy really had a knife. The odds were fifty-fifty, I figured.

I went back to the car and fell asleep. I woke up with my head on Sanchez's shoulder. The air inside the car was close and gamey. Even Emile looked wilted.

"What's up?" I said.

I realized that I'd been awakened by the crackle of a walkie-talkie.

"Childers has to fall back," he reported. "It's getting too light. We'd better get out of here, too. There must be a parking lot around here that isn't full of cars for export."

He found one, and he and Sanchez took binoculars and went off to see if they could find a vantage point from which the warehouse could be kept under surveillance. I got out to stretch my leg. Arriving dock workers gave the Jag looks ranging from suspicion to admiration to lust.

I'd found myself in many situations over the years that required patient waiting, sometimes in tight spaces and uncomfortable positions. So I'd learned to do it, but it had never been my favorite activity. And it was worse for me now, because I couldn't expect the waiting to end in action. My frustration was compounded by ignorance: I hadn't even laid eyes on the warehouse we were watching. At this point, with more people around the docks, everybody else could grab a windbreaker or old tee shirt out of the trunk and walk past the place. I remained too conspicuous.

At a little after 8:30, Didi showed up with Jerome Childers in tow.

"We need you on your motorcycle," he said to Sanchez. "They're loading a container from the warehouse onto a flatbed. We need you to follow it. We'll track you."

Emile handed Sanchez a small padded case. "See if you can get close enough to tag it," he said. Childers gave him a walkie-talkie.

"How you doin', M.J.?" Childers said as he replaced Sanchez in the back seat. He was a former basketball player who took up more space than Sanchez and I shifted my leg to give him more room. "Nice dress."

We ended up in another parking lot closer to the wharf. This one was a multi-story building, and we parked on the fourth level, overlooking the wharf. This time, I did get out and joined the others at the railing, where we could see a gray container being unloaded from a flatbed with a forklift. The container was huge, maybe twenty feet high, the size of a railroad car, I realized—plenty of room for a large Picasso or two. Emile handed me a pair of binoculars, since we were still a considerable distance away. The dockside was full of gray containers with white stars on blue backgrounds and the word "Maersk" prominent on their sides. I found a forklift stacking one of them on top of another just like it, and scanned them. Our binoculars were expensive and very good, but I couldn't find an address label anywhere.

"We're going to lose it," I said. "It looks just like all the others. And it's too high for Sanchez to reach. He can't climb up there without being seen."

"Why we sent Sanchez," Childers said cryptically.

"We should've sent you," I said. "What's your vertical jump?"

He just grinned at me.

"I can't even see a label anywhere," I said. I felt every muscle in my body tight as a drumhead.

The containers were being stacked next to a cargo ship—the

Maersk Montana. It was docked under a row of mammoth cranes that looked like Legos for giants.

"I've just asked Bernie to check the ports of call," Emile said.

We watched as Sanchez, who had picked up a steel pipe and a hardhat somewhere, passed behind the containers, between the containers and the ship, looking not at them, but at something he had in his free hand. He disappeared from view and I held my breath. Our GPS transmitters were small, powerful, and very sticky. Once one was in place, it would be hard to spot and hard to dislodge. A minute passed, then two, then three, then four. Now Sanchez reappeared on the other side, and Didi's walkie-talkie crackled.

"Tell Childers he owes me a case of beer," he said. "And I want Michelob, too, not none of that Bud Lite crap."

He sauntered on down the wharf.

Childers grinned at me. "My vertical jump ain't that good," he said. "But Sanchez used to pitch in the minors."

Emile's phone chirped. "Bernie says the unit is sending," he said. "She says that the *Montana* is headed to Miami and Houston."

"So he's sending the paintings to Fort Worth," I said, "probably mixed with drilling equipment for his company."

"Let's hope so," Emile said.

"Where are Ghaznavi and Rouhani?" I asked.

Childers took the binoculars from me and scanned the area. "Don't see 'em," he said.

"Rouhani will be here somewhere," Didi said, "watching from the shadows like we are. Ghaznavi is probably just hired help. He might have been paid off and sent home."

"What we need," I said, "is somebody on that ship."

"We're way ahead of you, M.J.," Didi said. "In fact, here he comes now, the old pirate."

I turned to follow his gaze and saw a familiar figure in the crowd of dock workers. I took the binoculars back from Childers and found the figure in their sights. He wore jeans, a plain white tee-shirt, sneakers, and a Yankees ball cap, and carried a duffel bag slung over his shoulder. He was lean and muscular and tan, his dark blond hair ruffled by the sea breeze. I couldn't see his blue eyes because they were turned toward the *Maersk Montana*, but I was sure they were bright and calculating.

A large knot behind my breastbone uncoiled and I felt my whole body hang from my crutches as it relaxed. Nothing would happen to the paintings on Lafitte's watch.

"Bernie got him a union card?" I asked.

Didi shrugged. "She got him something that could pass for one, at least."

Lafitte stopped to talk to someone with a clipboard who appeared to be a supervisor of some kind. The man pointed up at the ship. Lafitte nodded and crossed to the gangway, then climbed the steps like a fly on the wall. Someone on deck sent him out of our sight, and he didn't reappear.

"He'll try to mark the container so that we can locate it by sight as well," Emile said.

"Did she actually get him a job on board?" I said.

Didi shrugged again. "If she didn't, he'll talk his way in," he said. "They're usually short-handed."

His phone buzzed and he looked at the screen. After three rings, it stopped.

"He's in," Didi said. "Let's go home."

I took one last look at the temporary home of one of the most famous art collections in the world, and hoped it had been packed with loving care. If an industrial rock bit put a hole in a Picasso, I would strangle Sami Rouhani with my bare hands.

"You be surprised," Childers said, "how many containers get lost at sea. I read that all kinds of shit gets washed overboard, and then it all collects in this one place in the ocean—like a sea of plastic."

I caught my breath. Emile put a hand on my shoulder. "Jonas won't let that happen," he said, though he and I both knew that even Lafitte was no match for Mother Nature at her worst. "Anyway, this ship is hugging the coast, and Bernie says that the weather is expected to be calm for the next week."

I relaxed a little, but I wondered whether Bernie had really said that about the weather. It would have been like her to check, but it would have been like Emile to lie when he thought a lie would be helpful.

I glanced at his face, saw the lines of exhaustion around his eyes, and felt remorseful.

"Sorry I conked out on you," I said. "I couldn't keep my eyes open."

He smiled at me. "M.J.," he said, "you just got out of a nursing home yesterday." He glanced at his watch. "Well, the day before yesterday now. And you're on pain medication. You're entitled."

"I don't feel entitled," I said. "I feel old."

"You entitled to feel that, too," Childers said.

Emile frowned at him. "If you're in her condition at her age," he said, "you'll be lucky."

Childers showed us his palms. "I know it," he said. "I'm just saying."

"Besides, you need your rest," Emile said, "now more than ever."

"Why now?" I said.

"Because you'll have to go after the paintings," Didi said. "You'll have to steal them back."

11

I was still in bed later that day when the physical therapist showed up. Fina appeared in the bedroom door and asked if I wanted her to send him away, but I said no. She helped me into a pair of shorts and a tee-shirt, I brushed my teeth and ran a hand through my hair, popped a pain pill, and was ready to go.

An hour later, I called Bernie. "M.J., you're up!" she said.

"Not only am I up," I said, "I've already had physical therapy. Bernie, this isn't going to work."

"The therapist is treating you like an old lady with a broken leg," she guessed, "not like an Amazon who's had a temporary setback."

"Right."

"And you're in a hurry to get back to your fighting form so that you can go after the paintings," she said.

"Right."

"Okay," she said. "I'm sending Jasmine over. I've just been waiting for you to say you're ready. In the meantime, take a nap. You know she'll work you over."

"Okay," I said. "Thanks."

"But tomorrow, you have to go see Lydia," she said.

Jasmine Zidane had once played goalee on the French national women's soccer team. She was five feet, ten inches of muscle and grit, topped by an impressive head of thick black hair, sometimes braided and sometimes, like now, radiating from her scalp in an explosion of corkscrew curls. She had broad shoulders on her lean frame, and long, elegant fingers good for catching balls. She showed up toting a sports bag whose contents were suggested by the tautness of the muscles in her forearm.

"You've got a weight bench, right, M.J.?" she said. Sympathy wasn't her thing. She wasn't a hand-holder. She barely registered the crutches and cast, except to give them a brief assessing glance as obstacles to work around.

Nor was she a cheerleader, as physical therapists tended to be, cajoling and praising their victims as the going got tough and the whining increased. It did no good to whine in Jasmine's presence, she didn't hear it. So I gritted my teeth and shut my mouth.

Bernie showed up an hour later with a grocery bag in each arm. She looked at me and said, "That could be enough for today, don't you think, Jasmine? She had a rough night."

Jasmine, who was in The Zone, looked a little surprised, but consented to let me crawl out from under the barbell across my chest so that I could lean my back against the wall and pant.

"What's in the bags?" I croaked.

"Your new diet," Bernie said. "Anti-inflammatory and healing. I'm going to the kitchen to talk to Fina and make you a smoothie."

I felt a little uncomfortable about this. Fina wasn't my cook, and under normal circumstances, I cooked for myself and ate out, unless Fina felt inspired to make something special, either in my kitchen or in her own kitchen next door, and share it with me. Since I'd come home from the nursing home, Fina had been making meals for me, waving off my objections. But she hadn't signed on for a dietary consultation.

With Jasmine's help, I pulled myself up and fitted the crutches under my armpits. I plastered on a brave smile that might have looked more like a grimace. I hoped that gin counted as an anti-inflammatory food.

The next day I went to see Lydia Shaw, who had started life with a name more challenging for English speakers to pronounce. She worked out of a house on a quiet side street on Capitol Hill behind the Folger. Lydia had a medical degree from Boston University and a doctorate in acupuncture and oriental medicine from the Oregon College of Oriental Medicine. She had spent two years training in China. She had studied with a medicine man in New Mexico for a year—a rare arrangement made possible by mutual respect. She had studied with healers in Botswana, Japan, Korea, and Peru. But she didn't look like an overachiever, she looked like a pleasant Asian woman of indeterminate age who wore stylish pantsuits and kept her black hair, now threaded with white, cut short in a thick wedge that just covered her ears. Yet even the most resistant of her clients—and I might have been one of them—who didn't fully believe in auras and energy fields felt something in her presence that could have been either—the brush of a palpable force against the skin.

This appointment was a favor to Bernie, I knew, because it normally took at least three weeks to get an appointment with her, whether you were a Wal-Mart associate or a senator. I handed her my original x-rays, unclear on whether she could see the broken bone with her own x-ray eyes. She looked at them, which might have meant she couldn't, but then she nodded, which might have meant she'd anticipated them.

"Let's start with forgiveness," she said.

"Forgiveness?" I echoed. I was pretty sure this was not a topic covered at B.U.

"Have you forgiven the person who caused your accident?" she asked.

"I guess so," I said.

"Really?" she said.

"Well, no," I said.

"Then that's where you need to begin," she said.

"Do I have to stop using words like 'idiot' and 'moron' to describe him?" I said.

"That would be a good start," she said.

She had me lie on her table and took me through a visualization exercise in which I embraced the idiot with light from my heart chakra. She had me visualize all of my anger and resentment as dark matter rising from my body into a dense cloud, which she cleared away with her hands. Then she made a few passes with her hands over my body. By now I was beginning to feel heavy-bodied and light-headed. Next she got out the acupuncture needles, which is the point at which I normally start to feel nervous. But I barely registered them, even the ones in my hands. She turned out the light and I drifted into sleep. When I woke up, she was massaging my shoulder. It felt great.

"All done," she said. "Come back in three days and I'll give you some exercises to do at home."

Just what I needed—more exercises.

But I left feeling better than I'd felt since before the accident. Even my cast felt lighter and the itching, which sometimes drove me crazy when I wasn't focused on the pain, had abated.

So began my healing regimen. Jasmine came every day and finished what the physical therapist started, and every few days I went to see Lydia. Fina fed me salmon and trout—a big hit with the cats—and avocado and smoothies made with pineapple, papaya, and ginger. I took turmeric supplements and a Chinese herbal "tea" that was the consistency of toxic sludge and drank gallons of green tea. I agreed to trade gin for red wine and interpreted liberally the recommendation to eat dark chocolate in small quantities, especially after a dose of sludge.

The exercise sessions entertained the cats, who enjoyed demonstrating how flexible and athletic they were. Jasmine, it turned out, had a soft spot for cats, and won their hearts by bringing them treats. Allen, the physical therapist, told me he was more of a "dog person," and clearly thought cats were more appropriate companions for little old ladies than for macho guys like himself. I didn't bring up Hemingway's cats.

At night the cats and I curled up in a chair and read Bernie's reports on Sami Rouhani. He was the founder and CEO of Imperial Drilling, a name that was no doubt supposed to remind business associates of his royal connections. The company had ridden the current fracking boom into Fortune 500 heights, though as a privately owned company with undisclosed financial records, it wasn't on the official list. Rouhani's visible private assets, including a second home outside Paris and a villa overlooking Lake Geneva, testified to his personal fortune, as did his very public gifts to Fort Worth charities, and especially to art museums in the Dallas-Fort Worth area. But our intelligence also suggested that Rouhani's lavish lifestyle had hit the major speed bump of plummeting oil prices, and he might be experiencing some cash flow difficulties.

I spoke to Theo twice on the phone. Didi had called to tell her the likely whereabouts of the paintings and to reassure her about their recovery, but I thought I should call as well. Later I'd called to update her after Lafitte called from Miami, where he was still babysitting the container, and to get the autopsy results and the funeral information. I also wanted to find out how the meeting with the relatives and attorney had gone.

"Don't ask," Theo said to the last of these questions. "It wasn't pretty. The niece gets the house, and the boyfriend was pretty adamant about seeing the contents of the vault, but I put him off, saying that we had to inventory everything before we let anybody in to see it, which was tantamount to saying I didn't trust them not to make off with the valuables, but what could I do?"

I made sympathetic noises.

"I don't know how long I can keep him out," she said. "If we don't get the paintings back soon, I'm liable to get arrested for stealing them. Do we have a timeline on recovery?"

I told her it would happen as soon as possible, but not within the next week or two, probably, because Emile and Didi wanted me to go after them.

"You?" Theo said. What followed was a long silence while she processed this piece of information.

"I'm working on it, Theo," I said. "We have to act quickly in case he plans to sell them off. I'm aware of that."

I'd learned to be comfortable with silence. I'd learned that you were much more likely to get into trouble for the things you said than for the things you didn't say.

"Unless he already has a buyer—I mean, someone else who commissioned the theft, he can't sell them too soon," she said. "He'll expect the theft to be reported."

Another opportunity to keep my mouth shut, and I took it. Rouhani knew that the paintings were stolen to begin with, so he might not expect the latest theft to be reported. But did Theo know that? And was that the real reason she hadn't called the police? How much did she know about marketing stolen art based on her background as an appraiser? I didn't know.

"Anything useful in the autopsy report?" I asked.

She said, "Cause of death was suspected poisoning by an unknown substance, causing cardiac arrest. They found—hang on, let me read it to you so I'll get it right—acute pulmonary edema, myocardial infarction with cardiac tamponade. That's—."

"Fluid buildup around the heart," I said.

"Know-it-all," she said. "You probably also know it's consistent with alkaloid poisoning, which was your theory. We'll have to wait for the toxicology results to know more."

I wrote down the funeral information.

"Though between you and me," Theo added, "I don't think Dottie would have wanted a funeral. I'm sure she'll boycott it."

On Friday, I went into the office.

"Looking good, M.J.," Spike said as he passed. "Nice dress."

I was wearing a dress that had belonged to my late mother, a navy shift with white polka dots that begged to be worn with spectator pumps, not a single Saucony with arch supports.

Annie Vivian, another agent, said, "I hear Zidane's really kicking your butt."

I stuck my head in Didi's office. He was reading a printout with his feet up on his desk, idly scratching the ears of one of our canine employees, Dopey. Archie and Maisie were snoozing on the rug. Dopey cocked her head at me.

"Any news?" I said.

"Ship got into Houston this morning," Didi said. "Lafitte marked the container with white paint, dribbled to look like seagull droppings. He also—well, marked—the container with urine so that we could use a black light to find it in the dark, if we need to. He's pretty proud of that."

I realized that I had one eye closed as I conjured up a mental image of Lafitte hanging from the side of a shipping container like a spider, aiming his pecker at a corrugated steel canvas. But probably he'd collected the urine first.

"Don't they have a lot of thunderstorms on the Gulf Coast in July?" I said. "Won't it wash off?"

"Probably," Didi said. "The ship will take a while to unload. Our best guess is that the container will be loaded onto a flat car dockside. He'll let us know. Then things will get dicey because as soon as the paintings are unpacked from the container, assuming they're in the container to begin with, we'll lose contact with them. We're trying to work out a way to tag the crates."

The challenge, I knew, was to transfer the GPS units from a farther distance than Rafael Sanchez could pitch. If the container was unloaded inside an equipment yard or warehouse, we wouldn't be able to get that close. And our GPS units were sturdy, cushioned against impact, but they couldn't be fired from any kind of gun using gunpowder."

"Blowgun?" I suggested.

"We're working on it," Didi said.

Bernie had three files for me on Dottie's family members—nephew, niece, and niece's boyfriend. I opened the boyfriend's file.

As I did, Dopey, who had tagged along to Bernie's office, wandered over to inspect my crutch. She took it between her teeth, shook it, and sent it crashing to the floor.

"Dopey!" Bernie scolded her.

"Oh, let her have it," I said. "She can't hurt it."

"You'd be surprised," Bernie said, as Dopey flopped down next to the crutch and began chewing it like a bone.

"Neil Callahan," I read aloud.

"Keep reading," she said.

I scanned the page. "Neil Calloway," I said. "Callahan's an alias? Why?"

I kept reading. "Salesman. What's he sell?"

"Flimflam," Bernie said.

I kept reading. "Son of Kevin Calloway." I looked up. "Should that name be familiar?"

"Not necessarily," Bernie said. "He worked on the U.K.'s art recovery squad in his youth. Then he went to work for the Fibbies, moved to the States, raised his kids here. Don't ask me why—the Bureau didn't used to give a shit about stolen art, though they've gotten better in the last ten years. I cross-checked the addresses. It has to be the same guy."

I turned it over in my head for a while. "But what does it mean? If the Bureau knew that Dottie had the paintings, they would have gone after her."

"Unless—," Bernie prompted.

"Unless they only suspected that she had them," I said, "since, after all, the Iranians had never reported them stolen. And besides, we weren't doing any favors for the Iranians anyway. That makes sense. But between suspecting that the paintings had been stolen and suspecting that a particular elderly American lady had them stashed away in Bowie, Maryland, there's a gap you could drive a cargo container through. How would they get to Dottie?"

"Don't know," Bernie said.

"He must've known, Neil Callahan Calloway," I said. "I've seen the niece, who's at least five years older than he is, and it's hard to believe she ensnared him with her feminine wiles."

"Does she have feminine wiles?" Bernie asked.

"Not detectable ones," I said. "So unless he's working for his dad's outfit, he must've thought that the niece would inherit the paintings, so if he married her, he'd inherit them. It could explain why he's staking out Dottie's house—he doesn't trust Theo and he thinks he's protecting his investment."

"They'd bring in a fortune," Bernie said, "even if they were sold privately to collectors. More, of course, if they could be auctioned publicly."

"So the next question is, did he decide to hasten Dottie's death?" I said. "Did he try to get to her before she could get any ideas about changing her will?"

"Do you know the terms of the previous will?" Bernie asked.

"No," I conceded. "I don't. Theo gave me the impression that Dottie reduced the size of her relatives' inheritance, but that doesn't mean they would have gotten the paintings before. In fact, now that I think of it, I have to assume that Dottie would have always made provisions for the paintings that didn't include her relatives. What could they do with them, anyway? And she wouldn't want to take the secret of their existence to the grave with her."

"You're assuming that Dottie's paintings are genuine," Bernie said, "and that her motives for stealing them were benevolent."

"No," I said slowly, "I'm not assuming they're genuine. I'm trying to keep an open mind. Sometimes I think they must be, and sometimes I think that they can't be, whether Dottie thought they were or not. But I suppose the Calloway connection makes it more likely that they are."

"Best to keep an open mind," Bernie said. "For all you know, she could have invited him over one night to see her oil paintings. Maybe he could tell they were fake, or maybe she told him they were. Maybe the son got the wrong end of the stick."

I nodded. It made sense. But it reminded me what I really wanted to ask her.

"Bernie," I said, "you remember Birdman?"

"Of course," she said.

"He still alive?" I said.

"Don't know," she said. "Want me to find out? You think he was mixed up in this?"

"Don't know. Where was he living, last you heard?" I asked.

"Italy someplace, I think," she said.

I nodded encouragement.

"Tuscany, maybe?" she said.

I fished my digital camera out of my pocket and handed it to her.

"I want to bring up the pictures of Dottie's desk and enlarge them," I said.

She plugged in the camera and scrolled through my photographs. When she got to the first one I'd taken of Dottie's desk, she enlarged it.

We studied the results, which looked like a complicated jigsaw puzzle.

"Are we looking for Italian?" she said.

I put a finger on the screen, over a stamp with a colorful depiction of a canal lined with buildings. "That one," I said.

She isolated that area of the image and opened it in another program, then enlarged it further. We both leaned toward the screen.

"The stamp's Italian," Bernie said. "Isola di Burano, not Venice. Beautiful, isn't it? But there's no return address."

"And the cancellation stamp commemorates the pope's visit to someplace," I said. "Probably not the same place the letter came from."

"Pompeii," Bernie said. "Probably not. Wonder why he went there?"

"Wonder why they felt they had to commemorate it?" I said. "Do they design a new cancellation every time he steps foot outside of the Vatican?"

"Well," Bernie said, "you can see why they wouldn't want to commemorate their prime ministers, after the Berlusconi scandal."

I became aware of wretching sounds coming from the vicinity of the rug beneath our feet. I reclaimed my now damp and slightly mangled crutch, and departed.

Like me, Emile was supposed to be semi-retired, which meant that he came in an hour later every day. He was sitting in an armchair reading when I looked in.

"M.J.," he said, "you're looking well. Fully recovered from our all-night escapade, I hope."

I sat down in the armchair across from him as he set his book on the small table between us.

"Before I risk my neck in Fort Worth," I said, "I'd like to know if the paintings are genuine."

He steepled his fingers. "You know that as far as our clients are concerned, it doesn't matter," he said. "Those are the paintings they've hired us to recover."

"I know," I said.

"How can you find out?" he said.

"I might want to go to Tuscany," I said.

He frowned. "Birdman? Do you know if he's still there? Or even among the living?"

"Not yet," I said.

"And even if he is, why would he tell you anything?" he asked. "Assuming he knows anything."

I shrugged, then winced. Shrugging hurt my shoulders, which had been sore from the crutches even before Jasmine took over my strength training.

"Well, it's up to you, of course, M.J.," Emile said. "If you want to go, go. But you might not find the answers you're looking for."

I grinned at him. "Anything's possible," I said.

12

I made my way back down to the fifth floor, where I found my pal Grace Wang in charge of the monitoring center. The room consisted of four walls of monitors watched by six staff members sitting in well-padded red-uphostered roller chairs. Every thirty minutes, they rotated to the next station, like a volleyball team, until they completed the final station and went on break for thirty minutes. Then they repeated the procedure until their four-hour shift was up. All junior staff at Levesque Security, from the secretaries and mechanics to the guards and operatives, put in their time in the monitoring center. Even the dogs, who found the room restful, wandered in from time to time. At the moment, Happy, a hyperintelligent poodle, was napping, paws up in the cartoon roadkill position, in the middle of the room.

I snagged an empty chair and maneuvered it to sit close to Grace.

"Hey, M.J., how's it going?" she said. She did not compliment me on my dress.

"Not bad," I said. "I've been better. I've been worse." At this point, my leg had begun to itch like crazy but according to Lydia, I wasn't supposed to dwell on that, just think cool, soothing thoughts.

She nodded. "Some days 'not bad' is pretty good," she said. "What can I do for you?" It was characteristic of Grace that she didn't waste time with chitchat. People who sought her out in her work area usually wanted something from her.

"I need to get into the Rivers house in Bowie," I said.

"We just installed all the new equipment out there on Wednesday," she said noncommittally.

"I know," I said. "Now I need to know how to get past it."

"Will Didi authorize it?" she said.

"Probably," I said.

She grinned at me. "But Emile wouldn't."

"Probably not," I said.

"You can't ask the client—the executor?" she said.

"Rather not," I said. "Don't know yet how far I can trust her."

"She probably says the same thing about you," Grace said.

"Probably," I agreed.

"And you'd probably rather I didn't ask Didi," she said, "but I can't do that, M.J. I would be in sooo much trouble if you got caught."

"I won't," I said.

She looked pointedly at my cast. "You planning to beat off the responding officers with your crutches? Or just pass yourself off as a crazy old lady who wandered into the wrong house?"

She reached for the phone. She spoke to Didi for a minute, then handed the phone to me.

"Let's pretend I'm the judge and you're the detective asking for a search warrant," he said. "What, specifically, are you looking for?"

I sighed. "A letter in the pile on her desk," I said. "A letter with an Italian stamp. I have a photograph of it."

"Why is it important?" he said.

"I'm trying to find out if there's a connection between Dottie and George Finch," I said. "At the time of the Tehran debacle, I thought Birdman could have stolen the paintings we were after. I still think it's possible. Bernie thinks Finch lives in Tuscany. I want to look at the letter to see who it's from."

"On the strength of an Italian stamp?" Didi said. "It could be her art dealer. It could be her former neighbor. Hell, it could be her dressmaker."

"Yes, I realize that," I said.

"And you don't want to ask Ms. Underwood to just give you the letter because you recognize how lame this theory is, and you don't want to be embarrassed," he said.

"I don't trust her," I said. "I don't know why yet, but I don't."

"M.J.," he scolded, "it doesn't matter whether we trust her or not, she's our client. If you mean that you think she's going to set you up to take the fall for a major art heist, that's one thing. But I don't see that happening here. I'm sorry, but I can't authorize it. Ask her for the letter, or give up on the idea. Or have Bernie track down Finch and go ask him if he knows Dottie. Or if he did the Tehran job. Or anything else you want to ask him. That's fine with me."

If any other security firm had been in charge of the Rivers house—well, most other firms—I would have trusted my intelligence to figure out a way around it. But I was one of the people who had helped design the Levesque system. If it had any flaws, I didn't know them.

Well, okay, I knew one. And I would just have to exploit that one. But first, I knew that I'd better get the goddamned cast off my leg.

Dottie's funeral was on Saturday, and I went to study the family members and to see who else turned up. The niece Monica was sporting a new engagement ring, and was having a hard time matching her demeanor to the occasion. The boyfriend Neil was already behaving as if he was part of the family, which was probably just as well since Monica was inattentive and Steve, the nephew, was sulking. Neil was the only one of them who spoke, and he made a charming but highly implausible speech about Dottie's warmth in welcoming him into the family. A cousin who had been close to Dottie growing up spoke about how much fun she was to be around, and Ada talked about how knowledgeable she'd been in so many areas, though the areas themselves remained vague. Julius Radcliffe-Jones, who was looking worse than when I last saw him, gave a moving tribute to her spirit of adventure as he expanded on her involvement in the *Macbeth* performance. Her attorney spoke about the loss of an old and cherished friend. And that was about it. The minister served as a kind of hired emcee who kept calling the deceased "Dorothy." Theo didn't speak.

Over cookies and punch, I went around introducing myself in hopes of finding former coworkers, but didn't find any. Judy was there, and seemed from a slight puffiness around her eyes and a balled handkerchief clutched in her fist to be one of those most affected by the ordeal. I let her unload on me for a while, silently acknowledging that she was a good person who genuinely meant Dottie well.

Then I met a dapper gentleman in a three-piece suit who turned out to be an art dealer. He had a slight German accent.

"Did you sell Dottie a Toulouse-Lautrec sketch of a dancer with a cat?" I asked.

Yes, that was one of the pieces he'd sold her. Dottie had a good eye for art, he said.

"She once told me that she'd taken a painting class in college, and discovered that she didn't have an artist's soul—that's how she put it," he said. "That was why she admired people who could paint, she said. She had tried to do it, and failed, you see, so she knew just how difficult it was."

I didn't mention the paint-by-numbers kits. To do so would fall into the category of "speaking ill of the dead."

Theo looked harried and exhausted. I patted her elbow on my

way out and gave her a thumbs-up. But I felt a pang when I realized that the last time I'd seen that gesture was during the dress rehearsal for that damned Scottish play.

On Sunday, Bernie sent me images of crates being unloaded from a storage container. The container sat on a flatcar in a yard with a lot of heavy-duty drilling equipment. Nothing else in the yard could have fit inside the crates. But a Picasso? That would have fit. More tellingly, Sami Rouhani was supervising the operation himself. The crates were being stacked on a flatbed truck that had been well padded with what looked like air mattresses.

Lafitte rode in a half-full boxcar two cars back from the container, Bernie wrote. *He tracked its location on his GPS. When the train started slowing down on the far side of Fort Worth, he hopped off and then followed it into the yard. He hid behind a piece of equipment to shoot the photos. Afterward, when the truck was almost loaded, he walked into the yard and tagged one of the crates. Don't ask me how he did it; you can ask him yourself when you see him. Didi is sending Montoya, Estevez, and Sneezy to replace Lafitte.*

This was all good news—very good news. Rouhani was behaving exactly like a man who had stolen one of the world's major collections of modern art. And Didi had picked the right operatives to cover him. Veronica "Shorty" Montoya looked younger than sixteen until you got within two feet of her. In D.C., Pilar Estevez was a slightly plump and voluptuous fashion plate who liked to balance on three-inch heels, but by changing her clothes and shoes and letting her hair down, she could transform herself into a dowdy middle-aged woman who would be overlooked and underestimated. In fact, Pilar could outrun most of the male operatives, and in heels, nobody could touch her, a fact that was commemorated by the annual awarding of the Pilar trophy following a 100-meter dash at the company picnic. The contestants, many of them men, had to run in high heels and trained for weeks before the race. Pilar was not permitted to compete.

For her part, Sneezy could play the part of a dull-witted hound dog to perfection—chasing her tail, snapping at flies, lazing around in the shade. But like all the dogs at Levesque-Quixote, she was highly trained, a focused professional with a nose like a surgical laser. She, too, was likely to be underestimated.

I appreciated that Didi and Emile still considered the recovery mine—the logical follow-up to an old case. It was this respect for their operatives that kept me working for them after all these years. On the other hand, they wouldn't—couldn't—wait forever. That thought got me out of bed in the morning and helped me swallow the Chinese herbal sludge and think kind thoughts about the moron who had put me in a cast in the first place.

When I wasn't busy torturing my body, I worked on creating a new identity for myself, in case I needed one. The pictures coming in from Montoya and Estevez in Fort Worth suggested I might, since the paintings were now sitting inside a sprawling ranch-style house in the middle of a drought-depleted landscape of scrub and brush. My chances of getting them out would be greatly improved if I could get a closer look at the security set-up.

Since my own name was relatively common, and since I had worked hard to preserve my anonymity on the Web, I'd always used my own name when I went undercover, changing my middle initial to "T." Margaret T. already had some frequent buyer accounts connected to an address in Boston, as well as a membership in the Boston Museum of Fine Arts. But now I wanted to move her to a condo in Miami, so Bernie found one for me, and then ordered a fake driver's license and a Blue Cross Blue Shield card with that address, as well as a subscription to the *Miami Herald*. She arranged for an associate in Miami to acquire a Miami-Dade Public Library card, as well as some miscellaneous receipts for my wallet. A recent gas receipt would look suspicious, since I wasn't driving with a broken leg. But Margaret T. didn't join the Miami Art Museum or the Perez; we weren't sure we wanted her to know that much about art. Instead, we got her a country club membership. I found golf unbearably tedious, even when I had two good legs to play it with, but I knew how to impersonate a golf enthusiast, and could put in a moderately good performance on the links if it came to that. We also enrolled her in a riding club, which could explain the game leg. I'd ridden horses from time to time when they offered the best transportation available, and if I didn't belong to the horsy set, I'd learned enough from Didi to talk the talk.

On July 14th, Secretary Kerry announced a historic nuclear deal with Iran. If the Iranians wanted their paintings back, it wasn't in the papers. Of course, it was always possible that Sami Rouhani played both sides of the fence, and had stolen the paintings as an agent of the revolutionary government, or had stolen them in the hope of currying favor with the revolutionary government. Or planned to ransom them to the revolutionary government. Apart from his gifts to the Fort Worth art museum, Rouhani struck me as more businessman than philanthropist, but even if the paintings were a pawn in a bigger political game, at least he knew enough about art to understand how to take care of them.

On the four-week anniversary of my accident, a Wednesday, I went to see Leo Bonamy, a kindly orthopedist of medium height and build with a dense thicket of graying brown hair on top. Everyone called him "Dr. Bones."

"I want a walking cast," I said, then corrected myself. "I need a walking cast."

He tilted his head. "It's only been four weeks, M.J.," he said. "Four weeks yesterday."

I just looked at him. He can't have thought that this was news to me.

"You're not as young as you used to be," he said. "You can't expect to heal as quickly as you used to."

This was hardly news to me, either. "Just take the damn x-ray," I said. "I've been working on it."

So he did. And then he brought it back and clipped it to a light box. He studied it in silence for a long time. Without looking at me, he said, "What exactly did you mean when you said that you'd been 'working on it'?"

Crap, I thought. I've made it worse.

"Oh, you know," I said, "the usual. Working on forgiveness, things like that."

"You've been working with Lydia?" he said.

I nodded.

"Okay, M.J.," he said. "You can have your walking cast. But keep in mind that you're still going to be handicapped by it—probably more than you think. You'll need to learn how to walk in it. I'm going to give you a set of instructions that you and your physical therapist need to follow."

I just grinned at him.

"I mean it," he said. "No mountain climbing, no bungee jumping, and no motorcycles."

He was right. The new cast, or boot, took some getting used to, and he had me circle the PT room twenty times before he'd let me leave.

At the Levesque building, I hung out in a small conference room down the hall from the monitoring center and watched for Grace Wang to leave the center and head down the hall toward the restroom. Then I made my way down the hall and helped myself to a passkey from the small container by the door. I opened the red folder on Grace's desk, the one that contained all of the security codes for the locations we monitored. Nobody paid any attention to me, apart from a wave or a nod. The section of the list I needed was on top, which probably meant that Grace had left it there for me, since Dottie's surname started with "R." I blessed Emile's fondness for redundancy, which had created a hard copy of the list in the first place. I memorized the code, replaced the folder, and checked the duty roster. I knew that I couldn't exit any faster than I'd entered, so I was still standing there when Grace returned.

"Hey, M.J.!" she said. "No cast!"

"Now I have a shot at beating the tortoise," I said.

Her eyes went to the red folder, then back to me. "Just don't overdo it," she said.

"I'll be careful," I said.

From home, I called Lafitte, who was back from Texas and hadn't yet been sent out on assignment. "You busy tonight?"

"Not especially," he said. "What's the plan?"

"You up for a little B&E?" I said.

"My favorite thing," he said. "We doing this on crutches?"

"One crutch," I said, "and a walking cast." The single crutch had been a compromise with Bones. I'd lobbied for no crutches, but I was still sufficiently unsteady to give in and accept a single crutch. "Can you pick me up at one? And can you bring one of the dogs? Maybe Doc."

"No problem," he said. "You planning to look like any other neighborhood dog walker in a cast?"

"I'm working on it," I said.

When Jasmine showed up, lugging her bag of weights, I told her that what I really needed was to practice walking in the new cast. I put on a trench coat.

"M.J., this is July," Jasmine objected. "The temperature will be in the mid-seventies at one in the morning."

"Doesn't matter," I said. "When a dog needs to be walked in the middle of the night, and you don't want to get dressed, you just put on something to cover your nightgown."

I practiced for an hour, and then Jasmine told me I'd better rest. She unfastened the boot, slipped it off, and gently massaged my leg.

"What's the matter?" she said, catching a glimpse of my face before I turned it away.

"Nothing," I said.

"Yes, there is," she said.

I turned back and gestured at my bad leg where it lay, pale, inert, and shrunken on the massage table. I found I couldn't speak.

Jasmine grinned at me. "For a leg that just spent four weeks in a hard cast," she said, "it looks fabulous, M.J. It really does. You'll be surprised how fast it bounces back now, as long as you keep working."

I waited until seven to call Gunnar Halversen. Since he was working the late-night shift, I didn't want to wake him up if he was sleeping. I picked him because I knew him best of the people working the monitoring center tonight, and I knew I could trust him. The newer people didn't know me as well, and it wasn't fair to ask them to do something that would make them nervous. Also bad for me if their nerves got noticed, of course. Gunnar was a poker buddy with a face unreadable as a plaster wall, when he wanted it to be.

"I need you on monitor seventeen tonight between one-thirty and two," I told him. "I need you to turn down the sound and not notice if you see me or Lafitte on the monitor."

Turning down the sound was important, because if the house was entered during a time when the system didn't think anyone should be there, it would emit a warning beep audible to everyone in the room.

"Okay," he said. "Tell me you're not going to break the lock. That's one of our most expensive ones."

"I have a passkey," I said. "I won't break anything. And I won't take anything, just looking and leaving."

"And you won't attack the camera with your crutch?" he said.

"Promise," I said. "I won't attack the camera with anything."

"And you'll leave your cell phone at home so they can't track you," he said.

"Good thinking," I said, because I had forgotten about the cell phone, though I probably wouldn't have taken it anyway. "I won't take it."

"And you won't be arriving on the back of a motorcycle?" he said.

I promised. I'd already told Lafitte to bring the car. Doc was too old to ride in a sidecar, anyway.

"And if I do this for you, will you forget the $3.78 I owe you?" he said.

"What $3.78?" I said.

"Okay," he said. "Break a leg."

13

If we'd had a full moon to contend with, I would have delayed the operation, but the sky was overcast and the moon wasn't visible, although heat lightning occasionally flashed in the distance. It was a sultry night, and I'd put the trench coat on over a cotton bathrobe in case we got stopped by a cop, so I was drenched with sweat by the time we arrived on a quiet side street around the corner from Dottie's house. Lots were large, driveways were long, and houses were far apart in this suburban neighborhood, which made me feel exposed. I clipped the leash to Doc's harness. I took the leash, flashlight and plastic poop bag in one hand, and gripped my crutch in the other, though it was awkward. I tried to keep the flashlight trained on the sidewalk far enough in front of me to conceal the fact that I was only wearing one slipper.

Doc's stiff-hipped waddle showed his age, which contributed to the impression that he was a dog who might need walking in the middle of the night. We were neither of us in any condition for speed, which was just as well. We moseyed along at an enforced amble. I kept my eyes peeled for any curtain flutterings or silhouettes that betrayed a watcher, but I didn't see a thing.

When I reached Dottie's shadowy front walk, I reined Doc in and urged him toward the door. The front porch, hidden by shrubbery, was black as pitch, but I felt Lafitte's hand on my shoulder and I handed him the leash. I switched on my penlight, turned it on my face and looked up at the camera so that Gunnar could see that it was me, then shone it on the passkey. The lock made a faint snick, softer than a cricket's chirp, and I went in, opened the box and entered the security code. Lafitte pulled the door closed behind me.

I made my way to the study and checked to see that the curtains were closed. Finding the envelope I wanted on Dottie's desk took more time. Even though I'd studied the photograph to memorize its position, everything looked different in the near-darkness. Then I spotted the distinctive stamp and plucked it from the pile.

I took it to the kitchen, a room I hadn't seen before but guessed was at the end of the first-floor hall. The kitchen faced the back of the house, an advantage for me because the back yard was large and bordered on a tree-lined stream rather than another back yard. I didn't take the time to admire Dottie's décor, although what I could see of it looked surprisingly domestic—a flowered tea towel hanging from the oven handle, a scattering of refrigerator magnets on the refrigerator door, and, best of all for me, a tea kettle on the stove. It took less than five minutes to steam open the envelope. I took it into a windowless pantry and risked a light to supplement my high-powered flash, photographed the letter and its envelope, returned the letter to the envelope, and resealed it with a glue stick from my pocket. I had replaced it and was out the door, resetting the security system, within another five minutes. I'd spent sixteen minutes inside the house—an eternity for someone who could have managed it in half that time with two good legs.

Lafitte handed over Doc's leash, and I retreated the way I had come—down the front walk. As we stood screened by the shrubbery while I checked out the street, Doc gave a soft woof, his version of a whispered warning. We both froze. Then I heard it, the scrape of a shoe on pavement. It wasn't Lafitte; Lafitte would not be making any sound. The footsteps were approaching—too late to retreat. Best case scenario, it was the burglar returning. Doc and I could take care of him. Worst case scenario—.

A frantic yipping ruptured the silence. I emerged from the shadows to confront my doppelganger: a woman dressed like me, holding a leash and a flashlight like me, staring at me as I stared at her. Her flashlight was trained on my face, mine on hers.

"Oh, Judy!" I said, and put a hand to my chest.

"Marge, it's you!" she said, mirroring my gesture. "You gave me such a fright! Quiet, Pepe! You'll wake the whole neighborhood. My goodness! My heart's about to jump right out of my chest! Quiet, Pepe!" She aimed the admonition downward at a Chihuahua quivering with excitement and outrage, probably more excitement than outrage. "Whatever are you doing here at this hour of the night? I didn't know you lived around here."

"I don't," I said, "not right around here, but not too far away—maybe ten minutes. It's okay, Doc." Belatedly, I realized that I should be calming him or shushing him, though in fact he was standing placidly awaiting instructions. I stooped awkwardly and patted him on the head. I straightened up and bit my lip.

"Oh, Judy, I feel like such an idiot! I'm such a worrier." I put a hand to my cheek—the only hand available, the one holding the poop bag as well as the flashlight. "After all the things we said about burglars and break-ins, when I couldn't sleep and Doc wanted to go out, I thought, 'I'll just pop over to Dottie's and see if everything looks okay.' You know how it is when you get something in your head in the middle of the night, and the more you try to ignore it, the worse it gets? Well, that's just how it was tonight. I brooded on it and brooded on it and finally I thought, 'Well, if there *is* something wrong, and you could've gone over there and prevented it, you'll feel terrible later.' And then I knew I couldn't sleep again until I'd come over here to see."

"I know just what you mean!" Judy said, to my relief. "I've been feeling the same way—waking up in the middle of the night and dragging poor Pepe out for a late walk. Of course, I tell myself there's no need to worry. You know, a security company came over on Monday and installed all new equipment." She clutched her coat and looked around. "They're probably watching us right now, wondering what we're up to."

I looked around too, then at Dottie's house. "I don't really know what I'd do if I found a burglar here," I said. "But I have my cell phone, so I guess I'd just call 911." I hoped I wouldn't have to produce it, since I'd left it at home, as promised. I patted my pocket.

She held up her own cell phone. "Well, I sure wasn't planning to confront him if he was here," she said. "Pepe would do it, though, wouldn't you, Peps?" Pepe was busy trying to sniff Doc's hindquarters, which were firmly planted on the pavement. "He's not afraid of anything."

She looked around again. "But how did you get here?" she said. "You didn't drive, not with your leg. And what happened to your other crutch?"

I lifted the hem of my robe to show her the new cast. "I have a walking cast now," I said, "so just one crutch. I do okay. Just don't tell the cops. Of course, I'd never drive far, and not during the day, but this seemed safe enough."

She frowned. "But where's your car?" She seemed to be trying to penetrate the surrounding darkness.

"Oh," I said, and laughed, embarrassed. "I got turned around in the dark. It's around the corner up there."

She stared in the direction I'd pointed. "But how far did you walk? You shouldn't be walking so far with a bad leg."

I shrugged. "You know what they say, whatever doesn't kill you—."

"Well, I know, but I'd take it easy, if I were you," she said.

"I will," I said, inching away from her, pretending that Doc was pulling on the leash. He looked up at me, then obligingly got to his feet and ambled off. "Anyway, I'm so relieved that you told me about the new security system. That really eases my mind."

"It was a nice service, didn't you think?" Judy asked. She appeared willing to delay her own departure for a good gossip about the funeral.

"Yes, I did," I said, letting Doc pull me away. Now that he'd been given his cue, he was doing his beagle best to move me in the direction of the car. "It was so interesting, all the different kinds of friends Dottie had. Well, looks like we're going. I'll see you later, Judy."

"See you later," she said with a wave. "Sleep tight!"

"Trouble?" Lafitte said as I slid into the passenger seat.

Doc clambered into the back, circled twice, and flopped down with a grunt.

"Neighbor," I said. "Fortunately, one I know."

"She believe you?" he said.

I shrugged. "Hard to tell," I said, "but she didn't call the cops."

"Yet," he said.

The next morning I downloaded the photograph of the letter onto my computer. All of our cameras were state-of-the-art, so the image was, if anything, sharper than the original—or at least it was after I made a few adjustments. My Italian was a little rusty, but the handwriting was clear and the message uncomplicated. The heading read, "San Miniato, 27 May, 2015."

Dear Mrs. Rivers, it read. *I apologize for writing to you but I do because of your close friendship with Signor Giorgio and I did not know who else to write to. I am sorry to tell you that his health is not so good as it was. His body is strong enough but his mind grows weaker and I am worried about him. Sometimes he calls me "Vittoria," and once even "Dorotea," which greatly distressed me, as I am sure you will agree that we look nothing alike, Signora. And then a cousin came to visit, and Signor Giorgio talked of the old days as he never does, except with you,*

Signora, and I worried what he might say. That one is gone now, and never said a word about taking care of Signor Giorgio. Signora, we are still paid by the bank and managing the best we can, but it is not right that he is on his own. If you know his family, will you please tell them what I have told you? Or if you do not wish to communicate with them, I will do it if you would be so kind as to give me an address where I can write. Again, excuse this letter to one who is not his family, but I believe that you care about Signor Giorgio, and so even though my husband says I should not become involved, I am asking for your help. Most sincerely, Giulia Massini. p.s. Please excuse that I write in Italian, but I know that your Italian is better than my English, and I want to be clear.

I felt a pang. She had hoped for a prompt response two months ago, and now she would never receive one. Except from me.

I picked up the phone and asked Bernie if she could track down George Finch's family—the sooner, the better. She promised to try.

"And have you checked Dottie's phone records?" I asked. "I want to know if she's called Italy in the past, say, six months."

Then I had her transfer me to Kathy "K-Rod" Roddick, our travel coordinator.

That left me one more thing to do. I printed out several high-resolution images of the little golden bird. After lunch, Marco Antonio drove me to see a jeweler that Quixote favored.

Mr. Moulin was not merely a seller or appraiser of fine jewelry, but a craftsman. He was a tall man, with stooped shoulders, wispy white hair and a Bassett face. He studied the photographs in silence, lifting them one by one off the counter with fingers that looked impossibly thick and blunt for his line of work. Then he called one of his assistants, and they both examined the photographs, exchanging comments in French.

"How good does it have to be, the copy?" he said to me at last. "Without the original—."

"Not perfect," I said. "I'm hoping the old man's eyes are not as good as they used to be."

He nodded. "In that case, yes, I believe we can produce a credible facsimile. When do you need it?"

"Yesterday," I said.

He did not react. It was what I always said. "In that case," he said, his eyes moving to a calendar on the wall, "we shall do our best to have it by next Thursday."

"Make it Wednesday," I said, "and I'll put you in my will."

His eyebrows lifted in surprise. "But my dear M.J.," he said, "I am already there, five times over, by my calculation. What more could you have to leave me? That is a very attractive crutch, but I am not in need of a crutch."

"Not now," I said.

He conceded with a tilt of his head. "Oui, c'est vrai. Anything's possible."

14

The morning sun glinted off the Duomo in the rearview mirror and painted fingers of light across the blue Tuscan hills as we left Florence behind us. I had expected the stylish and vivacious Angelina Drago, but had been met instead by Aldo the Silent, a young man whose mission in life was to contradict all stereotypes about Italian expressiveness. I'd worked with him once before and found him competent, but as unimaginative as he was uncommunicative. That was fine with me; Angelina could be exhausting, especially after an overnight flight. Aldo glanced at my cast and picked up my duffel. He did not ask what had happened to me. He did not compliment me on my dress. These omissions were both points in his favor.

Aldo took me to a picturesque farmhouse—tan stucco, red-tiled roof, and a few trees I couldn't identify in the company of a tall pair of cypresses. In front was a dusty pair of apricot trees laden with ripening fruit. I hoped that my travel agent hadn't persuaded the owners to vacate the house for my convenience, but I didn't put it past her. It was too early to call on Finch, so I unpacked, a five-minute operation, showered, and explored the house while Aldo, to my surprise, sat on the patio and talked nonstop on his tele-fonino. July was the hottest month in Tuscany, and as I walked I felt the sweat dribble down my leg inside my cast. So I sat down in front of an anemic fan and reviewed the Finch file for the twentieth time.

Finch was credited with some of the boldest, most complicated, and most lucrative jewel heists ever committed, and he'd probably committed most of the crimes he was credited with. He didn't usually go after art—he liked his haul more portable—but he had been known to steal paintings and other art objects from time to time, probably just because he enjoyed the challenge and because they caught his eye on his way to the jewelry. He'd also been known to return a family heirloom if he believed the victim worthy and in genuine distress.

We had a lot in common, he and I, and though I'd never met the Birdman, I'd always admired his style. The Tehran job had somehow felt like him to me, but I'd had to agree with Emile that he was far more likely to call attention to the theft by leaving a calling card of some kind than to conceal it by leaving a fake.

He was in his eighties now, and had been living in San Miniato alone for ten years—quietly, as far as anybody could tell. I wondered how often Interpol or other agents had searched his house, looking for long lost treasures. Did I hope he had a good security system? Well, good enough to keep out everybody but me.

I had an e-mail from Bernie to tell me that Theo had called. She'd wanted me to know that she'd told the niece and nephew about the theft of Dottie's paintings. She'd added only that a private security firm was investigating the theft, and felt confident that they could recover the paintings. I wondered what the fallout had been. The paintings hadn't been left to Steve and Monica, but they probably expected to get their greedy mitts on the artwork nonetheless. That would be especially true if the boyfriend, Neil Calloway, a.k.a. Neil Callahan, suspected the value of Dottie's art collection.

Around noon, at the hottest hour of this blistering July day, Aldo declared that we could pay Signor Finch a visit.

Villa Offuscata was tucked low into a hillside in a small depression like a giant's footprint. With its overgrown shrubbery and earth-colored stucco, it lived up to its name, and I thought that this would be especially so on misty or foggy days, when it might vanish altogether like Brigadoon. Aldo offered to move the rusty wrought-iron gate that was blocking the drive so that he could deliver me to the door, but I thought it would be better for me to walk, so he parked the car in the shade and trailed me like a nonchalant cat. The still air was heady with the scent of cut hay baking in the sun, and closer to the house, I smelled lavender mixed with something more pungent, like mustard. Crowding the door were low bushes sporting a few delicate white-and-purple flowers like fairy skirts. In the glass on one side of the door was a sticker from a local security company, but it had faded, cracked, and partially peeled away. I didn't see a camera anywhere, or sensors around the glass.

The woman who answered the door had a youthful face under wavy dark hair with occasional strands of silver, cut short. She wore a full apron over a jade print cotton dress, and at first had the distracted air of someone interrupted in a task requiring her concentration. But then her keen dark eyes flicked to my crutch, and they clouded with caution and worry.

"*Sì?*" she said.

"Signora Massini?" I said, and when she nodded, held out my hand and opened my palm. In it lay the little goldfinch replica. I wished I had her letter to show, but this was the best I could do, and it was a gamble. But she gasped, and put a hand to her mouth. "I came in response to your letter," I said.

She reached out and took the necklace. To my surprise, her eyes filled with tears and she looked away. He's dead, I thought. George Finch is dead.

Her eyes returned to scan my face. "She is dead, yes?" she said in English. "*La signora?*"

I nodded.

"Oh!" she said, and crossed herself. Then she turned away, one hand still on the door and one to her forehead, the little bird hanging from her clenched fist like a rosary. "He will be *molto triste,* very—sad, *il Signor Giorgio.*"

Then she seemed to gather herself, and stepped back from the doorway. "Come in," she said. "That young man is your—?"

I followed her gaze to where Aldo leaned against a tree, talking on his *telefonino.*

"He's with me," I said. "But he's okay where he is. *Va bene.*"

"Oh, you speak Italian," she said.

"Sort of," I said. I held up a thumb and index finger. "*Poco.*"

I stepped into the cool hall and she led me to a kitchen flooded with light, slowing her pace and glancing down at my bad leg with concern. The worn marble floor had shallow dips and furrows, but it was not especially difficult to negotiate, unless you were furtively scanning the walls for stolen artwork and pretending not to. The kitchen smelled of lemon and garlic and rosemary—a scent barely stirred by a ceiling fan that made desultory circles overhead. She gestured me into a wooden chair beside a venerable wooden table and offered me lemonade.

"I don't want to interrupt your work," I said, nodding at the marble countertop where a dusty ball of dough sat awaiting her ministrations. I propped my crutch against a windowsill.

She brushed aside my comment. "It is not important," she said, and nodded in the direction of one of the windows. "He don't wake for lunch, only when I wake him." She sighed. "Now I don't want to wake him, I think."

She poured us both lemonade and sat heavily in the chair opposite me. The goldfinch lay on the table between us.

I touched the bird lightly with my forefinger. "He gave it to her, didn't he?"

"*Sì*," she said softly. "She weared it always when she came to visit. That is how I knew—*che era morta*. She didn't want to give it, you see—not to anyone, I think." She looked up at me. "How?"

"How did she die? We think she was poisoned," I said.

She gasped, and a hand flew to her mouth. Then she crossed herself again. I could have softened it. Before I'd arrived, I hadn't decided how much of the truth to tell—not to Giulia Massini or to George Finch. But now that I was in her presence, I felt that she needed to know—that we needed to be allies. "We think maybe she had something that somebody wanted."

Her eyes clouded again, and her eyebrows descended as she looked toward the window she'd indicated before. "*Tutti e due*—they have things that people want, I think—*la Signora e il Signor Giorgio*," she said. "I don't know all of these things, but they must have a big value. *Cose preziose*, you know?"

"After Dottie—*la Signora*—died," I said, "some paintings were stolen from her house."

"Yes," she said. "All want the paintings."

"The nephew, too?" I asked.

She sighed. "*Il Signor Giorgio* gave him a small one—not a very expensive one, I think, and he—he was happy—." She mimed delight. Then she waved a cupped hand in the vicinity of her ear. "*Capisce*? Do you understand?"

"*Sì, sì, certo*," I said encouragingly.

She continued. "But me, I don't believe that he was happy. After the nephew went away, some paintings—." She searched for the word. "Disappear." She closed and opened her fists, as if miming a disappearance into thin air. She pointed at first one wall, then another. "And—other things."

"You don't live here," I said.

She shook her head. "He is *solo*—alone. It is harmly—no, *peri-*

coloso, dangerous," she said. "*Per il Signor* Giorgio and for the thief. He has guns, and he walks at night. Someone can die. That is one reason I write to the family."

"Your English is very good," I observed.

She smiled. "I ask him always to speak English with me, so that I can speak better, but he like—liked—to speak Italian." She sighed again, and her smile became rueful. "Now he speak *quello che capita* —whatever come out from his mouth. He don't remember who can understand him and who cannot."

She straightened a little and folded her hands on the table. "But you were a friend *della Signora*?" she said. "Tell me how she is dead."

"I was a friend of hers, but not a close friend," I said. "I only knew her a little while. But I was there when she died."

I told her the story, and she only interrupted me once, at its weakest point. I would have interrupted me myself. She was holding the business card I'd handed her, but she wasn't looking at it.

"You say that your boss send you to this *casa di cura* to watch someone," she said frowning, "but they don't say who you must watch. Why they don't say?"

I shrugged. "They're men," I said.

"Ah," she said, throwing up her hands, and I continued.

When I'd finished, she said, "So you are *ingaggiata—come si dice?*"

"Hired," I prompted. "I was hired."

"*Sì*, to find the paintings, yes? But why you think that *il Signor Giorgio* know about these paintings?"

I hesitated. "How much do you know about Mr. Finch's past, Giulia?" We were Giulia and M.J. by this time.

She made a gesture of dismissal and shook her head. "I know nothing, and I don't want to know nothing. Some people, they say he was *un criminale*, a criminal, once, but—." She waved backwards

131

over her shoulder. "A long time ago. He has been always kind with me, and that is what I know," she said.

"But you suspect that they are right," I said. "What kind of criminal do they say he was?"

The corners of her mouth turned down in distaste. "Some say *un mafiosi*—a gangster. But I don't believe. Some say a thief. *Nessuno lo sa.*"

I noticed that she did not contradict this last theory.

"He was a very great thief," I said gently, "one of the greatest of them all. Mostly he stole expensive jewels from foolish rich people who could afford to lose them."

Her troubled eyes drifted to the window.

"Sometimes, he stole paintings," I said.

Her eyes returned to mine and her hands rose to plead with me. "But you can't think he has steal the paintings *della Signora!*" She made as if to rise from her chair. "I present you to him and you will see. He is a sick man. He can't—."

I put out a hand to restrain her. "No, of course not," I said quickly. "I quite understand that he's too ill to work. And in any case, I know that he retired some years ago."

Her eyebrows descended into puzzlement. "Then what you think that he know?"

"I have seen a list of the paintings that were stolen," I said. "They are all very famous paintings. And as it happens, they were all stolen from an Iranian museum, probably during the revolution. I know, you see, because I stole them myself."

She sat back in wonderment as if I had just announced that I was the Grand Duchess Anastasia.

"*Ma che cosa sta dicendo!*" she exclaimed, one hand, fingers to thumb, pumping in front of her mouth. "You?!"

"Well," I confessed, "I had help. We were stealing the paintings to protect them from the revolutionaries, who wanted to destroy everything Western. They were great treasures, and we wanted to preserve them. But the thing is, when we got them back to America, and showed them to our experts, most of them turned out to be forgeries—you know, not real paintings. Someone had been there before us, stolen the original paintings, and replaced them with fakes."

Her next question belied her look of confusion. "But how you can be sure that these paintings—they were not all—fakes"—she stumbled over the unfamiliar word—"at the beginning?"

"It was a famous museum, and many famous experts went there to see the paintings," I said. "I don't think they could all have been fooled."

"And you think that *il Signor Giorgio* steal the paintings?" she said. "But you said that he steal jewelry?"

"I think perhaps he also had help," I said, "perhaps from someone who cared more about paintings than he did."

"*La Signora* Rivers," she said softly. "*Sì, ho capito.*"

And to my alarm, her eyes filled with tears, and the tears began to slide down her cheeks.

I reached out to her. "Giulia, what's wrong?"

She stood and went to the window. Her back to me, she said, "I don't permit that the *Polizia* come and arrest him for the stealing. He is old now, he is *malato*, in his head. You can see what he has. He don't live like a rich man. I don't permit that he die in prison. If he confess this stealing, I will go to the court and say that he is not right in his head. The doctor will say the same." She made the palms-out Italian gesture for *basta*—"enough."

"Oh, Giulia," I said, "I didn't come to arrest him. I'm not a police officer. And anyway, even if I wanted to see him charged, I couldn't do it without admitting to theft myself. Don't you see? I'm in no position to cause trouble for him. I'm hoping he'll help me."

She turned back to me. "How? He don't know who steal the paintings *della Signora*. He don't remember the things that he knew before. He don't remember what he eat for breakfast."

"Yes," I said carefully, "but based on what I know of his condition, the people who have it may not know what they ate for breakfast but will remember the distant past with remarkable clarity. Sometimes they confuse the past with the present. That's what Mr. Finch does when he calls you by other names, isn't it?"

When she didn't respond, I added, "Actually, we're pretty sure we know who stole the paintings."

She spread her hands. "Then what he can do?"

"We know who stole the paintings," I said, "and we know where they are. What we don't know is whether they're the original paintings or whether they're fakes. When I return to America, I will have to go steal them back. It won't be easy. I'm trying to find out, if I can, whether it will be worth my trouble."

Comprehension dawned and her face relaxed. "*Ho capito*," she said.

"Mr. Finch may not be able to answer my question," I said. "He may not know anything about the paintings. He may not have been involved in the original theft, and he may not know who was. But I'd like to try."

She stood awkwardly, arms folded. "You tell him that—*che la Signora è morta.*"

"Not if you don't want me to," I said. "It's your decision."

"Don't tell him," she said, her voice a soft plea. "Maybe he don't understand, maybe he understand. It—." She pressed her hands to her heart and sighed. "I don't know how long he live, but I wish he believe that *la Signora* will visit him again."

I nodded. When I could trust my own voice again, I extracted two images from my pocket and laid them on the table. "Could you take a look?" I said.

She returned to the table and looked down. "*Eccolo qui*," she said, and put her finger on the image on the left.

"The cousin?" I said.

She nodded, and looked at me questioningly.

"His name is Neil Calloway," I said. "He's been dating—you know, romantically involved with, an *innamorato*—Mrs. Rivers's niece under a different last name. His father worked for Interpol, and now works for the Federal Bureau of Investigation. His specialty—the father's—is art theft."

She sat heavily and put her hands together, palm to palm. "*Madonna!* And he come to arrest *il Signor Giorgio*, the cousin?"

"I think he's after the paintings," I said. "He's never had a steady job, as far as we can tell. He's twice divorced, he's been arrested a few times for theft, and it's not clear how he earns his living. He doesn't seem the type that the Fibbies—the F.B.I.—would trust with an important mission. I think he's been listening to his father's stories, heard about Mr. Finch's condition, and saw an opportunity. I think he came here to find out what Mr. Finch had and how easy it would be to get his hands on that. But if Mr. Finch said anything to implicate Mrs. Rivers—that is, if he mentioned that she had once been his partner—he might have decided to take the lazy man's way out, and marry her niece so that he could inherit the paintings she had, or any profit he thinks she will make on their sale."

"So he has kill her?" she asked quickly.

"I don't know," I admitted. "Truly, I don't know. There are plenty of bad guys and potential bad guys in this story." I leaned a little closer and looked at her intently. "You know, Giulia, I could be one of them—one of the bad guys, I mean. I don't want to scare you, but you should be careful—and suspicious."

She laughed—a surprising burst of mirth that made me smile. "Don't worry, I am." She placed a finger below one eye and patted my arm with the other hand. "I put my eye on everybody. But I know always the people. I am never wrong."

"Not even about Signor Giorgio?" I asked.

She smiled ruefully. "Not even him," she said. She looked at me sideways. "He was good, *diceva*?"

"The best," I assured her. "They'll never get him, not even if

135

they raid the house and find a Titian on the wall over his bed. He never left anything behind that he didn't mean to be found."

"You have never met him?" she said.

"No," I said. "Not even when our paths crossed."

She put her palms on her aproned thighs and stood up.

"Then I must present you," she said.

I tucked the little goldfinch into my pocket and followed her out to meet its namesake.

15

The old man lay motionless in the shade of an enormous oak tree. He lay on a folding lounge chair, bony knees showing below khaki shorts and leather sandals on his feet. He wore a white shirt open at the neck, its sleeves rolled up to the elbows, and a New York Yankees baseball cap. His unruly white hair was damp with sweat. Curled on his lap was a black cat like an abandoned Cossack hat. The old man's head was turned away from us, and he was wearing earphones attached to a device that lay on a small wooden table beside him, so I didn't know if he was asleep or not.

Giulia tapped him on the shoulder to rouse him, and then gently removed the earphones.

"*Ha una visita,*" she said, "*un'amica della Signora Dorotea,* from America."

I was a little surprised that she'd mentioned Dottie at all, but I would take my cue from her. I waited for his head to turn in my direction before I offered my hand.

"Marge Smith," I said. "I've looked forward to meeting you, Mr. Finch."

"George," he said. "You can call me George." His voice was a little hoarse, but his grip was firm, and he studied me as I pulled up a nearby wooden chair and sat down.

"I bring some lemonade, *Signor Giorgio*," Giulia said, and retreated.

His smile was slow, but the wrinkles it exposed suggested that it was a habitual expression. "So you're a friend of Dottie's," he said. "What do you know about that? How is the old girl?"

"Fine," I said, feeling an unfamiliar twinge in my chest as I lied. "She sends her love."

He waved a hand at my crutch. "What'd you do to your leg?"

"Wiped out on my Ducati," I said.

"Bike look better than you do?" he asked.

"Worse," I said.

"Shame," he said, and shook his head.

"You have a bike?" I said.

"I do," he said. He looked around. "I wonder where they put it." He raised his voice and called, "*Giulia, dove sta la moto?*"

But Giulia, who hadn't yet reappeared, didn't answer, though I suspected that she was accustomed to these importunities *ad alta voce*. And so, apparently, was the cat, who didn't stir.

Finch put a distracted hand on the animal's back. "I'd like to show you my bike," he said. "I wouldn't mind taking it for a ride."

Imagining that Giulia had likely taken steps to insure that he wasn't racing around the district, getting himself lost, and concerned that I'd raised a ticklish topic, I changed the subject.

"You have a beautiful place here," I said.

He followed my gaze to take in the herb and vegetable gardens that edged the patio, and the row of cypresses behind them, beyond which the hillside rose up in a sloping wall thick with vegetation.

He put a thumb to a forefinger and made the horizontal gesture Italians use to designate perfection. "I like it," he said. "Always wanted to live here. Always knew I'd retire here."

"Have you lived in many places?" I asked.

"Not lived," he said, "but I've traveled all over the world. You?"

"I've traveled a lot, yes," I said. "But I might be inclined to agree with you. It's beautiful country."

Giulia delivered two glasses of lemonade. Finch showed no sign that he remembered what he wanted to ask her.

He took a drink. "Who'd you say you were now?" he said.

"A friend of Dottie's," I said.

"Oh, Dottie," he said, and smiled. "Dottie loved it here, but she couldn't live here, she said. She was a city girl. You know Dottie?"

"Not for long," I said, "but yes, I know Dottie. Did she always live in cities?"

"Yes, always a city girl," he said. "Chicago, Baltimore, and then Washington. Don't ask me why she wanted to live around all those corrupt politicians." He grimaced. "They foul the air." He took in a healthy lungful of Tuscan air with satisfaction, and inhaled the scents of tomato sauce and baking bread. "What time is it?" he asked abruptly. "Is it lunchtime soon?" He turned his head toward the kitchen window.

"Pretty soon," I said. "You know, the last time I saw Dottie, she was worried about the paintings. She thought someone was planning to steal them."

He turned a surprisingly sharp eye on me. "They were, were they?" he said. "Well, I wouldn't be surprised, if someone found out." He relaxed back in the chair. "But I wouldn't worry about it. Nobody will ever find out. Nobody knows about 'em but Dottie and me, and I'm not talking."

"Oh, that's good," I said. I leaned in, conspiratorially. "You're sure you haven't talked to anybody about the Tehran business?"

"Me?" he said. "Of course not. My lips are sealed." He mimed locking his lips and grinned at me. "Of course, there were those other chaps—they might've known something."

"What other chaps?" I said.

"The competition," he said in a stage whisper.

"The other ones who were there that night?" I asked.

"Hell of a night," he said. "Raining like a son of a bitch. Pardon my French. I was on the other side of the wall with the ladder, soaked to the skin, couldn't hear a goddamn thing over the rain. Couldn't even see the top of the goddamn ladder." He shrugged. "No going back after that. Our last night."

"Did you know who they were?" I asked.

"Nope, never knew," he said. "Never found out. There was this one outfit I found out about later—could've been them. Knights of the Round Table—some stupid name like that."

"Did Dottie have a theory?" I said.

"Smoke," he said. "She thought it was the one they called 'Smoke.'"

"But you didn't believe it," I said.

He shrugged. "I didn't believe it and I didn't disbelieve it."

"Did she know who Smoke was?" I asked.

He smiled. "Nobody knew who Smoke was. That fellow was like me—invisible."

"But Dottie saw him," I said.

"She saw someone," he said, "but she didn't get a good look at him."

"You've never talked to anyone except Dottie about Tehran?"

"Not me," he said, a little defensively. But he shifted uneasily, and I wondered whether a memory was struggling to the surface.

"I heard your cousin came to visit you recently," I said, as if I were changing the subject. "That's nice."

He frowned. "Which cousin?"

"I'm not sure," I said. "Giulia mentioned it. Nick, maybe, or Nathan? Something like that."

"What time did you say it was?" he said. "I'm getting hungry. Are you?"

In the end, I stayed for lunch. When I'd tried to beg off, Giulia took me aside and asked me, as a security expert, to assess the security system at the house, and I'd agreed. She delivered a plate to Aldo and a saucer of milk to the cat, and we ate outside under the oak, with the breeze rustling the cypress trees and stirring their heady scent.

Twice Finch asked who I was. "*Ma chi è lei?*" he'd say, scrutinizing my face, and then turning to Giulia, "*Chi è lei?*" When Giulia patiently explained to him that I was a friend of Signora Rivers, a light dawned in his face and lit up his eyes in a way that wrenched my heart. Once he reached over and patted my hand.

"How did you and Dottie meet?" I asked him.

"She didn't tell you?" he said.

"She told me to ask you," I said.

It was disconcerting to talk to someone in the middle stages of Alzheimer's, as I'd had occasion to notice before. Sometimes, they seem to understand nothing; others, they seem to understand everything. From sentence to sentence in conversation, you could not assume that the next sentence would be one of the former times when it could just as easily turn out to be the latter. Now, he began to repeat a story that he had told many times, if only to himself.

"It was at a big fundraising shindig at MOMA," he said. "They were opening some big cubism exhibition. She was wearing Dior. But it wouldn't have mattered if she was wearing a lampshade, she was still the most beautiful woman in the room." He raised a hand, forefinger and middle finger pressed to his thumb. "*Bellissima!*"

"And you were the handsomest man," I said. "She went to look at the paintings and you went to look at the women's jewelry."

He grinned delightedly and pointed a gnarled finger at me. "But you'll never prove it," he said.

"No," I agreed, "I never would."

While Finch took his postprandial *sonnellino*, Giulia showed me around the house. I checked the security sticker by the front door and wrote down the name and number, but its condition hadn't improved since I'd first spotted it. There were no cameras anywhere, or sensors, or a box for entering a code. The company had probably installed the locks—very good locks at the time they were installed—and promised to come immediately if they were contacted about a break-in.

"A painting was there," she said pointing to a brighter rectangular patch on the wall, "*e un altro qui*. One morning—no paintings. After the cousin visit, *capisce? Ho chiesto al Signor Giorgio* where were the paintings, but he don't say. Maybe he put them someplace."

"Were they valuable paintings, do you know?" I asked.

She shrugged. "*Sembravano di valore* ," she said, "but one of them *era della Signora*."

"It belonged to her?" I said.

"She made it," she said. She clasped her hands to her breast. "*Un'artista meravigliosa, la Signora*. I never see her do it, but Vittoria —she was here before me, you understand—say that she had a *cavalletto*—." Here she indicated a triangular shape with her hands.

"An easel?" I said. "For putting the painting on?"

"*Sì, sì,*" she said eagerly. "And also paints, that she keep in the *deposito*. When she come to visit, she take them—." Here she gestured toward the hills surrounding us. "Come, I show you. But —," she added, with a gesture at my crutch, "maybe you are too tired."

I shook my head, baffled. Surely you wouldn't come to Tuscany to paint the Italian countryside as a series of numbered blobs.

She led me to a small room off the kitchen.

"Someone has break the lock," she said, and showed me.

"Someone?" I said.

"Maybe *il Signor Giorgio*," she said, wagging her head to suggest possibilities. "But I don't ask, because when he remember, he don't speak." She touched her forehead to register the frailty of Signor Giorgio's memory.

She reached up to a high shelf and brought down an object wrapped in brown paper. She unwrapped it. "Maybe you saw *i paesaggi* in Signor Giorgio's room?"

"Those were Signora Rivers's?" I asked, surprised. "She painted them?"

"*Ma questo qui, è il mio preferito,*" she said, and handed it to me.

I caught my breath. It was an oil portrait of George Finch in his younger years—handsome, roguish, grinning, full of life. Like all good portraits, it captured the essence of its subject—it conjured his presence in the room. The style leaned toward the impressionistic, and relied on sure, deft brushstrokes for its effect. I took it into the kitchen where the light was better, and looked at it for a long time, trying to connect its creator with the painter of Scottie dogs I had known.

"Nobody steal this one," Giulia said, gazing at it over my shoulder. "I hide it because it make *il Signor Giorgio* sad. I don't know why, but it does." She tilted her head. "Maybe he know where it is. And maybe sometimes, when I am not here, he look. Maybe he has break the lock to look."

I nodded. "He would know how to get in," I said.

But he wouldn't have broken the lock. At least, Birdman wouldn't have broken the lock. The old man sleeping in the garden? About him, I wasn't so sure.

To Giulia, I said, "The security system is outdated, but it's not bad. It was good in its day. I will talk to my boss and then recommend a good local company for you to work with. They will need to take into account Signor Giorgio's condition in any system they design for you."

She nodded. "I want him safe, but I don't want him *come un detenuto.*"

"That will be the challenge," I said.

"I talk *con il Signor Manfredi, della banca,*" she said. "He is who pay the bills. I don't think he say no."

That might depend on how much he knew about the costs of high-end security systems, I thought.

What I didn't say was that I didn't see much left worth stealing. What I didn't say was that there had to be more somewhere. But where? In a bank vault? In a storage unit? He'd been a jewel thief primarily, not an art thief, so his cache of jewels could be secreted behind the bathroom plumbing, like Dottie's. And cat burglars didn't like to be burdened with bulky objects. Still, he'd been known to lift a sculpture or artifact or painting from time to time, and I didn't think I believed that he'd sold everything after he'd retired. Our best intelligence, which was quite good, suggested that quite a few missing objects attributed to Birdman had never surfaced, not even on the black market. Like so many jewel thieves, he didn't seem to steal because he was hard up for cash, he stole for the thrill of it.

I walked around the outside of the house and studied it. I leaned on my crutch and tried to put myself in the silent sneakers of a younger, sharper Birdman. I swung my gaze around and let it sweep the hillside.

Yes, I thought. That's what I would have done.

I only hoped that the path wouldn't prove too much for an old cripple to manage.

I stumped to the edge of the patio and looked past the cypresses, scanning the ground and the brush, until I thought I saw the traces of an old trail. I would have to return tonight, when Giulia was gone. If there was a cache hidden in the hillside somewhere, she might know about it, or she might not, but she hadn't told me if she did. Perhaps she thought secrecy was the best security system of all.

I didn't linger because I didn't want her to worry that I'd spotted something I wasn't supposed to see, if I had spotted something. I made one more circuit of the house and then took my leave and went back to the villa to exercise, nap, and drink my herbal sludge.

16

Aldo watched the house that evening, and once he saw Giulia leave, came and retrieved me. The sun was on its way down, but I still had an hour of golden light before dusk began to blur the outlines of things.

"Have your phone?" he said. "They told me to ask."

He waited until he'd pulled up outside the gate to say, "I'm not the only one who's been watching it."

I turned toward him and raised an eyebrow. "No?"

He shook his head and produced from his pocket a cigarette butt, which he handed to me. "It's the biggest one I found."

I was reminded, as I so often was when in the company of a relative stranger in a foreign country, that Quixote only worked with professionals. Usually, though not always, social skills were fairly far down on our list of priorities.

I examined the butt, and spotting the traces of a familiar logo, smiled at him. "American," I said.

He tapped his temple in a silent commentary on the insanity of a spy who would sneak around, find a place to observe without being observed, and then permeate the air with cigarette smoke and leave his cigarette butts behind.

I didn't waste his time or mine stating the obvious—that the butts could belong to Finch, even though I hadn't seen him smoke in the time I'd been with him. It was always possible that Giulia had removed cigarettes and matches out of concern that he'd burn the house down, and that he'd found a way to circumvent her precautions. But Aldo wouldn't have drawn the conclusion he'd drawn if he hadn't found a concentration of butts in a suspicious spot. And the feat of amassing a secret stash of American cigarettes seemed beyond the old man's capabilities now. This butt was fresh. I'd need to watch my back.

Aldo was extending a hand. In it was a Beretta subcompact. I waved it off.

"I don't want to get caught with anything," I said, "in case the security system is better than I think it is."

I was wearing a pair of khaki trousers that Fina had altered to accommodate the boot, and a loose-fitting shirt to hide the tool belt around my waist and the small field glasses around my neck. I had my phone in my pocket. I maneuvered my crutch out of the tiny car and got it positioned under my arm. A pistol was one encumbrance too many. The tools I could justify as a security consultant; the pistol I couldn't.

"You sure you don't want me to wait?" he said.

I shook my head. "I might be here all night. I'll call you when I'm ready to leave."

"Okay," he said.

Through the glasses, the house looked peaceful. A flickering of light in one window suggested that a television was on, but there was no way to know whether Finch was watching it or not. Giulia might have turned it on before she left in the hope that he would sit quietly and watch it until bedtime, but he might have other ideas.

I made slow and clumsy progress as I skirted the house, disconcerted by the noise I was making. I startled one or two small creatures in the underbrush, but they must have been deaf because everybody else could hear me coming from fifty yards away. I had to watch the ground, and then pause when I wanted to re-check the house. But despite my precautions, the bloody boot caught on things and threatened to trip me up. I had to clamp my lips together to keep the curses in. A red squirrel looked balefully down at me from an oak branch and chittered his disapproval, then followed me, leaping from one tree to the next. I might as well have hired a herald to walk in front of me and announce my arrival. Finch's mental faculties were failing, but his hearing might be fine.

I found the break in the undergrowth, where a narrow path led up the hillside. The surface of the path was worn hard, so there were no footprints to see, but the encroachment of weeds made it appear long undisturbed. Still, if the legend of Birdman was true, he wouldn't need a path. He could fly.

As I started up the path, I took care. If I fell and broke something else at this point, I'd be humiliated. Besides, I hated being rescued. Some day in the not-too-distant future, I'd be one of those old ladies found dead in her assisted living apartment, the emergency cord within easy reach.

I rounded an outcrop and found myself on flat ground—a space wide enough for Aldo's little Fiat to have spun around in—flanked on two sides by steep walls of rock covered by thick vines and the kind of hardy shrubs that thrive in the crevices of rock where wind plants their seeds. The path continued on the opposite side, but all of my alarms were ringing now. I slipped on a glove and studied the area. Then I approached a part of the wall where the mass of vines grew densest, uninterrupted by shrubs. I reached out, penetrating the thick cover of wild grape and probing its face. The surface under my touch was hard and flat—too flat and too smooth to be natural.

The susurration of brush behind me could have been a small

animal, but I didn't think so. I withdrew my hand and retreated, as quietly as I could, behind the cover of the outcrop. It wouldn't hide me, but it would give me the advantage of a few seconds to assess the situation.

I saw his shadow, long in the twilight, before I saw him. And then I saw the dull gleam of the pistol in his hand, held out in front of him like a divining rod. Neil Calloway.

He was dressed in jeans and a blue polo shirt that set off his blue eyes. He wore sunglasses atop his wavy blond hair—a look I hate in men.

I might have taken him then, but with my gimpy leg, the odds weren't in my favor. I'd have to wait.

His eyes made a circuit of the clearing and came to rest on me. He grinned. "I guess you really do work for a security outfit," he said. "I didn't believe it when Steve told me. I figured you were just hanging out with the old biddies. But then I spotted you at the airport, and I thought, 'Wait a minute! I know her. What's the old girl doing here?' And now I have my answer. Good thing I didn't leave yet. I don't know who figured this out and how, and I don't really care. You must've overheard something and said to yourself, 'Hey! Maybe I can beat everybody to the spot and get some of that for myself.' Am I right?"

"Pretty close," I said. He was underestimating me—good. I wanted him to go on underestimating me. It was always my trump card.

On the other hand, if he'd followed me from the airport without my knowing it, maybe he wasn't underestimating me. I resolved to double my daily dose of herbal sludge.

Behind my back, I slipped the glove off and dropped it in the undergrowth. It would look too professional.

"I have my ways," he said. His gaze made another circuit, but he kept the gun trained on me. "You think there's something here," he said. He studied the ground

I shrugged. "The path continues up the hillside."

"But you stopped here," he said.

"I'm tired," I said.

He glanced at my crutch. "Maybe," he said.

Daylight was slowly fading into dusk. That was in my favor, too.

"You must've searched the house today," he mused, as he crossed the space to the wall of rock with its curtain of vegetation. He began exploring the dense growth with his unarmed hand. "I'll bet you have a card with that security company's name on it. You probably talked old Giulia into letting you look around. That was pretty smart. But you didn't find anything."

I certainly hadn't found the items he'd already removed. But I didn't say that. I didn't say anything. I didn't want him to know that I knew who he was and what he'd been up to.

He was still grinning. "And you said to yourself, just like I did, 'There has to be more.' But where?"

He advanced along the wall. Then his expression changed as his arm moved slowly.

It was another missed opportunity. Two good legs, and I would have had him flat on his back before his attention could return to me. I edged closer—or rather, I made a move that would have been edging if I hadn't been planting a crutch.

His grin widened. "Looky what I found," he said.

He began tearing at the vines with his free hand, but they were thick and impossible to manage, one-handed.

"Come over here," he said, and backed away. His eyes never leaving my face, he removed something from his back pocket and set it on the ground between us: a pocket knife. "Go ahead," he said. "Pick it up. I figure you're as curious as I am to see what's on the other side of that door, so you can do the work."

I bent awkwardly, steadying myself with my crutch, and picked up the knife. Good to have this confirmation, in case I didn't know already, that he was not a trained agent of anything, and never had been, whoever his father was. This clumsy knife would not have been my preferred weapon to practice my knife-throwing skills on, but I could probably take out his gun hand with it.

He nodded at the tangle of vines and gestured with the pistol. "Go on," he said. "Find the door for me."

I hobbled to the wall and began cutting away at the vines, which were old and thick—a condition that made me wonder if we were on the right track. Nobody had been here in a long time. The vines had been permitted to grow undisturbed. I couldn't be certain in the waning light, but I didn't see evidence of old cuts, either.

"I don't suppose you brought a hacksaw," I grumbled, "or electric hedge trimmers."

It would be out of character for me to show no curiosity about him, and I suspected that he liked to talk about himself, so I said, "I heard he was some kind of master thief. He stole some of the world's most famous jewels—that's what they said. Somehow they knew he was a friend of Dottie's—that's how his name came up. They heard he wasn't in good shape, and my boss, Emile, he wondered what had happened to all that loot." I winced when I said it and mentally apologized to Emile, who would never use a word like "loot."

I didn't look back at him, but I could still hear the grin in his voice. "That's the big question," he said. "What happened to all that loot?"

"How did you hear about it?" I asked.

"Let's just say I have connections," he said.

I glanced back at him, trying to look impressed. "Oh, yeah?" I said.

The temptation to brag was too much for him. He said, "My old man used to be with Interpol. I read Finch's jacket, put two and two together, and here I am."

This confirmed my suspicions that he'd gotten to Dottie through Finch and not the other way around. According to Giulia's letter, he'd been hanging around, encouraging Finch to talk about the past, and Finch had been uncharacteristically forthcoming—perhaps because it gave him pleasure to talk about things he remembered more clearly than what he'd eaten for breakfast. If Finch had discussed the Tehran job, Calloway could have gotten Dottie's name out of him. He'd probably also learned Dottie's general location, or maybe he had just searched the house for Finch's address book. Dottie might have had her own Interpol and FBI files, but if so, her house would have been searched long ago, search warrant or not, and the paintings located because they weren't very well hidden. And I couldn't see her gossiping about Finch to Monica and Monica's new boyfriend.

On the other hand, I couldn't believe that a true Interpol agent, now a Fibbie, would leave a file like that lying around for anybody to read, so unless his father deliberately set him on Finch's trail, he must have done some sneaking around.

I felt something under my right hand—a circular protuberance. A dial.

"But how'd you get together with Dottie's niece?" I said. "Is that connected to Finch?"

I didn't want to call him "Birdman." I didn't want to betray how much I knew about him.

He didn't answer the question. Instead he said, "She's my fiancée. Old Aunt Dottie had some nice things, and Monica will inherit them."

"Did she leave everything to Monica?" I said, surprise in my voice. "I heard she left a lot to some foreign government, which sounded totally crazy to me."

"We'll get everything that's coming to us," he said with confidence. "That's why I'm around—to see that we do."

I was curious to see whether he'd mention the theft at Dottie's house. But now a beam of light hit my hand, and he gave an exclamation. "Hey! You found it."

He moved forward and gave me a shove backward. The damn boot caught on something, and I went down with a thud and a faint metallic clink. Belatedly, I yelped and tried to roll in the direction of the sound, but my legs were tangled under me and he'd already heard it. A small object rolled toward him, and he picked it up. If I'd recovered faster, I could have taken him down then, while he studied it, but I didn't know what I was going to do with him. Even unconscious, he'd be a body that needed to be dragged, and I was incapable of dragging him in my current condition. Meanwhile, I was about to lose some of my advantage.

A slow grin broke over his smug face. "It's a picklock," he said. "You know how to use it?"

I shrugged. "I'm not very good with it," I said. Just as well I was on a reconnaissance mission. I hadn't brought the drills or any other bulkier equipment, and it hadn't occurred to him that I might be carrying more. The other picklocks and bump keys were still snug in their case under my shirt. But I already knew that a picklock would do us no good.

He mimed opening a lock with the little blue tool, imagining himself in the role of master criminal. Then he handed it back to me. "Go ahead, open it," he said.

"Can't," I said, gesturing at the lock. "It's a combination."

To cover his stupidity, he said, "Yeah, okay, I guess you do know something about lock-picking."

I didn't bother to point out that any idiot could tell that you couldn't open a combination lock with a picklock.

But apparently, he took my point as a sign of unsuspected intelligence on my part. He looked at me speculatively and said, "Can't you open a combination lock? You must've picked up a thing or two working at that security place."

Okay, so here's the thing. Much as I wanted him to go on underestimating me, I wanted to see what was on the other side of the door as much as Calloway did. And what I didn't want was for him to decide to just shoot me and go looking for a drill.

"I could give it a try," I said, doubt in my voice.

He waved the gun at me. "You do that," he said. "Try real hard."

By now I'd climbed up my crutch and was standing more or less upright again. I went to work on the lock, bending my head close to listen. I hadn't done this in years, not for real. But I did practice from time to time, because I didn't like to over-rely on technology. In many parts of the world, security measures were still low-tech. Lucky for me, Finch either hadn't trusted the modern electronic locking systems or hadn't bothered to update, just as Dottie hadn't. He had once invested in a high quality lock, one that he was probably arrogant enough to believe couldn't be opened by anyone less skilled than he was, and he'd relied upon the concealment of the heavy curtain of vegetation. But this was going to take time. It used to be easier somehow.

"You ever opened one of these?" he asked.

"Shh," I said. "I have to concentrate." I wasn't about to close my eyes on him. Sweat tickled my temple and time passed. Then, on my third time around, I felt the first tiny shiver in my fingertips as the dial passed a gate. I eased it back.

There was more ambient noise than I would have liked, including the noise of his shoes scuffing the ground impatiently. I couldn't stand it. I threw him a look.

"If you can't stand still," I said, "move farther away."

"Sorry," he said, chastened.

My first attempt failed. Less sure about the second gate than the third, I turned the dial back to try again. Now I was in the zone, all of my awareness shrunken to focus on the sensations in my fingertips. I found the second gate.

Eventually, I heard the faint click as the final gate aligned with the other two, and I said a silent thanks to my old partner Brian—a safecracker from a long line of safecrackers whom Emile had bribed to switch sides not with the dental plan or even the shiny blue Maserati but with the promise of a life so thrilling and perilous that it made safecracking look like insurance sales. Brian had been with me on the Tehran job, and taught me almost everything I knew about opening locks—at least, the old fashioned kind —and I liked to think he was still taking an interest from whichever camp he was occupying in the afterlife. "Age and experience still count for something, Bri," I said to him.

I took a deep breath and pulled the door handle, which didn't budge. I tried again, using all my weight against it until I felt it give with the complaint of metal on metal. The door was thick and heavy and I wondered whether we'd get it open at all without a crowbar, then the seal popped. But the vines wouldn't release the door, clinging to it like jilted lovers. I began sawing at the vines, making the whole operation look as awkward as possible.

He stepped forward in impatience. "Jesus Christ, we'll be here all night!" he said. "Give me that."

I let him have the knife and stood back to give him room. I didn't mind letting him do the work.

Finally, the last severed vine released its grip and the door swung open with a metallic scrape and groan. I stepped forward, crowding Calloway. As he rushed the door, trying to shove me aside, I chopped his gun wrist and used my good foot to shove him inside, ignoring the complaint of my bad leg when it felt all my weight come down on it. As he went sprawling, I stooped, awkwardly, stepped through the doorway, and picked up the pistol at my feet, checked to see that it was loaded.

Now I wouldn't have to drag him anywhere. Good.

He had cried out in pain and shock and when he sat up, his mouth still hung open, which was not a good look for him. He gaped at the gun in my hand.

"Why'd you do that?" he said.

I considered the question rhetorical, since the answer was obvious. You don't have to be a trained agent of anything to know that in any given situation, if somebody's holding a gun, you want that somebody to be you. Fewer accidents that way.

I was conscious of things behind him that bore investigating, but he needed to be dealt with first. At that point, the lights went out, leaving us in the shallow, dusty dusk of natural light from the open door.

Then he charged me.

He couldn't believe I'd use the gun, and he was right. The room appeared to be lined with solid steel walls, floor and ceiling, and I wouldn't risk the ricochets. I just managed to thumb the safety on when he slammed into me, knocking the crutch out from under me. The pistol slipped from my hand. I inhaled the odor of cigarettes and sweat as he crawled over me to reach it, but I managed to get a hand on my crutch and used it as an awkward hockey stick to send the gun skittering across the room and into the shadows on the far side. He scrambled after it, but I caught hold of his foot with both hands and twisted. He yelped and kicked free as I got the crutch under me and hauled myself up. But in the dim light from the doorway, he'd spotted something and reached for it—an antique sword from a nearby display rack of antique swords. He turned toward me, sword in hand, grinning. I scooped up a small bronze bust from a nearby shelf and flung it at him.

"Here, catch!" I shouted.

He didn't drop the sword, as I'd hoped, but it staggered him, and he stumbled backward, nearly knocking himself out with the cross-guard when he flung his sword hand up to protect his face. When he focused on me again and saw the sword in my hand, he grinned.

Don't ask me why, but most men seem to think that the Y chromosome makes them natural sword handlers. This delusion is no doubt encouraged by Hollywood movies, in which skilled swordswomen are few and far between. But contrary to popular masculine belief, sword fighting has little to do with physical strength and everything to do with precision, training, and practice. I let the crutch fall and balanced on my two feet as best I could.

He came at me like a drunken samurai—the samurai who had flunked out of samurai school—slashing haphazardly, all flash and no force. I stepped in, parried, slid my blade past the guard to nick his fingers, and then, when his grip loosened, sent his sword flying. It arced above his head, rang against the steel wall, and clattered to the floor. Calloway crumpled, put his bloody fist to his mouth, and wailed.

"Don't be such a baby," I said. "It's just a nick."

I heard a sound from the doorway and turned.

The old man stood looking at us. He wore an open cotton bathrobe over a baggy pair of shorts. His smooth crown and wispy hair were silhouetted against the dying light outside. His expression was unreadable. Before either of us could speak, he turned and left, closing the door with a hollow metallic sound that reverberated off the stone walls in the sudden blackness.

A few seconds of total silence passed, and then Calloway's voice spoke huskily out of the void, not far from my ear. "*Now* look what you've done," it said.

17

The light from his cell phone flickered on and glinted off his eyes as he moved toward the door. He was fumbling to wrap his injured hand in a handkerchief. I climbed to my feet and started in the direction of the gun, as quietly as I could manage. But he wasn't thinking about the gun.

"It's locked!" he said. "Goddamn the bastard, he locked us in!" His voice quavered.

The small light streaked and grunts and thuds told me that he was throwing himself against the door. I slid a penlight out of my tool belt and found the gun on the floor. I bent and picked it up again, broke it open and pocketed the clip.

He didn't register the sound until he heard the metallic click. As he wheeled around, I extinguished the penlight.

The light he was holding showed him peering nearsightedly into the darkness, and I could tell that he couldn't see me. Sweat shone along his hairline. With the light below him, he looked like a ghoul—if ghouls are ever sweaty and panic-stricken.

"Oh, right," he said. "I guess you got the gun. I guess you think you'll shoot me now. Well, go ahead, shoot me! We're going to die in this hellhole anyway—you and me both."

"Oh, give it a rest," I said.

I'd been trapped many times with people who had more to fear than he could even imagine, and most of them had shown more bravery than he could muster in the face of a minor setback. I slid my hand in my pocket and felt my cell phone there, but I doubted any signal could penetrate these walls of thick rock and I didn't want to run down the battery against tall odds.

"Maybe we could shoot the lock off," he proposed.

"It's not a lock you can shoot off," I pointed out, "because it's not *on* anything. It's embedded in a concrete panel covered in cast iron or steel. If you fired at it, the ricochet would probably put a hole in your chest the size of a fist."

"Well, there has to be a way to get out," he said. "You can get us out, right?"

"Safes aren't meant to be opened from the inside," I said. "And besides, there's a time lock on the door." I pointed.

He turned his head to see the small window embedded in the door, behind which three brass cogs were visible.

"What's that mean?" he said.

"It means that the door can't be opened again for as long as he has the time lock set for," I said. This wasn't true. I had seen at a glance when I'd first stepped inside that Finch hadn't stopped to set the time lock or activate the current settings in any way, but Calloway didn't know that.

"Well, how long is that?" he said.

I shrugged, though I knew he couldn't see me. "Could be as much as seventy-two hours," I said.

There was a silence while he did the math in his head. It took a while.

Then he burst out, "But that's, like, three days!"

"Yep," I said. He was right to be afraid. If I had to put up with him in close quarters that long, he'd probably be dead inside of twelve hours.

"Well, can't you break the glass and screw up the timer or reset it or something?" he said.

"No," I said. "And anyway, like I said, I can't work the combination lock from the inside."

At that point, the light on his cell phone wavered and died.

"Fuck!" he shouted, and went on shouting it.

He wore himself out at last, and turned his fury on me. "I don't see what you're so calm about," he said. "Maybe being buried alive is your idea of a good time, but it's not mine." His voice dropped into the self-pity register. "Or maybe I'll bleed to death before I starve or suffocate. I'll probably get blood poisoning or something."

He was struggling to light a match, and I thought that if he lit a cigarette, I'd break his neck and his worries would be over.

It was cool inside the room, and the air was close, but not as musty as it could have been, and I was sure there was a ventilation system of some kind. From what I'd glimpsed before the lights went out, I was sure Finch would have installed some kind of climate control.

"Or maybe you know something I don't," he said. "Is that it? I don't hear you making any suggestions." He was holding a lit match.

"Okay," I said. "Here's one. You might start by flipping the light switch you're practically leaning against."

A motion detector had turned on some lights when we entered, but they were designed to go out in short order. The main lights needed to be turned on manually.

He said nothing, but I heard him fumbling, and then the lights came on.

He gasped when he saw the gun in my hand again.

"What I really want to know," I said, "is whether you killed

Dottie to get your hands on her estate." I kept it vague. I still didn't want to betray that I knew what the house had contained.

I thumbed the safety off. "I think I'll start with your right knee. Then we'll be evenly matched."

"I didn't kill Dottie," he squeaked. "I don't know who killed her, honest to God. I don't know. I was as surprised as everybody else when the old bag popped off."

It was as much a measure of his fear as of his stupidity that he would disrespect one "old bag" to another.

I moved the gun up and over. "On the other hand . . ."

"No, wait!" he cried. "You've got to believe me. You want to know who killed Dottie, you go ask Steve and Monica. You ask them! They were both dying to get their hands on her dough, believe me."

"But they'd get it anyway," I said.

"Not soon enough," he said. "Those two, they just wanted to live the good life, and they were tired of waiting around for it."

And you didn't? I thought.

"And anyway, they were afraid she'd change her will," he said, "which, it turned out, they were right. She didn't like them all that much to begin with. Another year and she might've given it all away to, like, homeless cats or something. You never knew."

I surprised myself by believing him. In spite of his recent samurai impersonation, I wasn't sure he had the sangfroid needed to poison someone and watch her die. I thought he probably had enough to pull a trigger, though, so I'd keep an eye on him.

"Hey!" he said. "Look at all this stuff!"

His eyes were finally scanning the room, and its contents were distracting him from his fear of imminent death. It was larger than the average living room, and it was a genuine strong room, with walls and floor made from sheets of steel, strategically placed pillars and braces to push back against the weight of the hill pressing down on it, and a quiet, compact air conditioning unit in a back corner. Otherwise, it looked like a storage room, with two venerable wood cabinets the height of my shoulder and stacks of wooden and cardboard crates and a couple of wooden chairs the same vintage as the kitchen chairs standing against one wall. There was a workbench in the middle, illuminated by brighter overhead lighting, a couple of sword racks, and a few small metal sculptures, like the bronze bust I'd thrown, decorating various surfaces.

But the most visible treasure was hanging on the wall, illuminated by its own spotlight. It appeared to be a Chagall, moderate-sized, depicting a couple floating in a flowery sky while an amiable cow and some kind of fat yellow bird looked on. Even from across the room, it was dazzling, as if it was a source, not a mere reflector, of light.

"A Chagall," Calloway said, with something that could have been reverence but was probably cupidity in his voice.

He approached the painting and extended a finger to touch it, like a chimp confronting an alien object.

"Don't touch it!" I snapped. "Don't you know anything about art?"

He grinned at me, but he withdrew his finger. "I know what it's worth. A Chagall about this size just sold for a cool thirty-two million at an auction in Seoul. It was, like, the most expensive painting ever sold in Asia, or something like that. Even on the black market, this baby would sell for megabucks."

I winced. The painting would be better off in his hands than in the hands of revolutionaries dedicated to destroying Western art, but if those were the only alternatives, Western art would be in very bad hands indeed.

All I said was, "Probably that one didn't have bloody fingerprints all over it." I put the safety back on and slipped the gun into my trousers pocket. His eyes followed it there, then turned to the nearest cabinet. I retrieved my crutch, keeping my eyes on him.

He pulled out a drawer, and said, "Holy shit!" He whistled.

I took a few cautious steps forward, planting my crutch and

careful to stay out of range of a sudden lunge, but he seemed genuinely transfixed by what he was looking at. He extracted a box and turned to show it to me.

The box, which was lidless, seemed more like a display case than a box. Nestled in its black velvet lining was a collar of gold fili-gree and pearls, embellished with rubies and emeralds. It was what Sophia Loren would wear to the Pope's Christmas party.

"Very nice," I said.

"You better believe it," he said, turning back to the drawer. "Man, this place is like a pirate's trove, huh? X marks the fucking spot. I bet all those boxes are crammed with valuable shit. This place must be worth billions, am I right?"

The door groaned. We turned toward it. The old man stood there, the same as before, except for the gun he was pointing.

"Hey, George!" Calloway said, and started toward him.

Finch fired. Whether he intended to hit Calloway or not, the bullet whizzed between us and I heard the ping of three ricochets before sound yielded to silence.

"What'd you do that for, Cousin George?" Calloway said, and his voice wobbled.

"Missed," Finch said, and moved farther into the room, stop-ping about five feet away from us so that he could still cover both of us with the gun.

From where I was standing, the gun looked like the Sig Sauer P226 that ex-Seals like to carry. Looking down the barrel, I couldn't really tell whether it had a .40 S&W or a .357 SIG round chambered, but it didn't matter since either could do the job.

"I won't miss again," he said. "I shoot thieves, and I shoot to kill."

The words sounded ludicrous coming out of the mouth of a man wearing nothing but a pair of shorts, a bathrobe, and bedroom slippers, but I knew that I was hearing an echo of the legendary

Birdman, the one who had coolly escaped from every trap Interpol had ever set for him.

"Ladies first?" he said. He turned the gun on me.

I fumbled in my pocket, and brought out the little yellow bird. I held it up. "I came from Dottie," I reminded him gently. "I really did."

He froze, his eyes on the pendant, his lips parted but speechless.

Calloway bolted. He bounded across the line of fire, past the old man, and out the door. I heard the door thud shut. I heard the ominous sound of the dial turning.

Finch didn't register Calloway's departure. Instead, his face collapsed and his gun hand fell. "What—what happened to her?" he choked out.

"What do you mean?" I said cautiously, still hoping that I wouldn't have to tell him.

"She's dead," he said, blinking. "Isn't she?"

I took a deep breath. "Yes," I sighed. "I'm so sorry, but yes."

His eyes melted. He looked down, raised both hands in a gesture of futility, let them drop.

I hobbled toward him and put an arm around his shoulders. I wasn't much of a comforter, I knew that. Quixote had never offered a class in it, so while I knew how to handle rage and hostility and violence, I'd never been coached in how to handle grief. I'd seen a lot of it in my work, but it was usually a luxury we didn't have time for. Nevertheless, I had observed the soothing effects of an arm across the shoulders.

"I'm so sorry," I repeated. "I was hoping I wouldn't have to tell you. But how did you know?"

He found the hand with the necklace and I let him take it from me. "She wouldn't have given it to anyone—not anyone, ever. It was special to us," he said, his voice thick with sorrow and memory.

I removed the gun from his other hand, ejected the clip, and set it on a nearby cabinet. He didn't protest. I led him to the chairs and we both sat down. I rested a hand on his. My own chest was tight, my heart a lead weight.

"Who did you say you were?" he asked. "I don't remember."

"A friend of Dottie's," I said. "But I didn't know her very long. How long did you know her?"

His moist eyes sought the distance. "Oh, I don't know," he said. "I don't know anything anymore. I—." His shoulders heaved. "I thought I'd be the first to go. That's how it was meant to be." He took a ragged breath. "I wanted to see her one more time—just one more time before—."

I patted his hand.

"When did she come to see me?" he asked. "Was she here?" He looked around.

"I don't know," I said. "We'll have to ask Giulia."

"Did she suffer?" he asked, and turned eyes on me that were unsettling in their clarity. Just now, in this moment, he understood everything.

On firmer ground now that all I had to do was lie, I said, "No, it was very peaceful. Her heart gave out." True. "She was acting in a play at the time."

"A play? What play?"

"She was playing one of the witches from *Macbeth*," I said.

He smiled then. "She would have made a good witch," he said. Then he startled me by intoning, "Double, double, toil and trouble, fire burn and caldron bubble."

"She was," I agreed, "a very good witch."

"I like your painting," I said, nodding at the wall opposite. "Is it one of hers?"

He smiled fondly at it, then turned back to me. "It's a—a—oh, hell, it's by what's-his-name," he said.

"Chagall?" I prompted.

"Chagall," he repeated to himself. "Did she give it to me?"

"Dottie?" I said. "I imagine she did, if you liked it."

"It was my favorite," he said, admiring it. "We didn't get that one, you know." His voice trailed dreamily. "It was one of the ones that got away."

I looked at the painting, then back at him. "You didn't get it?" I echoed. "In Tehran, you mean?"

He grunted. "Had to leave it behind, didn't we?" he said. "When the others came."

"You mean, when the other thieves came that night? And took all the paintings?"

He huffed. "Not all of them," he said, a little testily. "We had—." He looked around the room, as if searching for the stolen paintings. He rose in agitation. "We had—."

I was hanging on to this conversation by my fingernails. "Dottie took the rest, didn't she? To the States?" I said.

He shrugged. "I don't know," he said. "I don't know anything anymore." His eyes snagged on my face. "Who are you?"

"A friend of Dottie's," I reminded him gently.

He looked around in confusion. "Where is Dottie?"

"Back in the states," I said, then added reassuringly, "You know that."

"Do I?" he said.

"Why don't you show me the painting?" I suggested. I hooked his elbow and led him to the Chagall. It was in a thin gold frame of carved wood.

He gazed at it fondly. Then he reached out and removed it from its hanger and turned it over to look at the back. He pointed at something there.

"What is it?" I asked and leaned forward to look.

He continued to point, looking up at me. I understood that he'd lost the words for what he was showing me.

I squinted at the label. "*Certificat d'authenticité*," I read. "From the Comité Chagall. And there's an image of the painting on it." I looked up. "It's real."

He beamed at me and shook his head.

"The certificate is a forgery?" I said.

He shook his head again.

I looked at the painting in his hands. "The certificate is genuine," I said slowly, "but it's been removed from the original painting and attached to the forgery."

He grinned at me, then returned his attention to the painting, which he turned over again and replaced on the wall. He sighed. "She added the finch after. She was the best," he said. "Dorotea." He raised a hand and mimed painting with a brush.

"The best?" I repeated. I had to make sure I was getting this straight. "The best—painter? The best forger? Dottie?"

Dorothy Rivers. The one who had taken a painting class in college and discovered that she "had no talent." But talent at what? At painting? Or at innovating, imagining, creating a unique vision and style? You wouldn't need imagination if you dedicated your life to copying the works of others. Or maybe you did, but it was a different kind of imagination. Maybe she hadn't intended it as a career at first. Maybe she'd been like every other painting student, copying the masters to learn her craft and find inspiration. And maybe she'd found it—in the quest for the perfect reproduction. But to succeed in that quest, she would have needed more than a college painting class; she would have needed a historian's and chemist's understanding of materials. How could someone with that kind of encyclopedic knowledge and skill be content to paint Scottie dogs by number? Did it permit her to satisfy her addiction to the cherished scents of paints and turpentine and give her the tactile pleasure of holding a paintbrush between her fingers without betraying her true calling?

When he didn't respond, I said, "Dottie forged the paintings in the Tehran collection. You were in the process of replacing them, one by one, when another team broke in and stole some paintings, except that they didn't leave any forgeries in their place. So you had to suspend operations."

"She grieved for them—the ones we didn't get," he said.

"And she was there that night—at the museum," I said. "The night that the others came. Dottie Rivers was there."

He turned to me in surprise. "You know Dottie?" he said.

"Not as well as I wish," I told him truthfully.

18

I patted him on the hand again. "It's time to think about getting us out of here, George," I said. "You're losing your beauty sleep." I tugged at his bathrobe sleeve to recapture his wandering attention. "Hey!" I said. "I don't suppose you installed an escape mechanism on your vault door."

He smiled at me sweetly and shrugged.

I smiled back at him. "No," I said, "you wouldn't have. Not Birdman. That would have been too easy. But you would have had another exit in mind—a backup plan. You wouldn't have survived as long as you did without a certain amount of caution."

He surprised me by saying, "I was lucky."

"Yeah," I said. "You and me both, George."

I made a circuit of the room, looking for any anomalies that might signal a hidden door or movable panel, or any buttons, levers, or dials whose purpose wasn't obvious. Since the walls were made of steel panels, seams were visible, but I couldn't see any way to move any of them. I used my flashlight and looked behind stacked crates as best I could, but I was hampered by my game leg and crutch. It would take me hours to move all the crates and the furniture away from the wall, and I would have to work carefully. Who knew what these crates contained? I doubted I'd find the Mona Lisa, since as far as I knew Dottie had specialized in modern art, but I might find a Picasso.

Every now and then, I'd stop and say, "Am I getting warmer, George?"

He would just shrug. He was distracted by all his loot.

I turned my attention to the intake and outtake ducts on the air conditioning unit. These looked like my best bet for communicating with the outside world, even though I couldn't quite believe that Finch would have built a room without an escape hatch. I used a screwdriver from my tool belt to begin dismantling one of the ducts, explaining to Finch what I was doing and why. I retrieved the longest sword I could find and laid it on top of the unit. I stood on a chair to reach the top screws on the lower section, leaving my crutch leaning against the unit.

Finch stood below. "Be careful," he said. "Don't fall."

I removed the section of ductwork, and, looking up, saw stars. That was reassuring, since I thought it likely that I wouldn't see anything because the opening would be completely obscured by vegetation.

Standing on tiptoe, I inserted the sword into the shaft. The sword wasn't long enough. With trepidation and a little help from Finch at the end, I wrestled the chair on top of the unit and tested it with my weight. It seemed stable enough—more stable than I was.

I used a small length of wire from my tool belt to attach my cell phone to the business end of the sword. I switched the phone on, and noticed that my battery was half dead—or half alive, if I was inclined to optimism, which I wasn't. Optimism could get you killed. Quixote phone batteries were incredibly long-lasting, and they even had a solar recharge option, but you still had to make a conscious effort to recharge them.

I pushed the distress call button on the phone.

"Well, here goes nothing," I said to George. I clambered awkwardly onto the chair, used a hand on the chair back to steady myself as I stood up, and raised the sword, fitting my arm into the opening.

God, how I hated being rescued!

Now I blessed Jasmine for all the weight training she'd made me do. At the time I'd objected that I had no plans to walk on my hands until my leg healed, but now the arm strength was coming in handy, though the cold air blowing on me from below wasn't helping.

I wondered what Calloway would do next. Since he didn't have the combination to the lock, he'd probably return with an acetylene torch, but would it be tonight? He might worry that the old man would be missed, and that a search party would find the strong room if he waited until tomorrow. But surely it would take him some time to score an acetylene torch and a floodlight, and if he went looking for another gun, even longer. I angled my wrist to look at my watch: it was almost ten o'clock. He'd probably wait until at least midnight, I thought, even if he already had his equipment together. That should give Quixote plenty of time to get me out of here. I switched arms.

I heard Finch opening drawers behind me, and assumed that he was taking the opportunity to examine his treasures.

"Look!" he said, and I screwed my head around to see that he was holding up a beaded gold broad collar in the shape of a bird with its wings spread. It was probably Egyptian, probably ancient and genuine.

"Very nice," I said, though it wasn't my cup of tea.

I wondered when he'd last inspected his trophies. Not for years, probably. I wondered if he'd remembered that they were here. If I thought that I was destined for Alzheimer's in another ten years, I'd use the sword—probably also ancient and genuine—to cut my throat now. In my experience, this long middle stage, the mental limbo in which Finch now existed, was the most agonizing. The snatches of rational conversation and flashes of intelligence hinted at a greater understanding that he was rarely capable of expressing. I switched arms again.

He was back. "Look at this one," he said, holding up something too small for me to make out.

"I can't see it from here," I said.

He raised it two inches. "It's a—a—." He inspected it, frowning. "It's a—a bug," he said.

"A scarab?" I said.

"Yes," he said, excitedly. "A scarab. In —in—blue."

"Lapis lazuli?" I asked.

He nodded and went away. His voice was more distant now. "She said I ought to send it all back to Cairo," he said, and sighed. "Well, maybe I will, some day. She didn't want it."

"She preferred the goldfinch," I said, but I couldn't tell if he heard me.

Of course, I wanted to see all his loot. I was curious—sure. But every time I turned my head to look at what he was showing me, the chair wobbled, so I hoped he wasn't planning to show me his collection, piece by piece.

Now he tapped me on the foot. "Hey!" he said. "I have to go back now. You have to leave, too."

"That's what I'm working on, George," I said, looking down at him.

"You have to leave," he said. "I'm going to bed." He ran his hands through his hair in agitation. "It's time for you to go home."

"Okay," I said. "You go, and I'll follow."

He marched to one corner of the room, shifted a pile of crates resting atop a dolly, put a palm to the wall, and stood watching while the wall slid away in front of him.

I lowered my aching arm and dropped my sword. I eased myself down from the chair and then used my crutch to help myself down to the floor. I unfastened my cell phone from its improvised boom and replaced the sword. Then I limped after Finch.

At the opening, I stared down into a dank, dimly lit stairwell containing a set of crudely built wooden stairs.

"Come on!" Finch's voice rose from below and echoed off the walls.

I put a hand on the stair rail, feeling the faint, sticky resistance of a spider web against my fingertips. The fusty smell of mold made me feel light-headed. I tested a step with my crutch, and when it held, started down. The air was close, hot and humid here where it hadn't been disturbed for years, and an overhead light flickered like a strobe. Step by cautious step, I descended.

I heard voices, paused, and fished the pistol out of my pocket. I took the time to reload the clip. The voices were speaking Italian, which was probably a good sign. I stepped out into the warm night air, my hand on the pistol in my pocket.

"Ah, M.J.," Aldo said, as if I'd just arrived late for Happy Hour. "*Bene, bene.*"

We were standing in a dense patch of brush, and a rustle to my right drew my attention to the figure of Finch, dim in the moonlight, disappearing around the bend, talking to himself.

"Yes, yes," Aldo was saying, and I saw that he had his *telefonino* to his ear. "She's fine. At least I think she's fine." He raised his eyebrows at me and I nodded. "She just walked out of a hill. Yes, with her crutch. Yes, okay, boss." He handed the phone to me.

"Didi?" I mouthed, and Aldo nodded.

"I'm fine, Didi," I said into the phone, "really." All of our cell phone conversations were cautious. Nobody knew better than we did how easy it was to listen in on them.

"I'm glad to hear it," Didi said. "What now?"

I gazed out over the landscape. I could see Villa Offuscata below, a faint blue light still flickering in one window.

"We'll have to dogsit," I said, using our code for staying in place. "Tomorrow someone else will need to do it."

"I'll talk to Aldo about it," Didi said. "Call me in the morning, anytime."

"Didi," I said, "I can't guarantee payment."

"Well," he said, "let's call it a favor for an old competitor."

I wanted to ask about Dottie's paintings, but I couldn't think of a way to do it that wouldn't give away what we knew about them to anyone listening. I handed the phone back to Aldo.

The conversation with Aldo was brief. When Aldo hung up, I asked, "How did you get here so fast? And how did you find the back entrance?"

He shrugged. "I was parked up the road. When they called me, I set my phone to pick up your signal. I was about to start up the hill when I heard something crashing around. It could have been a wild animal, but wild animals don't speak Italian, so I followed the noise and found Finch."

"Well, thanks," I said. No point in saying more. I had sent him about his business, but he was a professional, and his business was watching my back, so that was what he'd done. I would have done the same, and so would any Quixote agent.

"You didn't need my help," he said.

"This time," I said.

He looked around, hands on his hips. My watch told me that it was after midnight. "So what do we do now?"

"We wait," I said. "Your cigarette-smoking friend saw the strong room crammed with valuables that Finch installed in the hillside. He'll probably be back with a torch. He might decide to get the old man out of the way first."

He nodded. "Shall I take the house?"

"Sure," I said.

He started off, then turned. "Oh, I forgot, I have something for you in the car," he said. "I'll get it."

I trailed him to the foot of the path that led up to the main entrance to the strong room. I found a rock nearby, uncomfortable but concealed by shrubbery. Aldo returned shortly and offered me a cold San Pellegrino and a brown paper bag that turned out to contain biscotti.

"Remind me to recommend you for a raise," I said.

"A Maserati," he said. "Tell Didi I want a Maserati for my company car."

For the rest of the night, I fought to stay awake, but the orange soda and biscotti helped. I thought about the crates stacked in Finch's strong room, and wondered what they contained. In the world of art theft, Birdman was known as an opportunist, not a major player. Stealing a handful of jewelry and stealing a bulky, often well-guarded canvas typically involved a very different set of skills, even a different personality type. But if Finch had worked with Dottie on the Tehran heist, perhaps there had been others. If so, where was Dottie's portion of the take? There were four additional paintings in Dottie's catalog, paintings that didn't appear to have been hung with the rest in Dottie's vault, and Bernie had texted me while I'd been snoozing over the Atlantic to tell me that all of them were from the Tehran collection. How many had they stolen to begin with? The fifteen on Dottie's list, or more? Finch had perhaps thirty crates squirreled away. Had he kept some paintings for himself? Or was he keeping some for Dottie? He certainly had a better storage space than she did—more secure and better equipped.

My imagination returned unbidden to the mental image of Dottie in her witch's hat, bent over a folding table in the garish artificial light of the day room at The Elms, daubing pink paint on a Scottie's nose, her own nose pink from blowing. I'd had the fleeting thought at the time that she had saved this spot of color for last—as a reward for the tedium of hours of variations on beige and gray. But for someone who had painted Chagall and

Picasso and Monet and Gaughin, how was that monotony bearable?

Come to think of it, when had she painted the forgeries? Had she foreseen the trouble in Tehran long before Emile had, or the U.S. State Department? I was having enough trouble reimagining her as a master forger, but as a visionary political analyst as well? Anything was possible, but how much lead time would she have needed to produce eight forgeries? More than the eight we'd stolen and identified, actually, since she must have substituted forgeries for the seven additional paintings on her list, if they had all come from the Tehran collection. And Finch seemed to be implying that they were prepared to steal more of the paintings until we showed up and queered their pitch. The small Chagall in the strong room tended to back him up. How long did it take to paint a credible medium-sized Picasso? I had no idea. The museum had opened on the queen's birthday in October of 1977 and the first demonstrations against the shah had taken place soon afterward, though he hadn't left the country until early 1979. If she was exceptionally prescient, that would have given her a little over a year to produce at least fifteen high-quality forgeries, which would certainly explain her four visits to Iran in 1977 and 1978. Those visits would have given her an understanding of the worsening political situation there and a consequent sense of urgency. Perhaps she was already an experienced forger who had painted many of these artists before. But it just didn't seem possible.

Eventually the night noises died down, the birds began their morning serenade, the sun came up, and we were relieved by two serious-looking women with high-tech binoculars and slender rifles with high-powered scopes. When Aldo dropped me off at the villa, I'd long since put my brain on hold. I stumbled into the house and crossed the main salon on my way to the kitchen, head drooping.

So it was the movement that first caught my attention—the

busy flickering of light and shadow on the pale tile. When my brain processed what I was seeing, I looked up at the glass-paneled doors that led to the courtyard. Morning light flooded in. But silhouetted against it was a confusion of small, dancing creatures—much smaller in fact than the shadows they cast. Fogged by exhaustion, I moved toward them. They were on the other side of the glass. And when I came closer they resolved into flies—dozens of flies. Jolted awake, I looked down.

There, sprawled across the stones of the courtyard, was the figure of a man with a neat hole in the back of his shirt and a dark pool under his chest.

I slipped my cell phone out of my pocket, thumbed it on, and called Aldo.

"We need to reassess the dogsitting operation," I said.

19

"So what do we think?" Aldo said, staring down at the body. "That he had an accomplice who now knows what he knew about Finch's cache?"

"Seems likely, doesn't it?" I said. I was executing a kind of one-legged squat—something I hadn't wanted to do without a spotter to help me up—and extracting his wallet from his back pocket with gloved fingertips. From this distance, I could see that the back of his head was sticky with blood, indicating a second bullet: someone had wanted to make sure he was dead. I didn't plan to be this close when the *Polizia* turned him over and exposed the exit wounds, if there were any.

Aldo raised his palm in Italian disbelief. "What kind of idiot keeps his wallet in his back pocket like that? In Italy? He was asking to be robbed."

"But probably not killed," I said. "Convenient for us, though." I felt a twinge of guilt when I said it, but not a very big one. I'd seen dead people that I'd liked better.

I examined the wallet. "Driver's license is genuine," I said. "Didn't bother with one for his alias. Address is probably genuine as well. No pictures of Monica, but they'll probably find her on his phone. It won't take them long to get to Kevin Calloway and the whole Interpol-FBI connection."

"True," Aldo conceded with a flick of his shoulders, "but then they'll say, 'Wait, we know about the infamous Birdman—we have a file on him. So if we found this guy dead in Finch's courtyard, we would understand that he was going after Finch's stash. But what's he doing in the courtyard of this visiting American lady?'"

"Wrong address?" I suggested.

He didn't bother to answer. Instead he said, "So what's your story? Do you know who he is or don't you?"

I was easing the wallet back into Calloway's pocket.

"I'll have to talk to Emile and Didi," I said, "but I think I don't. I would only have seen him maybe twice before, and I doubt that his girlfriend even noticed me noticing him. Even if they show me his driver's license, I can honestly say that there's something familiar about him without coming up with a name. I'm not supposed to know him as Neil Calloway, anyway."

"And what is the purpose of your visit, *signora*?" Aldo said, in the polite, detached voice of a *poliziotto*. He got a hand under my shoulder and heaved me to my feet.

"*Grazie*," I said. "I work for a security firm, Levesque Security. In the course of another investigation, I came across a letter from Giulia Massini pleading for help from my late client. Because I thought it might be connected to my investigation, and because the letter suggested that the writer might be in need of security services, I came to Italy to meet with her."

"And what investigation would that be, *signora*?" he said. "What investigation would have any connection to San Miniato?"

I smiled the smile I liked to think of as "charming." "All that I am at liberty to say is that the investigation concerned some stolen art," I said. "But recently stolen, you understand."

I would add that in the hope of staving off a renewed search for

Birdman's storehouse of stolen goods. If they spoke to Giulia, she would confirm my story, and would tell the cops that several paintings had disappeared from Finch's house.

"As you know," I continued, "Mr. Finch is an internationally recognized expert in the area of art theft. I hoped to consult with him. But sadly—." I gestured with my outspread arms.

"You found that Mr. Finch was not well enough to consult with," Aldo said. "*Ecco*, you made the trip for nothing, *signora*."

"One never makes a trip to Italy for nothing, *signore*," I said. "One is always rewarded." I turned and indicated the landscape visible through the open end of the courtyard with a sweep of my hand.

Aldo nodded his head to acknowledge the truth of this statement.

"But this young man," he persisted. "He is from Alexandria, Virginia. Is that not close to Washington, D.C., where you live, *signora*?"

I frowned. "Yes, it is. Are you suggesting that he might have seen me there? That even if I don't recognize him, he may have recognized me, and followed me?" I broke off. "Hell, this story is full of holes. Can't we just move the damn body and be done with it?"

"Did you bring a gun with you, M.J.?" Aldo asked.

"No," I said. "I wasn't expecting trouble."

"That's good," he said. "Well, at least whoever shot him had the courtesy to shoot him from behind. Nobody will believe that you could have sneaked up on him with your crutch."

"If he was shot at close range," I pointed out. "No powder burns on his shirt, so it wasn't close."

Aldo smiled a little. "Even from across the courtyard, M.J.," he said, "he would have heard you coming."

I sighed. "They're going to suspect something, the *Polizia*," I said.

"Yes, of course, they'll suspect something," Aldo said. "They always suspect something. And they will suspect that the something is relevant to Calloway's death, whether or not they suspect that you killed him."

"And even if we move the body," I said, "they will discover in short order that an American lady from a place near the dead man's address was staying at *Villa De Luca* at the time he was killed. If I dump him and run, I'll look even more suspicious."

"*Ecco*," Aldo said, raising his palms. "Why *do* you think he was here? What was he after? Was he trying to find out more about you?"

"Beats me," I said. "He didn't show that much curiosity about me earlier. But that was before I disarmed him twice. Maybe he decided that I was more of a threat to him than I seemed. Or maybe he was looking for tools or weapons. He knew I had picklocks and he saw me open a combination lock. Maybe he figured I had an oxy-fuel torch in my suitcase."

"The police will ask why you didn't hear the shots," he said.

"I'll say that something woke me up, but I don't know what it was," I said. "The shooter probably used a suppressor, though, don't you think? He or she."

Aldo's eyebrows rose. "You think it could have been a woman?"

I shrugged. "There is a woman in this case—more than one, in fact. So yes, it could have been a woman."

"They might not be able to tell if a suppressor was used," Aldo said, "though they will, of course, consider that possibility."

"And the possibility that the suppressor absorbed most of the gunpowder, which would make it impossible to tell if he was shot at close range," I said. "So we're back to square one. We don't know who shot him, from how far away, and why.

"He saw me at the airport," I said, "and it sounded like he was departing at the time. I wonder how long he'd been here, and whether there was anyone else in his party when he booked. Can you find that out?"

"Maybe," he said, "but it will cost you."

"Worth it," I said, "to identify another player with a gun they like to shoot."

In the end, I had to remain in San Miniato for another three days before the *Polizia* let me leave the country. I had to move to a hotel not only because the villa was a crime scene, but also because moving out of it was the kind of practical precaution any other elderly American lady traveling alone would take. I was accustomed to conforming to stereotype when it suited my purposes.

I spent a good part of the three days being grilled by the police, who were infallibly polite but relentless. They knew I was hiding something, not only because my story was weak but also because everybody is hiding something. Giulia confirmed the part about the letter, and about the security consultation, but they wanted to know why Aldo, my local business contact, hadn't toured the property with me. I told them I felt that Giulia would be more comfortable with a woman at first, which was lame, and they knew it. But wasn't Signor Berti's firm going to be taking over the security at Villa Offuscata? Surely it would have been better for Giulia to spend time with Aldo in my company. I told them the truth—that I was only assessing the situation, and that if I believed the current security arrangements to be perfectly adequate, I would not have recommended a change. But they argued that it would not have required more than one question and a cursory glance to recognize that the security was not adequate, and I had nothing to say to that.

In the end what saved me was Giulia's identification of Calloway as a cousin of Mr. Finch, and her insistence that the young man was up to no good. He was the cause of her concerns about security, and although she couldn't prove it, she suspected him of theft. Finch identified Calloway as his cousin, though he was vague about the exact connection, and then five minutes later denied ever having seen the man. That Calloway had observed me and gone to the villa because he worried that I posed a threat to his ongoing looting of Villa Offuscata would have been more plausible if he hadn't already removed the most valuable objects on display in the house. Also more plausible if I'd been a man my age with the same haircut and a suit; then I would have looked more like a security consultant. As it was, in spite of my business cards, you could tell that my interrogators couldn't fathom why a reputable firm would send me as its representative.

The way I looked during my first interview, nobody could picture me sneaking up behind somebody and plugging him, as Aldo had predicted. After a sleepless night of hill climbing, hand-to-hand combat, and dueling, not to mention the quarter-hour I spent posed with my sword up, I looked every minute of my seventy-two years. Everything ached. What hurt the most was my game leg, but my good leg had objections to the uneven distribution of labor. By the time the cops got hold of me, I didn't look like I could lift a feather, much less hoist a gun above my waist and aim it with deadly accuracy. I sat in an interrogation room, leg elevated and shoulders slumped; I had a death grip on a ceramic mug of strong coffee that I didn't have the willpower to lift as far as my face. I needed to wake up and stimulate my brain, but I didn't want to have to drag my carcass all the way to the end of the hall for a call of nature. I could see a reflection of my state in the eyes of every inexperienced cop I encountered. My clothes looked slept in. If only.

They identified Calloway senior as an FBI agent within twenty-four hours. The Alexandria police had searched Calloway's apartment and found several paintings and a sculpture matching Giulia's descriptions of stolen objects, but no jewelry.

So they knew what Calloway was doing in San Miniato. And they suspected that he kept returning because he, like everyone else who knew about Birdman, believed that there was a cache of jewelry somewhere that was worth millions. What they couldn't figure out was what connection Calloway had to me. They would have suspected me of being his partner, but my story checked out with Levesque Security, a firm with an international reputation. They knew that Calloway had a girlfriend named Monica Jeffries, and they would have been happy to involve her, but she hadn't left the country in the past week. Monica didn't tell the Alexandria police about her recently dead aunt, whose paintings had been stolen, so the trail ended with her. With great reluctance, the *Polizia* gave me permission to leave the country.

I went to see Giulia before I left. I wasn't sure what kind of a reception I'd get, but she welcomed me into the kitchen and gave me another glass of lemonade.

"They find some of Signor Giorgio's things, the *cose preziose*," she said excitedly, "in the cousin's *appartamento. Certo, mi dispacie*—regret—that he is dead." She crossed herself, then leaned toward me and dropped her voice. "You do not kill him, M. J.?"

"No," I said, "it wasn't me. I thought about it a few times, but no."

She laughed. "I, too. With my *padella*." She mimed taking a swing at Calloway with her frying pan. "Easy, no? But probably he just wake up, and then I must hit him again."

I nodded. "I think he had a thick skull, that one."

"*Ecco, il Signor Giorgio* get his things again," she said. "But if the one who kill the cousin come here?"

"You know that I work for a security company, right?" I said.

She nodded, her brow knit. "A famous one, they say. But is it—."

"Is it what?"

Her eyes searched my face. "Is it like the Blackwater?"

I shook my head. "Not anything like. Those guys work for assholes—bad guys, while we try only to deal with good guys."

"'Asshole,'" she repeated carefully, nodding. "Then how is that you are famous?" she asked.

I laughed. "It's a very good question. We don't have the most promising business model. And we don't court publicity. In fact, I'm a little surprised that the Italian police have heard of us. We try to keep a low profile." When she frowned, I added, "You know—*molto segreto.*"

"Ah, *sì, sì,*" she said. "*Ho capito.*"

"Anyway, my friend Aldo—the one with the red Fiat and the *telefonino* attached to his ear?" I cupped my hand to my ear. When she nodded, I continued, "He works for an Italian company that is associated with my company. People from Aldo's company have been guarding your house around the clock—all the time—since the morning I found the cousin dead." I gave her the shortened version. No sense in alarming her with an account of Signor Giorgio's nocturnal wanderings with a gun, especially since she was the one who had predicted them. I'd given the gun to Aldo, but I doubted that it had been the only firearm on the premises, and I instructed him to search for the rest before Finch did.

Giulia looked amazed. "All the time? *Qui?*" She stood and leaned across the table to peer out through the window. "*Dove sono?* I see nobody."

"They're around," I said. "They aren't supposed to be seen."

She turned to me with her hands clasped to her bosom. "You do this for us? *Per il Signor Giorgio?*"

"For the friend of Signora Rivers, yes," I said.

Her eyes misted over. "That is *molto gentile,*" she said, "*molto generoso.* But the bank can pay. I talk with them."

"Why don't you talk to Aldo first?" I suggested. "Show him around and explain to him all the things that worry you. He'll take good care of you. And in the meantime, we're trying to locate Signor Giorgio's family." I leaned forward. "Do you have any old address books or letters or cards that I can look at? I promise I'll return them."

She got to her feet. "*Certo.* I see."

While she was gone, I looked out on the courtyard where the old man snoozed in the sun. I found myself wondering if his nights were full of nocturnal adventures that wore him out and made him sleep all day. All in all, it wasn't a bad life. Maybe I'd be ready for it in another ten years.

Giulia returned with a box. "Everything is here—*tutto*," she said, setting it down to show me. "Photo book and letters—*molto vecchie, sa*? They are all dead now maybe—the people in the letters. And here, *sopra*, is a book of *indirizzi*—how do you say?"

"Addresses," I said. "This will be very helpful. Thank you."

She waved a hand. "No, no, you are doing the favor."

"Actually," I said, "I'll probably give it to our computer whiz. She can find anybody on the Web."

"*Il Signor Manfredi* at the bank, he pay, M.J., *sono sicura*," she said. "We are all worry *per il Signor Giorgio*. I wish to find a true cousin—*un vero parente*."

"We'll do our best," I said. "And now I have a favor to ask you. I'll ask Signor Giorgio if you want me to, but I'm not sure he'll understand what I want and why I want it. It's something I want to borrow."

"*Certo!*" she said. "What you want to borrow?"

"There is a certain painting I've seen, hidden away," I said carefully. "Maybe you've seen it, and maybe you haven't. It appears to have been painted by a very famous painter, so it looks very valuable. But I think that Signora Rivers painted it a long time ago and gave it to Signor Giorgio as a souvenir. I'm not sure that he remembers it's there. I would like to borrow the painting and use it to catch a thief—the thief who stole Signora Rivers's paintings from her house."

"The paintings they steal, *la Signora e il Signor Giorgio*, long time ago in Iran," she said.

"Exactly," I said. "Signora Rivers said in her will that she wanted the paintings returned to Iran. I believe that she and Signor Giorgio stole them to protect them, as I did. I want to recover them so that Signora Rivers's wishes can be carried out."

"But you say, *prima*, these paintings—they may be—*contraffatti*, not real," she said.

"They might be," I acknowledged. "But we will need to get them back in any case, and then we'll know. But now that I know more about Signora Rivers from talking to you and Signor Giorgio, and now that I've seen her work, I think maybe these paintings are the real ones."

She gazed out the window. "You know where is this painting, the one you want?"

"Yes," I said.

"How long you need?"

"Two months, I think," I said.

She roused herself. "What happen to the little bird?"

"I gave it to Signor Finch," I said. "He can keep it. Signora Rivers wanted him to have it."

Later we would sort out the fake bird and real bird; it seemed too much to ask of her at this point.

She returned her attention to the courtyard. "Don't ask him," she said. "To ask, it confuse him. If you know where is the painting, take it. You take good care and send back when you catch the thief." She sighed. "Only promise that you leave that old thief there—." She pointed with her chin. "Leave that old thief in peace."

"I promise," I said. "I have a soft spot in my heart for old thieves."

20

"So Mrs. Rivers was the one who forged our Tehran paintings?" Emile said. He was standing by the window, examining Dottie's Chagall in the light. He was wearing his reading glasses. "I'm no expert, of course, but the visible brushwork must be authentic."

The rest of us—Didi, Bernie, and I—were sitting in red leather chairs in Emile's office, the place we gravitated to when we wanted to confer without the formality of a conference table. Archie and Maisie were stretched on the Persian carpet nearest Didi, whom they knew to be a softer touch during cookie breaks than Bernie was, and Bashful the bloodhound, who had apparently blissed out on the aromas emanating from my crutch and sneaker, was snoozing with his nose against them, one paw draped coyly over that vital organ as if it had been overwhelmed. We were drinking tea from English porcelain that went with the leather chairs and Persian carpet, but it was black and strong and I was so grateful to taste something unadulterated by obscure Chinese herbs that I didn't even miss the alcohol. The late morning sun streamed in through the tall windows. The throbbing in my leg, which had kept me awake much of the night, had settled down to a dull ache and become part of the background noise of my body's chorus of complaints in its eighth decade.

"She's the one," I said.

"The other paintings on Mrs. Rivers's inventory," Bernie said. "The seven we didn't steal—they were all from the Tehran collection."

"So, let me get this straight," Didi said. "Rivers and Finch stole fifteen paintings, we think, and we're inclined to believe that because our research confirms that all fifteen of the titles on the Rivers inventory came from the Tehran collection, and because we stole eight of the forgeries from Tehran ourselves. As far as we can tell, eleven paintings were subsequently stolen from the vault at Mrs. Rivers's house. That leaves four unaccounted for. That's four treasures of Western art. I'd say they were priceless, but of course, they'd be worth millions."

"We can't say for sure how much they're worth," Bernie said. "We can research the titles and find out the measurements of the canvasses, and then compare those measurements with the outlines on the walls of the strong room. But without knowing the frame sizes, our guesses would be just that—guesses. We don't know for sure which eleven were stolen from the Rivers house."

"With regard to the four-painting discrepancy," I said, "Dottie could have given four paintings to Finch. They could represent his cut of the take."

"But you didn't see them?" he persisted.

"No," I said, "but I didn't look at everything, and there were crates in Finch's strong room that certainly could have contained them. Or we may find out that Calloway stole them from the house. Or Giulia could remember that they're stashed on a high shelf in the storage room. I don't think that likely, by the way—that last possibility. Finch was clearly careful with the climate control in the strong room.

"Here's another complication." I pointed at the Chagall forgery, which Emile was handing to Didi. "I'm guessing that this one was meant to be used in the Tehran theft. She must have prepared additional forgeries that they didn't get the chance to substitute because we showed up and spoiled everything. But how many and where are they now?"

"Yes, I take your point, M.J.," Didi said. "They could be in Fort Worth."

"So she recognized you, after all, Mrs. Rivers?" Emile said, turning toward me. "When she called you 'Smoke'?"

"Apparently," I said. "What I don't know is whether she knew who I was all along, or whether it had something to do with the light behind me and the way her mind was wandering when she was dying. The way I looked at that moment—it might have triggered something."

"Or could she have known that you worked for Levesque when she contacted us?" Didi asked.

"I really have no idea," I said. "But there's no indication that she told Finch who I was. He called Smoke a 'fellow,' and claimed that nobody knew who he was. Unreliable evidence, I know, given Finch's mental capacities now, but I'm inclined to believe that she didn't tell him everything. I find that interesting, and maybe kind of —I don't know—touching? As if she were acknowledging a bond between us?"

Bernie nodded. "Forget the brotherhood of thieves. Sisterhood is powerful."

"Let's talk about Calloway's murder," Didi said. "You and Aldo didn't—?"

"Tempting, but no," I said.

"Do you believe that he was murdered by a partner?" Didi asked.

"Or a rival?" Bernie added.

"Aldo hasn't found any witnesses who saw Calloway with anyone," I said, "and he says that the police haven't found any either. He sent me the passenger list for Calloway's inbound flight, and I didn't spot any names I recognized. So if there was a partner, we should probably assume that the partner was also a rival, even if Calloway didn't know that. But what did killing him accomplish? Unless somebody was waiting for him with a car, and drove him to my villa, he hardly had time to report what he'd found in sufficient detail to make it expedient to kill him sooner rather than later."

"Yes, I see what you mean," Didi said. "The killer would have to know not only that there was more to steal, but where it was located and how to get to it. He might or might not know that you and Finch were locked inside the strong room, but it would still be in his best interest to have Calloway show him where it was and help him break into it."

"Unless he followed Calloway to the entrance to the vault?" Emile put in.

"God, I hope not," I said. "I don't like to think that I led a parade to the site. We do know that he probably didn't drive Calloway to my villa because the police found Calloway's rental car nearby. The freshest prints on the wheel belonged to Calloway. There were other prints in the car, including around the passenger seat, and on the underside of the passenger handle, but it's a rental car, so there would be. Aldo thinks someone was following Calloway in another car and stopped up the road from the Villa Offuscata to wait for him. This person smoked Turkish cigarettes—Samsuns. Calloway smoked Winstons."

Emile frowned. "But why would he wait outside the Villa Offuscata and then attack Calloway at his next stop, unless he'd heard something in between that motivated the killing?" he asked.

I shrugged. "Maybe he did. Or maybe he knew that the Finch place was occupied, since the television and lights were on. Or maybe he even followed Finch up the hill and retreated when he heard our voices, and waited, smoking, for a more private opportunity."

"Calloway was shot in the back, right?" Didi said.

I nodded. "At mid-range. Then again in the head at close range —to make sure he was dead."

"Sounds like a professional hit," Didi said, "except for the cigarette butts left at the scene. And Samsuns? Give me a break."

"Not at the murder scene," I corrected. "At Villa Offuscata."

"Still," Didi said. "A Middle Eastern cigarette brand? A sloppy professional hit, maybe. In which case, we have a theory for that as well."

"The Iranians?" I said.

Didi nodded. "It looks like Calloway might have been the one to tip off Rouhani about the paintings. Maybe he got tired of waiting for Monica's inheritance, so he sold his information to Rouhani. Then after the burglary, he decided to put the squeeze on Rouhani. We intercepted a phone call while you were gone, M.J. Someone calling from Calloway's number told Rouhani, 'The situation has changed. The police might be involved. So the price has gone up to one hundred thousand.'"

"That would have been after Theo told Steve and Monica about the theft," I guessed.

"Yes, and it probably cost him his life," Emile said gravely.

Didi said, "We know that Rouhani met with an Afghan thug and sometime hit man named Sahar Aziz. Rouhani called the meeting because he said he had a job for Aziz. Rouhani gave him an envelope. Nothing was said, but it didn't look good."

"Because neither man mentioned the envelope," Emile said, "that suggested that the transaction was routine for them. But it could have been a payoff of some kind. Aziz has worked as a collector or messenger sometimes in the past."

"We've sent Aldo a photograph of Aziz," Bernie said. "We should know soon enough if he was spotted in the vicinity."

I shifted to find a more comfortable position, and my leg objected. "I think Calloway got hold of a file on Finch—maybe even an old paper file, who knows?—and went to see Finch in San Miniato," I said. "From Finch, he found out about Dottie, probably even found out that she had the paintings. He must have concluded that Dottie was worth a fortune, and went after Monica. But you're probably right, Didi. In the meantime, to improve his cash flow, he sold the information about the paintings to Rouhani."

"You think Calloway was clever enough to get all that information out of Finch?" Bernie asked.

"It wouldn't have taken a great deal of finesse," I said. "Trust me. Finch is sufficiently addled to be super-secretive one minute, and giving away the store the next. The minute after that, he has a vague sense that he's said too much to the wrong person, maybe. It's heart-wrenching, actually."

All of their faces registered comprehension and sympathy. Secrecy was the bedrock of our enterprise. We knew that we could rely on every Quixote operative and each other to guard our secrets with their lives. None of us wanted to contemplate the possibility that we might someday lose control of our minds and our tongues. If that day came, we'd likely find ourselves exiled to a remote Quixote property where we would be well cared for and well guarded. It would be a pleasant exile, as exiles go, but exile nonetheless. On the other hand, senility is itself a kind of exile—a stranding of the essential self on a desert island, with no means of communicating with the outside world.

"We could check the passenger list on Calloway's flight again," Bernie said, "but Aziz probably travels under an alias and may not have taken the same flight."

"Especially since Calloway was probably in Italy when Theo made her announcement," I said, "because I got the impression that he spotted me in the airport when he was leaving, and decided to stick around. That would mean that he called Rouhani from Italy. We have a recording of that call, right? Did he say where he was?"

"Yes, we have a recording," Bernie said, "but it wouldn't matter. He wouldn't be hard to locate. Rouhani might have had his cell phone tapped, just like we have Rouhani's tapped. If somebody were blackmailing me with the threat of jail time, I'd sure want to keep tabs on him."

"Right," I said.

"Aldo can tip off his colleagues in the police, and they can check the cigarettes for fingerprints and DNA, if they're so inclined," Didi said. "Maybe Interpol has a file on Aziz. If so, they'd probably welcome the chance to put him away."

"They'll still need to put him at the crime scene," I said. "But if he tended to be careless, they might be able to do that. It's a start."

"We could be wrong," Emile cautioned. "Instead of a careless or incompetent professional, we could be talking about an amateur. And if Calloway was blackmailing one person, why not several? Especially if he had access to his father's files. I admit that the timing is suggestive, but we didn't have Calloway's phone tapped, so we don't know how many threatening calls he made."

"Okay, but the timing *is* suggestive," Didi said. "I say that Rouhani was behind the hit. And I don't think Rouhani deals with top-drawer professionals. Look who he hired to steal the paintings. I suspect that he's too cheap to hire the best talent. But yes, I take your point, *Père*. The job Aziz was doing for Rouhani might have had nothing to do with Calloway, or it might have been simply a payoff. We'll keep an open mind."

"How did your leg hold up?" Bernie asked, turning x-ray eyes on me.

"Fine," I lied.

"Hmm," she said.

"So Shorty and Pilar are still sitting on the paintings, right?" I said.

"Yes, we've set up cameras and a remote mike," Didi said, looking around. "Emile, do you have those pictures?"

Emile leaned forward and handed me a small pile of 8 x 10 photographs.

Didi gestured at the pictures as I leafed through them. "Hard to keep under surveillance because it's out in the middle of nowhere and surrounded by an electrified fence, so we're doing it electronically, but we haven't been able to plant any bugs. It's not a neighborhood where anybody goes door to door, not even Girl Scouts or Mormon missionaries."

Most of the shots showed a sprawling ranch house complex with outbuildings, including a barn with a stable and a garage closer to the front of the house. I squinted at a lower, closer shot of the entrance. It showed a wrought-iron gate surmounted by a wrought-iron arch with the name "Lazy R Ranch" and an elaborate crest featuring two lions armed with swords guarding a crown—the Pahlavi family crest.

The next shot was a night shot taken overhead of the house itself, showing a central courtyard.

"It's hard to find anything out there to mount cameras and equipment on," Didi said with a gesture at the photograph. "We can use a drone, but only at night, when it won't be seen. We have equipment in a mesquite tree that gives us access to the living and dining rooms, but not Rouhani's home office."

"Probably not much of a problem unless he takes a lot of clients out there," I said. "And even then, he's likelier to entertain them in the living room than in his office. As long as you have his cell tapped, you've probably got it covered."

"We've rented a nearby ranch that's for sale," Didi said. "Shorty and Pilar are supposed to be caretakers while work is being done in the house. They ride horses by the Rouhani place every day so that he can get used to seeing them. They've befriended the watch dogs."

That was Shorty's specialty—animal relations. It was partly because she was too short to intimidate the average Doberman, but she also had a gift with animals. She could communicate with them, even put them to sleep. She was the first to be tapped if we had a particularly challenging animal rescue to mount.

"Do we have anybody in his office?" I asked.

Didi shook his head. "It didn't seem worth the trouble," he said. "He seems to use his cell for everything."

"Is Rouhani really a Pahlavi?" I asked, returning to the picture of his gate.

"Only by marriage," Bernie said. "His uncle married one of the shah's sisters."

"Then I guess his own family crest wasn't as impressive," I said. "Probably no crown."

"Or lions, either," Bernie said, smiling.

I looked up. "Who's our Persian speaker?" I said.

"We sent Lafitte back with J.K. and the sound and video equipment," Bernie said.

I started to object to J.K. because a new Iranian in the neighborhood would look suspicious, but then I realized that he'd just pass himself off as a Pakistani, as he'd done before.

"And before you object, M.J.," Bernie said, reading my mind, "Fort Worth has a huge Muslim population, mostly Pakistanis, but enough so that another Middle Easterner more or less wouldn't draw attention."

I grinned. "Nice match," I said. J.K.—Jamil Kamaliazad—was dark and handsome just as Lafitte was blond and handsome. Lafitte looked powerful and rugged, while J.K. was wiry and debonair. A smile from either had been known to make strong women faint. Both men had been known to make use of this tendency.

Didi grinned back. "Ready to join them, M.J.?"

I opened my mouth to speak but Bernie answered instead. "Next week, I think."

"Next week?" I objected.

At this point, Bashful woke up with a snort, bumped my crutch, and sent it crashing into my bum leg. I yelped.

"Next week," Bernie repeated.

21

"We want to help," Ada said.

"We want to go with you," Theo said.

Outside, a lanky teenager was mowing Ada's front lawn, and the annoying buzz of the lawn mower assaulted us through the open windows, along with the heady fragrance of cut grass. The living room, which was comfortably furnished, was a minefield of children's toys, some of which were being played with by a pair of sweet-faced but jelly-smeared tots in diapers and tee-shirts. One of the shirts said, "My grandma spoils me," and the other said, "Grandma's little angel." I'd observed that the tots were not too steady on their pins but they made up for it with the inventiveness they applied to their play. They ignored all conventions and manufacturers' intentions and viewed every piece of molded plastic with unprejudiced eyes.

"You can't go with me," I said.

Ada cupped a hand to her ear, and I realized that with the competition from the lawn mower, I was going to have to shout. So I shouted.

"We can help," Ada said. "I have very useful skills. We both do."

I sighed. "You can't come," I said. Then, remembering, shouted it, sounding harsher than I intended to sound. "You hired Levesque to get the paintings back, and now you have to let us do our jobs."

"But we can help," Theo said with the kind of quiet persistence that carves canyons and caves out of solid rock. To Ada, she shouted, "I told her we could help."

"Look," I said. "I appreciate it, Theo. I really do. But this won't be a slumber party. You're smart women. I appreciate that, too. But unless you're the world's greatest second-story man, you'll only be in the way. You must see that—." I broke off. Theo was looking at me. Ada was looking at her. Suddenly, the room was quiet, and I realized that the lawn mower must have finished.

"Go on," Ada said to Theo. "Tell her."

"Tell me what?" I said, looking from one to the other. Nobody said anything. Then I held up a palm. "Wait, don't tell me. You *are* the world's greatest second-story man."

"I wouldn't go that far," Theo said.

"Oh, for Pete's sake, Theo, this is no time for modesty!" Ada said. She turned to me, clasping her hands primly in her lap. "Theo probably *is* the world's greatest second-story man. And I am the personal apparel and equipment designer and consulting electrician to the world's greatest second-story man."

I was thunderstruck. I flashed on an image of them in their witches' hats, rehearsing for the Scottish play. To Theo, I said, "And that's how you came to know Dottie Rivers, the world's greatest art forger."

Theo grinned at me. "Well, it's not like we attended a support group together," she said. "Our paths crossed, that's all."

"So you know about the paintings we're trying to recover?" I said.

"No," Theo said.

"Dottie never told us about them," Ada said. "She could be

really close-mouthed about things, you know? Well, we all have our secrets, don't we? We wouldn't survive if we didn't."

"But *you* know something about them, don't you, Marge?" Theo said, her eyes narrowed. "There was something about the look on your face when you saw that list. Not shock, but a stillness that was trying very hard not to register shock."

"Please tell us," Ada coaxed. "We really can help, you know."

I stared out the window. I wasn't big on sharing—never had been. Like most Quixote agents, I carried a lifetime of secrets stored in my memory. Not even Emile and Didi knew everything about the jobs I'd done. Only my partners at the time, when I'd had them, knew that. The question was whether I was willing to extend that trust to Theo and Ada, who hadn't been cleared by Levesque or accumulated the experience there to work for Quixote.

"Excuse me just a second," I said, reaching in my back pocket and extracting my cell phone. It was awkward, because I had to turn the damn thing on before I could activate the RF detector. No bugs in the room. Of course, people my age could still be relying on a battery-operated voice-activated recorder—something my younger colleagues never even considered.

"Sorry," I said, returning the phone to my pocket. "I'm expecting a message from Didi."

They exchanged a glance that said they knew exactly what I'd been doing, but refrained from comment. I decided to risk it.

"In 1979," I began, "in the early days of the Iranian Revolution, just after the shah left the country and Khomeini returned from exile, Quixote, Limited, a sister company to Levesque Security, sent a team to Tehran to steal paintings from the Tehran Museum of Contemporary Art, which had one of the best modern art collections in the world."

Ada nodded politely. Theo appeared to be concentrating.

"The idea was to preserve the paintings as part of the world's cultural history," I continued. "They'd been moved to the museum's basement to protect them from radical Muslims who wanted to destroy all Western art. But they were still threatened by extremists, so it was deemed safest to remove some of them." If they noticed that I was using the passive voice so common among diplomats and others with something to hide, they didn't say so. They didn't ask, "Who deemed it safest to remove them? Whose idea was it to steal them?" And I didn't answer.

"I went with a partner," I said. "We couldn't possibly take all of them, so we had to choose. We chose twelve—as many as we could fit inside a trash bin—and we went in the middle of the night and took them. Oddly enough, the guard was asleep at his post, so we just walked in, found the ones we wanted and walked out with them."

"Just like that?" Ada said.

"Pretty much," I said. "It was pouring outside. At one point I turned to look back at the exit door, and thought I glimpsed someone watching us, silhouetted against the light coming from the hallway. Then, the person was gone. We were almost done at that point, so we just finished up and left. When we got the paintings back to the states, we found that eight of the twelve paintings were forgeries."

Light dawned in their eyes.

"It wasn't obvious, you understand," I said. "The paintings had to be scrutinized by experts, who concluded that they were excellent forgeries, but forgeries nonetheless."

"And what did you think?" Theo said.

"Well, there were three possibilities," I said. "The first was that the paintings had always been forgeries—unlikely given the local expertise and the number of international experts who had viewed them since the museum opened. The second was that someone else —that is, another outsider—had stolen the originals and carefully replaced them with forgeries. They might have been taking advantage of the chaos to pull off the most profitable art heist ever executed, or they might have the same motivation we did—to preserve the paintings for posterity. The third possibility, and a likelier one, was that someone inside the museum was in the process of removing the paintings for safekeeping or to sell on the black market. In either case, we had queered their pitch because we left blank spaces on the walls instead of forgeries, and four of the paintings we'd stolen had been genuine. Now, the disappearance of the paintings had to be investigated. It seemed possible—even likely—that additional forgeries would be discovered."

"But I never heard anything about it," Ada said. "Did you, Theo? A theft that big, you'd think we would have heard something, unless it was an inside job. You'd think the revolutionaries would have used it somehow."

"The Iranians never acknowledged the theft," I said. "That inclined us to believe that the substitutions had been made by an insider, perhaps with the blessing of whoever was in power at that point."

"But now you think Dottie was involved," Ada said. "So if it wasn't an inside job, why didn't the Iranians go public with the thefts?"

"I don't know," I conceded. "Maybe they were embarrassed, or maybe even the revolutionaries weren't willing to risk all foreign investment at that point by acknowledging how little security they could provide, even for national treasures. The American Embassy hadn't yet been occupied, remember, so they hadn't yet cut all their ties to the West."

"And the figure you thought you saw, the one in the doorway," Theo said. "You think that was Dottie?"

"At the time," I said, "I thought it could have been anybody. An insider wouldn't have wanted to call attention to the thefts then any more than an outsider would. Better to 'discover' the thefts next morning—especially if most of what we'd stolen was fake. It seemed too coincidental that another thief would happen to be there when we arrived, all of us intent on the same task. But on reflection I realized that the substitutions had to be accomplished over time, because paintings had been removed from their frames and the forgeries substituted. That favored an insider. But if an outsider was involved, that person would have to return many times over the course of the job. In that case, their presence inside the museum on the same night that we chose to pay it a visit seemed less coincidental."

"You said the guard was asleep," Ada said, "but surely there was more than one."

"We only saw one," I said, "and I now suspect that he'd been drugged."

"Only one guard for such a famous collection?" Ada was shocked.

"Maybe it wasn't a very appealing job in those days," I said, "guarding the queen's collection of decadent Western art from the radicals."

"Did you have a suspect, if it was an outsider?" Theo asked.

I smiled. "It was such a complicated scheme that I was bound to suspect the only person whom I thought capable of pulling it off, even though he didn't usually steal art."

"George Finch," Theo said.

"Yes," I said. "The one they called 'Birdman.'"

"But Marge," Ada said, "couldn't you tell whether the person you saw watching you was a man or a woman?"

I shook my head. "Not really. The viewing conditions weren't ideal—it was raining hard. What I saw was a backlit form, in motion."

"But now you think it was Dottie?" Theo asked. "Because she recognized you at The Elms?"

My eyes drifted to the window again. "I'm not sure if she recognized me or not," I said. "I'm really not sure. But yes, I think she did."

"At your office, they said you were out of town and couldn't be reached," Theo said.

I drew a breath. "I went to Italy to talk to Finch," I said. "I wanted to find out whether Dottie's stolen paintings were genuine."

"But how did you connect Dottie to Finch?" Ada asked.

"Was it the necklace?" Theo said. "The little goldfinch?"

I nodded. "Pretty circumstantial, I know, but—." I wasn't about to add breaking into Dottie's house to this confession.

"So by then you knew they were partners?" Ada said.

"No," I said. "I knew they were friends. But that increased the likelihood that Dottie's paintings were genuine."

"What did Finch tell you?" Ada asked.

"Finch has Alzheimer's," I began. "His awareness is spotty. But he said enough to convince me that Dottie had been with him in Tehran, and that Dottie had created the forgeries. So there's a strong probability that the stolen paintings are genuine. Unfortunately, I ran into Neil Callahan/Calloway in Italy, where he was looking for Finch's cache of stolen jewelry."

They both looked startled. "Neil Callahan?" Ada said. "Monica's fiancé? What does he have to do with George Finch?"

So I explained about Callahan/Calloway, his background and his interest in Finch.

"Unfortunately, we'll never know how he knew what he knew about Birdman," I said, "because Calloway was shot and killed while he was trying to break into the villa where I was staying." I held up a hand. "And before you ask, I wasn't there at the time and I didn't shoot him."

I explained our theory about Calloway's plot to blackmail Rouhani.

Theo had gotten up and crossed the room to stare out the window. Now she turned angry eyes on me.

"And you were planning to tell us when?" she said. "About the trip to Italy and Calloway's death?"

"I'm telling you now," I said.

"Oh, cut the crap, Marge," Theo said. "If Calloway hadn't died, we wouldn't have heard anything about Italy and Finch, would we? You're only telling us now because you figure we'll hear about Calloway's death, and wonder what it has to do with anything, including Dottie's murder." She crossed her arms and regarded me with eyes the color of a thunderhead. "I wonder what else you're not telling us about Italy. Damn it, you work for us!"

Ada squirmed. "Theo, your lungs," she said.

I crossed my own arms. "And I assume that you hired Levesque Security because you'd heard that we get results," I said evenly. "We do our jobs in our own way, and clients who don't like it don't hire us. You hired us to recover the paintings. Fine. We know where they are, and we're in the process of recovering them."

"We're not a pair of doddering old biddies with a lost pussycat," Theo said.

"Theo, Marge didn't know that," Ada said, holding out her hands. "How could she know that? We haven't exactly been forthcoming with her."

"She's not telling us everything, Addie," Theo told her. "Not even now."

"Of course, she isn't," Ada said. "We're not telling her everything, either. She just told you that she once stole twelve of the world's most famous paintings, and you're complaining because she's not being candid with us?"

Perhaps the emotional intensity in the room caused the quarrel to break out in the diaper set, but Ada was called upon to broker a truce, and returned from the other end of the room to settle a red-eyed, snotty-nosed Grandma's Little Angel on her lap.

"For the record," I said, "I give you credit for being every bit as intelligent as I am. What I didn't know was that you were every bit as crooked as I am. But that doesn't mean I want to swap diaries with you."

Theo fought to repress a smile and lost, though her smile was grudging. "That would be a fun read."

I smiled back. "Likewise, I'm sure."

The Little Angel gummed a cookie noisily.

Ada said, "So how are we going to get the paintings back?"

"It won't be easy," I said. "They're inside a ranch house surrounded by a barbed-wire fence and acres of nothing but scrub and jackrabbits and gas wells. We haven't been able to bug the place and our external surveillance is limited to a few windowed rooms." I looked at the two of them. "As everyone is fond of pointing out to me, I'm not in top form. The three of us together don't make up a single able-bodied person."

"I love a challenge," Ada said brightly.

"You're looking at it the wrong way, Marge," Theo said. "What the three of us make up together, if we pool our experience, is one big, bad-ass dude."

Suddenly, she swung her cane up so quickly that it cut the air with a whoosh. When it stopped, a sharp metal blade at its tip gleamed in the light.

"Plus," she said, "we have all the best equipment."

22

"I was better at this when I was younger," Theo admitted.

We were sitting in the back of a panel truck like an oven, clinging to metal protrusions like oven shelf supports. We were sitting on pads, but they were no match for the road in a vehicle with no detectible shock absorbers. Theo looked semi-conscious, which was to say semi-unconscious, and Ada was fanning her with one of those in-flight magazines the airlines hope you take with the intent of ordering a sommelier's washing kit or an inflatable bar. We were on our way to the Quixote surveillance post so that I could see the set-up and Ada and Theo could meet the other team members.

As it turned out, I didn't get the week off that Bernie had prescribed for me owing to a Saturday gala at the Modern Art Museum in Fort Worth. Today was Friday. By five o'clock Saturday we were supposed to be ready to rub elbows with Fort Worth's art patrons. We were supposed to look presentable. Right now, it was even money we'd all be alive at five o'clock the next day.

The truck hit an especially nasty bump and we groaned in unison.

"Where'd your driver get his training?" Theo asked between gritted teeth.

"Baghdad," I said.

She nodded, and decided to save her breath.

The truck jerked to a stop, and our suitcases came sliding toward us like a cement tidal wave. We braced ourselves, our backs against the wall, and took the force flatfooted, absorbing the impact and then shoving back. A minute later, the doors opened and J.K. stood grinning at us.

"Everybody still alive?" he said cheerfully. "That driveway is pretty rough, but I missed most of the potholes."

"There were more?" Ada said in wonder.

The Texas heat made a frontal assault on us, as if someone had opened the door to a blast furnace. We scrambled out awkwardly, and J.K. gave me the bone-crushing embrace he hadn't given me at the airport, where he'd stood with a bored expression on his face and a hand-lettered sign that said "SMITH."

Then he held me at arm's length and said, "I have to admit, M.J., you've looked better."

My hair was frosted and permed over big white clip-on earrings that hurt like hell. I was wearing a beige suit skirt, now rumpled, and a sweat-stained white blouse, my suit jacket draped across my elbow like a limp flag of surrender. I also wore a pair of fake designer bifocals with gold filigree frames, which I didn't need because I'd already had cataract surgery in both eyes. Thank god the boot precluded any consideration of pantyhose; I wore a sneaker and sock instead—the only items in my ensemble that didn't come from the Quixote wardrobe department. Around my neck I wore a gold heart framing a miniature photograph of somebody's grandbaby, on one wrist a gold bracelet watch, and on one finger a rather large tourmaline set off by fingernails painted a glossy peach. Our wardrobe head JoJo Chen always said, "It's the small touches that create authenticity."

I thought my red lipstick had probably long since melted into oblivion, but now I saw its imprint on J.K.'s cheek and found a flowered handkerchief in my pocket to rub it off with. I made introductions, and J.K. retrieved our canes from the panel truck. I'd been ecstatic to see the last of the crutch, but now I felt a little unsteady and wondered if it had been a mistake. Surely things would improve now that I was on *terra firma* instead of *terra in movimento*. Besides, my new cane was custom made.

I noticed two other vehicles parked in the garage—a filthy beige pick-up truck and a Yamaha. The panel truck from hell had painted on its sides, "A-1 Painting—First in Quality, Dependability, and Price." The happy painter next to the slogan held a dripping, multicolored paintbrush. For the purposes of authenticity, we'd included a website and phone number, both of which were monitored by Levesque operatives.

The command center was inside a sprawling ranch house that was otherwise mostly empty, but as soon as we opened the door we got an earful of hound dog. Sneezy rushed me, tail wagging. I was gratified that she recognized me.

"Good to see you, too," I told her, bending awkwardly to accept the sloppy kisses that marked me as a member of her human pack.

"How did they find a place so close to Rouhani's?" Theo asked, looking around. "That was lucky."

"Not very, apparently," I said. "Most of the ranchers are giving up and selling because of the drought. The only people who can afford to keep these big spreads are oilmen like Rouhani, who are taking advantage of the fracking boom."

Ada started. "Do they have a lot of earthquakes around here?" she asked.

"More than they used to, or so I've heard," I said.

Pilar was in the kitchen making tuna fish sandwiches. Her black hair—or somebody's black hair, since hers was usually cut shorter

—was braided down her back, and she wore an embroidered peasant blouse, a colorful skirt, flat sandals, and no makeup.

"*Mamacita!*" I said when I saw her.

She flashed me a grin. "I know, right? There's a shawl around here somewhere that I wear for my nightly *paseo*." She wiped her hands on a dish towel and gave me a hug. "How you been, girl? You look pretty good to me."

"I looked better before I got in the back of the panel truck," I said.

"I know what you mean," she said, extending a hand to Ada and then Theo as I made introductions. To Sneezy, she said, "Go get Shorty, please. Lunch is ready."

I filled a kettle at the sink and looked out the kitchen window. "Is that Rouhani's place over there?" In the distance, I could barely make out some kind of structure.

"Use the binoculars," Pilar said, aiming her chin at a pair resting next to the sink. She set a bowl on the table and came to look over my shoulder. "He's got two live-in caretakers, the Rashidis. Neither one of them has a record. The locals say that she doesn't have much English, but he gets by. Plus, nobody wants to cross him, apparently. They're all afraid of him."

I moved the binoculars. "Is that a drilling rig?"

"Yep," Pilar said. "Sure is. Probably the reason this place is for sale. Rouhani has eight of them on his property, but this is the one closest to his house, just over the property line from this place. He's put up acoustic panels to block the noise, but you can still hear it, see it, smell it—hell, probably taste it. I'm not inclined to drink the well water here to find out."

"Fracking?" Ada said.

"Right," Pilar said. "Isn't that what you'd do in the middle of a drought? Encourage an industry that consumes and pollutes millions of gallons of water every year, including the local ground water? Never mind the noise and what it does to local roads when you triple the traffic of semis and tankers."

"I minded it," Ada said ruefully, rubbing her hip.

"Well, hell, I mind it, too, Ada," Pilar said. "I'm a native Texan and I mind it a whole hell of a lot. And I haven't even mentioned the earthquakes."

"Well, can't we blow up the rig while we're at it?" Ada said, turning to me.

"Wouldn't be worth the risk," Pilar said. "He'd only collect insurance money and repair it or build a new one someplace else."

"Is it manned, the rig?" I asked.

"Doesn't appear to be," Pilar said. "Sometimes trucks show up, but always during the day. Shorty and I have ridden over there in the evenings, and we've never seen anybody there. You can walk right in on the side without the wall, and we've yoo-hooed till we were blue in the face, but never raised a soul. It's hard to hear over the noise of the drill, but—well, you've heard Shorty at softball games. She's short but she's all voice when she wants to be."

"Is the fence barbed wire?" Theo was squinting over my other shoulder, so I handed the binoculars to her.

"No," Pilar said, "but electrified. Taller than most fences around here, too—maybe six feet."

"Electrified." Theo grinned at Ada. "How convenient. We brought our own electrician."

When the water boiled, I poured it over a packet of Chinese herbs in a mug. Pilar gave it a dubious look. "Anti-inflammatory," I told her. "For my leg."

"Lydia?" she asked. When I nodded she bent over and sniffed, then made a noise in her throat and wrinkled her nose. "M.J., are you sure you need that leg?"

"Estevez," I said, "I hope you never have occasion to find out how much."

Sneezy returned with Shorty, and I introduced her around. She had dark blond hair pulled back in a ponytail and wore jeans and a tee shirt that she probably bought in the children's department. Laugh lines etched into her tanned face around humorous dark eyes were the only thing that gave her age away. She and J.K. worked together often, and they entertained themselves by scrapping like sister and brother.

Lafitte, who was on the night shift, was asleep, but the rest of us sat down to eat and I put my finger on what was bothering me as I looked around the crowded table. It was the crowd. I was used to working alone or with a single partner. Sometimes, there was another intelligence-provider onsite—someone who was monitoring the situation as in this case. Often these days, Bernie was doing the monitoring from D.C. Occasionally I had worked on a larger team, but it always made me a little nervous. And now, two of the team members were unknown quantities. The clatter of dishes and silverware, the banter and laughter, even the backbeat of Sneezy munching kibble—these were the sounds of teamwork, and I'd have to get used to them.

"Sorry you can't meet Lafitte," J.K. said to Ada and Theo.

They exchanged a look. "We haven't met him," Theo said, "but we've seen him."

"Yes," Ada said, "and we wouldn't forget him."

The control room was set up in a windowless room down the hall—a room impervious to remote listening devices of the kind we were using to eavesdrop on Rouhani. It was considerably less cluttered than control rooms used to be because now every external device was connected to a computer, or in this case two computers, which recorded both audio and video. A third computer was using voice recognition software to convert sound recordings into printed transcripts. The VR software Quixote used was the best on the market, and could be set to transcribe dozens of languages, but it wasn't perfect, and it often produced howlers that entertained drowsy operatives reading at their posts late at night. Still, it served its purpose; if we needed evidence that would stand up in court, we used the original recording.

"Can I take these?" I asked Shorty, indicating a pile of transcripts in a box.

She nodded. "Knock yourself out, M.J.," she said. "Pretty boring stuff, unless you're into proppants, shear stimulation, virgin permeability, tensile failure, and microseismic bursts."

"Sounds like stuff I don't want to know," I said.

She grunted.

"Who's he met up with?" I asked. "Anybody interesting besides Aziz?"

"Business associates and women he sees socially, as far as we can tell," she said. "He's quite the ladies' man. Quite the man-about-town as well, though the locals say he's out of town a lot. Has an ex-wife and two kids in California—but you probably know about them. He went there last week, so he could have met up with somebody there and negotiated a sale of the paintings, but Didi didn't consider it cost-effective for us to follow him out there, unless we heard something on his cell tap that made it worth our while. His shadiest connections all speak Farsi, but we haven't caught him discussing the paintings or arranging any more hits, if that's what he was doing when he met up with Aziz. I'd guess that insurance fraud would definitely be up his alley—a little sabotage on a well that's losing him money."

"Aren't they all losing money these days?" Theo asked.

"There's that," Shorty conceded. "You've read the file?" She included both of us in her glance.

"We have," I said.

"Then you know he's treading water," Shorty said. Nodding her head at a screen showing various camera views of the ranch house, she added, "Takes a lot of money to keep up a place like that. He hasn't suffered from the drought like the farmers and ranchers around here, but cheap oil is biting him in the butt. You can see it in the flaking paint on the barn and a few wonky fenceposts. Has expensive tastes, too—a Beemer and a pick-up in the garage. A wine delivery from a gourmet food store last week. He could sell the Beemer and pay child support for a few months."

"I've seen his bank accounts," I said, "including the one in the Caymans. It does make me nervous. We're going to try to sell him a painting. He might not go for it."

Shorty cocked her head, considering. "He'll go for it, I think," she said. "My read? He's in denial. He's sitting on a priceless collection, telling himself that he can always start selling it if the end is in sight. But he doesn't see the end yet."

I respected her opinion. After a few weeks of surveillance, you tend to feel a kind of intimate connection with your subject. You've spent so much time with them, you start to believe that you can predict their next move. That can be dangerous, of course. But Shorty wasn't just basing her opinion on what she could see and hear going on next door, she would have read all the other material Bernie sent, from Rouhani's extensively researched file to his e-mails. And Shorty, like all the other members of the surveillance team, had very good instincts when it came to human behavior.

"What's his security set-up?" I asked, scrutinizing the images on the screen.

Shorty sat in front of the monitor so that she could illustrate her report with images. "I'd rate it as average," she said. "Electrified fence, not old, not new, somewhat neglected, as I said. Speaker phone at the front gate and a remote gate release. Floodlights all over the place, with motion detectors. He has a security service, and they're also about average, according to Bernie. That means the doors and windows are wired, but apparently not the outbuildings. One night Lafitte watched a raccoon who looked like he knew what he was doing climb a fence post and push his way into the barn. Either he accepted the electrical shock as part of the price of a meal at his favorite restaurant, or—." She shrugged.

"Somebody forgot to turn it on," I finished. "Interesting."

Unenthusiastically, Theo, Ada, and I piled into the panel truck once more for the trip to the hotel, where Bernie would have a nice, cushy, air conditioned rental car waiting for us. Pilar made J.K. rig up straps for us to hold onto, and secure our luggage to the truck walls with rope and a bungee cord. As the rear doors closed, she stood smiling, holding Sneezy and using one of Sneezy's paws to wave goodbye.

23

I was planning to make a rather daring fashion statement at the
art museum gala on Saturday night, and also to attempt a bold
experiment in footwear: I would trade my sneaker for a sandal.

When I'd shown them the invitation to the art museum gala,
Theo had announced her intention of wearing a caftan that Ada
had made for her, with sandals, no pantyhose.

"You should get Addy to make you one," Theo had suggested,
"her being a couturier and all."

The couturier, who now went by the single name "Ada" on the
website Bernie had set up for her, said, "Sure, Marge, I could do
that."

"Do you know how hot it's going to be in Texas?" Theo said. She
gathered up her reddish-gray hair and held it on top of her head,
fanning herself with the other hand. "You'll be grateful for the air
circulation. And you can carry all sorts of shit under a caftan." She
broke off a little self-consciously and let her hair fall. "Well, you
probably already know that."

I did know it. Caftans were like burkas: you could wear a second
outfit under them, and have room left over for a tool belt, water

supply, and, if you didn't mind looking pregnant, your brown bag lunch.

"But Theo," I objected, "we don't have time. We're leaving tomorrow."

Theo waved a hand. "Hell, Addy can run up a caftan in a few hours, can't you, Addy?"

Ada leaned on her cane, her head bent forward a little as if to hear better. To me, she said, "Oh, it wouldn't take long. It's just a length of cloth folded over with a hole in the middle for your head. But I have to finish little Bella's ballet dress first because she needs it on Saturday morning for dress rehearsal."

"That's okay," Theo said. "They're getting you a sewing machine. Isn't that what you said, Marge? A sewing machine just like the one she has? That's what we asked for."

"Whatever you asked for," I said, "it'll be there."

Once we arrived at the Omni, it took us a while to find the sewing machine in our suite, which might have had more square footage than my townhouse, but we finally found it in what I later discovered was called the "entertainment room."

"It's a bit much, isn't it?" Theo said, looking around. "Who do you suppose usually stays in a place like this?"

"I'm afraid I'll get lost walking from our room to Marge's," Ada confessed. "You might have to get Sneezy over here to find me."

I sighed. "I suppose it fits our profile as wealthy widows," I said. "But honestly, sometimes Didi goes overboard." I knew that our travel coordinator, K-Rod, wouldn't have booked this on her own. She would have consulted Didi, and he would have chosen the most expensive suite in the most expensive hotel in Fort Worth.

"Spa's a nice touch, though," Theo said. Both bathrooms were furnished with whirlpools tricked out to look like claw-footed bathtubs.

"Yeah," I said. "They're afraid my joints will freeze up, and they'll have to send a rescue squad."

"I approve of the fully stocked bar, too," Theo said. "We can oil our joints there."

The massage therapists showed up around four, while Theo and I were poring over the Rouhani transcripts and Ada was working on my caftan. They were powerfully built young women with prominent tattoos to call attention to their muscles and they were each toting a massage table as if it weighed no more than the average briefcase.

Theo and I both accepted massages, and then talked Ada into getting one while Theo played foosball with the other therapist in the entertainment room.

"I shouldn't really be encouraging this much activity right after your massage," the young woman said.

"So let me win," Theo said, whacking the ball into her opponent's goal.

But you could tell her adversary wasn't the type to yield gracefully, not even to a 73-year-old woman with a cane at the ready.

Much as we longed to stay in and order room service, we had to live up to our impersonation of visitors to the city, and K-Rod had booked us a table at a place called the Reata, which specialized in Southwestern cuisine.

"At least we don't have to stay out late," I said. "Nobody will expect us to do that, at our age."

So we made an early night of it, slept in, and ate a leisurely breakfast. Or rather, Theo and I ate a leisurely breakfast; Ada was hand-stitching trim on my caftan, a beautiful creation in light-weight gray, white, and beige polished cotton.

"It's going to wrinkle, Marge," she said. "But you won't have to wear it that long at a stretch and in this heat, you'll thank me for not making it out of silk or, god forbid, polyester. Plus, it's got vents." She showed me the slits on both sides. If I'd had two good legs, it would have accommodated running flat out—always a consideration in my line of work.

217

"I'm thanking you already," I said, watching the Texas sun beat down on the concrete maze that was downtown Fort Worth.

We had a date to go shopping and sightseeing with our local host, Pinky Devereaux, at ten. Pinky proved to be a chatty, good-natured, stylishly thin woman of average height augmented by a quantity of teased and frosted blond hair. She wore a brightly flowered sundress that showed a lot of tanned and freckled skin and sandals. The sandals, although freighted with large, fluffy red flowers, did not hide her matching toenails and indicated that she was not yet old enough to have her fashion choices constrained by orthotics. Faint laugh lines showed pale through her make-up, and mascaraed lashes framed lively violet eyes. She brought with her the light scent of a pleasant floral perfume. She brought us—what else?—flowers.

"Wow! Didi doesn't mess around, does he?" she said, looking around after introductions. "Would you look at this place?"

"How do you know Mr. Levesque?" Ada said. Then she looked at me and added, "Am I allowed to ask?"

I shrugged but Pinky was already answering. "Honey, Didi got my kids out of Libya. I'd walk through fire for that man, him and Bernice, I really would. Whatever he's up to in Forth Worth, it's all right by me. He said y'all needed to meet Sami Rouhani at the museum gala tonight. That's fine." She raised her manicured hands to show how little they would interfere with whatever we had going on. "If y'all want to meet the Sultan of Kumquat, it's a-okay with me.

"Now, speaking of Libya, I feel like I should make the obligatory apology for the Texas heat, though at least we don't have *giblis*, thank the Lord. God, Marge, you must be dying in that contraption you've got on your leg. Well, it's Texas in August, what can I say? Y'all will just have to come back in January, when you can play a round of golf and drink bourbon on the patio at the nineteenth hole."

"Where are we going?" Theo asked, adjusting her carryall to wear as a backpack.

"We're going down to the Stockyards," she said, anticipating Ada as Ada reached for her purse and handing it to her. "That's the Fort Worth national historic district, with shops and restaurants and things." She made a face. "There's a cattle drive every day at 11:30 and 4, and I'm afraid you'll have to watch those poor old longhorns poking along, pretending to be driven"—here she made air quotes—"by men on horses wearing leather and bandannas and handlebar moustaches—the men, not the horses. Well, I suppose there are worse ways to make a living if you're a longhorn. Anyway, everybody will ask you about it tonight, so we might as well get it over with, and then we can drink margaritas and eat guacamole and shop." Her eyes lit up on the last word.

She surveyed us. "Everybody got everything?" she asked. "Canes all round? Good."

Despite her chatter, she had taken an inventory of our needs, and her tone suggested not solicitude, but efficiency. If she wondered why Didi had sent what must have been his three most decrepit operatives for this job, she didn't say so.

I had not only a cane to wrangle but also a purse, something I never carry in my everyday life. It was a white boxy woven affair, meant to hang from my elbow like a Christmas ornament, and I was bound to leave it somewhere before the day was over. I felt like the Queen.

The margaritas and guacamole were definitely the high points of our first day in Fort Worth. It was a hot day, and we found it hard to watch the ambling longhorns and not wish them a speedy return to shade and whatever was the longhorn equivalent of margaritas. None of us shared Pinky's enthusiasm for shopping, but Didi had given me a wardrobe allowance and instructed me, at Emile's insistence, to make purchases suitable to my persona. Given this directive and the obvious limitations on my reserves of interest and patience, not to mention my physical limitations, Pinky decided we'd be better off at a mall, so we ended up at a Dillard's store. Ada and Pinky proved valuable consultants in this endeavor, and they mostly agreed. Theo went in search of a jewelry store, which made me a little nervous. After a while, I just camped out in the dressing room with my leg up and waited for my consultants to bring me another batch to try on.

An hour of shopping was all I could stand, and Pinky didn't need a second hint to return us to the hotel. On the way home, she eyed Theo in the rearview mirror. "If you're interested in jewelry, Theo, some other day I can take you to my favorite stores."

"She's not that interested," I said.

At the same time, Theo said, "That would be nice."

I wanted to scowl at her, but I was in the front seat and didn't have a rearview mirror to scowl in.

Ordinarily, Theo didn't look like somebody who would be interested in jewelry. She hardly wore any, and what she wore tended to be rudimentary—a watch, at most, a gold chain. Like me, she'd probably spent her professional career avoiding things that set off metal detectors, caught the light, or made noise. Now, however, in honor of our masquerade, Theo wore two rings, a bracelet, and a watch. Of course, male cat burglars don't steal jewelry to wear it, either. I assumed that Theo, like her male counterparts, saw jewelry as a commodity. I was hoping that Theo wouldn't take Pinky up on her invitation to return in cooler weather to collect some of her favorite pieces as souvenirs of Fort Worth, but really, it was not my problem. I closed my eyes and drifted off, the rising and falling cadences of Pinky's voice like a lullaby in my ears.

24

———

Roy Devereaux, Pinky's husband, was a big, slow-talking oilman with skin like tanned leather, keen blue eyes that didn't miss much, and an attitude of affectionate indulgence toward his wife. He wore a Western-cut tuxedo and a Stetson, and made the obligatory remark about accompanying not one but four beautiful ladies to the party.

I was gratified that both my caftan and Theo's gave credence to Ada's persona as a designer, as did her own outfit—a loose-fitting pair of pants out of some woven fabric in a plum color, a capped-sleeve shell in peach, and an over blouse in muted peach tones draped over her arm. On her head Ada wore a turban made from a colorful gauzelike fabric that included plum and peach but also brighter variations of those colors. She looked every inch the fashion designer.

Roy apologized for "stuffing" all three of us in a backseat the size of my kitchen, and we didn't confess to the panel truck we'd arrived in.

The Modern Art Museum of Fort Worth, a.k.a. "The Modern," is an impressive building—not so much from the front, which is a façade of ultramodern glass and concrete, mostly concrete, accented by a huge spiraling wood sculpture. But as we approached it from the back, we could see the series of glass pavilions that appeared to be floating on a lake, their roofs supported by enormous Y-shaped columns.

"It's supposed to be one of the most beautiful art museums in the world," Pinky told us. "A Japanese architect designed it, Tadao Ando."

Inside, it was clear that Pinky was in her element, and well known to museum staff as well as to just about everyone else. "I used to serve on the board," she told us. "I still volunteer in the gift shop." She waved at someone across the room, and lowered her voice. "Working in the gift shop is way more fun. You wouldn't believe how bent out of shape some people get about where we hang their favorite painting and what we hang it next to. We practically went to war over what to put in storage to make space for the Calder exhibit. And when Francie May Grand found out we were going to store the Barnett Newman she donated, they say she rose up off her deathbed and came down here to yell at the director." Pinky sighed. "Do y'all know Newman's work?" We all shook our heads. "You're not missing a thing. Brown canvas with yellow stripe, red canvas with blue stripe. I'm not kidding! Of course, working in the gift shop does cost me more than being on the board." And she turned to greet a group of newcomers.

The crowd got thicker and the three of us split up to look for Rouhani. Then I felt a tap on my shoulder and turned to find his smiling face not two feet away. He was with Theo.

"Oh!" I said, "You startled me." I slapped a palm to my chest, slipped my index finger under the neckline, and pressed the Record button on the small device secreted in one of Ada's handy pockets.

"Marge, I want you to meet Sami—," she said, and hesitated.

"I'm sorry," she told him, "I didn't hear your last name. It's so noisy in here."

He smiled affably. "Rouhani," he said to me, extending his hand. "But everybody calls me Sami. It is noisy in here."

He was dressed in a white tux and looked handsome, urbane, and thoroughly at ease. He was a little shorter than Theo, and might have been even shorter except for a pair of tooled-leather cowboy boots. He wasn't wearing a Stetson. He was, however, wearing the Pahlavi family crest on his lapel.

"We were just looking at a picture together, you know," Theo said. "And I said that I thought your painting—the one you brought with you—was much nicer. Because of the cow and all. And we got to talking, and Sami said he wanted to meet you."

"Oh, yes?" I said politely, marveling at the deft efficiency with which Theo had arrived at the point of the encounter. Watching her play her part, I was reminded that jewel thieves were accustomed to mingling with their wealthy prospective marks; that was how George Finch had met Dottie. She was smiling at Rouhani but I saw her appraising eyes drift to the lapel pin. She caught me looking and winked at me. "It's a beautiful museum, Mr.—Sami. Do you come here a lot?"

"I like to come, yes," he said. "And also to the Kimbell." He gestured over his shoulder. "Have you seen it?" His English was fluent, almost unaccented.

"No, we just got here yesterday," I said.

"We saw the cattle drive, though, didn't we Marge?" Theo said.

"Oh, yes, that was exciting," I said. "But I just don't see how those steers can stand to carry around so much horn." This much was true; I couldn't. "You'd think more of them would get hurt—the other steers and the cowboys, I mean."

I spotted Ada a little distance away, over Rouhani's shoulder. She raised her eyebrows at me and turned away.

"So you participated in a little history, and now you're soaking up some culture," Rouhani said. "Not bad for your first day in the city."

"So far, so good, huh, Marge?" Theo said.

"Oh, yes, Pinky is showing us a wonderful time," I said.

Rouhani smiled politely but I detected some edginess in his eyes and posture. He wanted to get back to the painting. Good.

"You brought a painting with you, I understand," he said.

"Yes, a Chagall." I slaughtered the name, giving it a hard *ch* and two flat Midwestern *a*'s. "Do you know his work at all?"

"Oh, yes," he said, "very well."

"I don't really know much about art," I said. "I mean, I like it and all. I just never studied it, you know?" A waiter appeared with champagne, and I beamed at him. "Oh, good," I said. "Champagne." This time I pronounced the *ch* correctly to indicate that I was more familiar with alcoholic beverages than art.

"Tell me about your painting," Rouhani said, leaning forward. I had the impression that he wanted to wall me off from all intruding presences until he got this story out of me.

"Well," I said, "there's not much to tell. My late husband, Gus, he inherited this painting from his uncle, who was in France during the war. This uncle was pretty young at the time. I don't think he knew any more about art than Gus and me. But somehow he acquired this painting and brought it back with him."

"Do you know if he purchased it?" Rouhani pressed.

I put a hand to my cheek and considered. "Well, seems like he said he did, but you never know, do you? The spoils of war and all. He was my husband's favorite uncle, but who knows what he did over there?"

"Isn't that the truth!" Theo put in. "They all did things they don't like to admit—that's what I hear."

I went on. "Will that be a problem if I want to sell it? I don't have any records of a sale or anything."

"It could be," he said. "Do you know if it's genuine?"

"Oh, it's genuine," I said. "Gus had it appraised this one time when he was thinking about selling it. But then someone told him that the price would just keep going up, so he decided maybe he'd better hang onto it. Seemed to me a shame to spend all that money having it appraised and then not sell it, but it was Gus's decision, not mine."

"That's very good, Mrs. Smith," Rouhani said, "but an appraisal is not an authentication. Who appraised it?"

As someone jostled me, Rouhani laid a hand on my free arm and urged me away. Our little group edged toward the wall and Rouhani backed me against it, blocking out the crowd by standing in front of me.

"Oh, I don't remember his name," I said, "but I imagine it's on the certificate—the one the appraiser gave us, I mean, not the French one stuck to the back. Why? Do you know any appraisers in Miami?"

"I might," he said. "But what do you mean about the French certificate?"

"There's this old piece of paper on the back," I said. "I can't read it, because it's in French. But the appraiser said that it was from some Chagall committee, and it meant the painting was genuine."

"I see," he said, eyes glittering. "And now you want to sell it?"

"Well, yes," I said. "I mean, it would be one thing if Gus had been fond of it. Then I'd keep it, you know, as a memento. But it hasn't been out of the box in, oh, thirty years maybe. I just ran into it the other day. I saw the box and thought, 'What in the world is this?' And there it was."

Rouhani winced. "You know, Mrs. Smith, fine art needs to be taken care of. There are optimal conditions for storing a painting or the painting will get damaged."

"Well, I didn't remember that it was there, now, did I?" I said. "And it doesn't look damaged to me. It's been sitting in the same closet my furs have been hanging in. So my daughter said, 'You're going to that gala in Fort Worth with Pinky, and Pinky has lots of connections to the museum. So why don't you take that Chagall painting along with you and see if you can sell it to the museum?' They don't have any Chagalls, do they? So maybe they'll want one."

"No," he said, "they don't, but—."

"I could try to sell it in Miami, I suppose," I said. "But I don't know anybody in any museum there. What would they think if I just walked in off the street with a painting under my arm and nobody to vouch for me? I probably couldn't do that, could I?" I was treating him like an expert, someone who could advise me, and I could see that he liked that.

"Perhaps not," he said. "What about paperwork to establish the painting's provenance?"

"Provenance—what's that?" I asked.

"Documents that establish its bona fides," he said. "Anything that helps to trace the work from the artist to its current location. You know, a letter from your husband's uncle describing where and under what circumstances he acquired the painting. Anything like that."

I shook my head. "I don't have anything like that. I never saw any letters. I could maybe write my husband's cousins—well, not Linus and Betty, they're both dead, but Eugene and Gloria might know something."

"Your uncle must have written letters home during the war," Sami said. "Who in the family would have them?"

"Well, if anybody would have them, we probably would," I said. "But I don't know. I suppose I could look."

"Do you know the title of the painting? Did the appraiser check to see if it was reported stolen?"

I frowned. "The title's in French, so of course, I can't read it. How could somebody tell if it was stolen? The appraiser couldn't find anything at the time, I don't think."

"That's good," he said. "It's not hard to check these days on the Web."

"Oh," I said, "I don't know much about that. I know how to find my grandbabies on Facebook, and I can read my e-mail, but that's about it."

"I keep telling you, Margie," Theo put in, "you should take a class."

"What for?" I said, turning to her. The glint in her eye suggested that she enjoyed making Rouhani suffer by derailing the conversation.

"As long as someone has checked for you, an expert," he said. "But perhaps I could check as well. If I—."

I cut him off. "Oh, it's nice of you to offer, Sami," I said. "But I imagine that if I show it to someone here at the museum, they'll look it up. They must have resources that ordinary people wouldn't know about, right?"

He put on an expression of concern. "But I'm afraid there is another problem with your plan, Mrs. Smith."

I turned to a passing waiter, snagged a small quiche, and took a bite before turning back.

"What's that, Sami?" I said.

"Look around," he said, with an expansive gesture. "The Modern only collects postwar art. If your painting was acquired during the war, its date will be earlier. Although I'm sure the director would admire the painting, I don't think the museum will be interested in buying it."

I looked around to take in the art he was indicating.

"You mean this museum only shows paintings that were painted after the war?" Theo said. "But weren't there some people —famous artists, I mean—who were painting before the war and after? Like Picasso?"

"Yes, of course," he said. "But the only Picasso owned by this museum is a later one."

"And you mean to say," Theo said, disbelief written in her eyebrows, "that this museum would turn down an earlier Picasso if somebody offered them one?"

"I'm afraid they would, Mrs. Underwood," he said. "Every museum specializes. So perhaps Mrs. Smith should reconsider—."

"Well, then, how about that other museum across the street?" I asked. "What's it called? The Kimbell? Maybe they'd want to buy it."

The alarm that flared in his eyes told me I'd hit home. "Possibly," he said, "but what I'd like to suggest—."

This time the interruption came from outside our little triangle. Given the crowd, we'd been lucky to manage such a lengthy conversation uninterrupted.

A heavyset balding man slapped Sami on the back. "Sami, you old rascal!" he said. "I knew that if I wanted to find you in this mob, I just had to find the best-looking women, and there you'd be!" He roared with laughter at his own joke, and I wondered how many times he'd laughed at it before.

The new man brought with him an entourage, to which we were introduced. But before we managed to slip away, satisfied with what we'd accomplished, Sami managed to turn me aside and say in my ear, "I'll call you. Where are you staying?" When I told him, he nodded and said, "Don't talk to anybody else about your painting until we've had a chance to chat. I think I can help you."

"That's awfully sweet of you," I said.

Theo and I went off to rescue Ada, who was probably having a hard time hearing anything in the crowd. Besides, my leg was killing me and I needed to sit down.

We refrained from reporting on our encounter with Rouhani until the three of us were back in our suite.

When we finished with our tag-team account, Theo said, tears of laughter gleaming in her eyes, "The best part, Addy, was the way his eyebrows jumped every time Marge pronounced 'Chagall'!"

25

We had Rouhani hooked, but not landed, and I was interested to see what he would do next. I thought that he would want to keep us away from art museums and galleries, and I was right. He called on Sunday to invite us to dinner on Wednesday night at his house, and he asked me to bring the painting. He told me that he would also invite the Devereauxs.

"It's short notice, I know," he said, "but I'm going out of town on Thursday and I hope to see your painting before I go."

I assured him that we would be happy to come, and that we were looking forward to seeing his art collection—all perfectly true. I didn't add that the part of his collection we were most looking forward to seeing was the part he wouldn't show us.

"He's in a hurry because he's leaving town?" Theo said. "Couldn't be better."

Pinky called to say that she'd accepted Rouhani's invitation, but Roy had a zoning board meeting and couldn't come.

"Let's see how he handles a mob of women in his bachelor pad," she said.

"Did you ever meet his ex-wife?" I asked.

"Anousha? Yes, I met her," she said. "I liked her a lot. She was one smart cookie—educated at Oxford. She's an investment banker. No way they're going to get that one to wear the veil."

I'd read about her in Rouhani's file, and been impressed. "So Sami's not afraid of smart women?"

"Honey, I don't think Sami's afraid of any kind of women," she said. "With his looks, I bet he has to fight them off with a stick, especially now that he's single again."

"She's in San Francisco, right?" I said. "Do you know why she moved there? She's taken the kids a long way from Daddy."

"Let me think," she said. "I believe she has a sister out there. And if I'm not mistaken, she wanted her daughter to go to the San Francisco conservatory. She's a gifted pianist, the little girl. The older brother's good, too, but seems like he's more interested in computer games, so maybe he can go to a school and study that out there. These days, who knows? He'll probably invent a game and be a gazillionaire before he's reached puberty."

I told her we'd meet her at Rouhani's to save her the drive downtown to pick us up.

"Are you sure you'll be able to find it?" she said. "It's way out in the middle of noplace."

"We have our ways," I said.

"Of course you do," she said. "Forget I asked. You're probably watching his every move on some kind of spycam."

The worst part of a job like this is the waiting. Visiting the surveillance center meant a ride in the panel truck, which we weren't eager to repeat, and we didn't have any reason to visit in any case because not only could we communicate with our colleagues electronically, but they could give us remote access to the equipment at any time so that we could monitor the cameras and laser microphone. They could even send us the translated cell transcripts electronically, which is how we knew that Rouhani hadn't mentioned me and my painting to anyone.

"He says he's going out of town," I said to Pilar on the phone. "Where's he going?"

"New York," she said. "He must have had his secretary make the reservation for him, because we didn't see it, but he mentioned it in a couple of conversations."

I think that if Theo had had her way, we would have skipped all the socializing and just gone over the fence at night and wandered around until we found the paintings. But even she had to concede the advantage of waiting until Rouhani vacated the premises.

Ada, meanwhile, had several business cards from prospective clients, and I predicted that once they'd looked her up on the Web and read the testimonials from celebrities—all of them one-time clients of Levesque or Quixote—she would have her hands full, if she wanted them full.

"I wish I could remember them," she said, sighing. "But I couldn't hear their names in the crowd at the art museum, so I don't know who's who."

We knew that we should behave like tourists, but a trip across the street from our hotel to the Water Gardens on Sunday morning told us everything we needed to know about ambulatory tourism in Texas in the summertime. We sat on a bench and rested our various compromised body parts.

"I can hardly see the fountains for the sweat in my eyes," Ada complained.

Theo was breathing through her mouth in a way that suggested a return of the oxygen tank was in order. "It's just the heat," she said. "We're not used to it."

"So nobody wants to move on to the zoo or botanical gardens after this?" I said.

"Who wants to go watch those poor animals and plants suffer in this heat?" Ada said.

"Maybe there's a cold front due," Theo said.

"Up from the Gulf of Mexico?" I said. "Yeah, I could see that happening."

"Anyway," Theo said, "You're going to the gym."

"*We're* going to the gym," I said. "When we go over that fence, you'll have to keep up with me."

"Eat my dust, granny," she said.

We sat dripping and contemplated our fate. In this heat, it was hard to motivate yourself to walk across the street, so the prospect of a workout was not a happy one.

Jasmine and Bernie had made the gym arrangements. I drove our nice comfy rental car five blocks to a parking garage under a 10th-floor facility with a panoramic view of the city. Theo and I were assigned to Manny and Carlos, who looked like Cowboy linebackers. Ada came along to watch and to join us in the sauna afterwards. The boys tried to show her some moves but she waggled an index finger at them.

"I have a note from my doctor," she said. "No gym class for me."

When the boys were satisfied that they'd left no muscle untormented, they peeled us off the floor and delivered us to the sauna, where a serious young woman handed us each a smoothie.

"Don't forget!" Carlos admonished us as he waved goodbye. "Yoga tomorrow at three."

"We followed Ms. Baptiste's recipe," the young woman said, unsmiling. "Be sure to tell her."

Theo regarded hers with suspicion. "Why is it red?" she said.

"Beets," said the barrista.

"For inflammation," I clarified, when Theo raised her eyebrows at me.

"Oh," Theo said. "I got plenty of that."

"Your piss will turn red," I added, as she took a swig.

"How interesting!" Ada said, tasting hers.

"Better with a shot of rum," Theo grumbled.

I didn't say anything because I agreed with her.

Over our protests, the Devereauxs had us over for a barbecue in the evening.

"Don't be silly," Pinky said. "Roy likes y'all. And besides—." She dropped her voice. "Whatever y'all are up to, it'll be more authentic if we have y'all over for supper."

We went and had a good time. To the other guests, I repeated the story I'd concocted about meeting Pinky "oversees" when my husband was in the diplomatic service. In my line of work, I'd encountered more diplomats than oil men, so diplomacy seemed a safer bet if I was interrogated about my spouse's line of work. Ada traded a few additional business cards.

We spent the next three days working out and attending yoga classes (Ada watched), exercising in the hotel pool (I swam laps while Theo did water exercises that were easier on her lungs), and visiting selected indoor tourist attractions, including the Kimbell and Amon Carter art museums and my own sentimental favorite, the National Cowgirl Museum and Hall of Fame. None of us was a big fan of Western art, the Amon Carter's specialty, but we figured that someone with a painting to sell might make the rounds of the museums simply for the education. I Skyped with Fina and the kitties, who always appeared to recognize my voice but not my image on the screen. Ada Skyped with her husband and grandchildren. We caught up on our reading.

"Does Ada's husband know what she's up to in Fort Worth?" I asked Theo while she was on the phone with him.

"Probably," she said. "Or maybe he has a general idea, but no specifics."

"We don't have any specifics," I pointed out.

"That could be why," she said.

On Tuesday afternoon, Theo surprised me by proposing a trip to the firing range.

"You carry a gun to work with you?" I asked.

She shrugged. "It never hurts to practice," she said noncommittally.

The place we picked was huge, with a large main building in something resembling corrugated steel like an ultra-modern factory.

"Oh, shoot!" Ada said, as we passed a poster in the lobby. "We missed Full-Auto Friday!"

I glanced at her to make sure she was kidding.

Theo pointed at another poster. "Yeah, but we could still get in on the Simunition."

"'Military-grade paintball?'" I read. "That sounds scary. I've never known anything 'military-grade' that wasn't overpriced and undereffective."

"And I've never heard of military-grade paint," Ada said. "Do you suppose it doesn't cover anything or it's the wrong color or what?"

"Maybe they lace it with BB's so that it feels more authentically painful when you get shot," Theo offered.

I rented a Colt Defender, Theo a Glock, and Ada, to my surprise, a Smith and Wesson, after examining the selection with a critical eye that indicated she knew what she was doing. Theo was a crack shot, but Ada wasn't bad and complained that she was out of practice. Then Theo insisted on renting a Remington rifle, and we each took a turn.

"Not bad," Theo said to me when I'd finished and handed it off to Ada, and I realized that she'd probably been worrying about my skills as much as I'd been worrying about hers.

"Having a broken leg doesn't affect my aim, Theo," I said.

On Tuesday evening, Lafitte arrived in the guise of a pizza delivery man, right down to the pizzas in their insulated carriers.

"Ah, Smitty, I couldn't stay away," he said, grinning. "Besides, I was going stir crazy."

I relieved him of the pizzas and he extended a hand, palm up.

I looked at the hand. "Take it up with Didi," I said.

"I'd accept a beer," he said hopefully.

"Help yourself," I said, "if you can find the bar."

I made introductions, and we took him on a tour of the apartment.

"How come I always draw the assignments that involve sleeping on hot sand next to a camel, and you get the luxury suite at the Ritz?" he said.

"When you're my age, Lafitte," I said, "maybe you'll get the luxury suite at the Ritz. I've been intimate with plenty of camels in my day, and if you think I've forgotten the smell of fresh camel dung in the morning or the prick of sand flies on my neck or the gritty blindness of a *haboob*, you've got another think coming."

While I set out plates and napkins, he investigated the "entertainment room."

"Smitty!" he called, his voice excited.

He appeared in the doorway to the dining room, holding up a box. "Look what I found." He waggled the box enticingly: Risk.

"Which version?" I asked.

"40th Anniversary," he said, admiring the box.

As Theo and Ada entered the room, he looked around. "I challenge everybody in this room," he said.

"Don't you have to work tonight?" I said.

He shook his head. "I have the night off," he said. "I'm all yours."

"Secret Mission rules?" Theo asked.

"No fair!" Ada complained.

"You're on," I said, and picked up a piece of pizza.

Lafitte set the box on the table and rubbed his hands together. "The last time we played Risk, we were waiting for that courier in Savannakhet, remember, Smitty?" he said.

"No fair," Ada complained.

In the end, she won, of course. Theo predicted it as soon as Ada took control of Australia. "She plays games all the time with her grandkids," she said.

"No fair," I grumbled.

Ada beamed at me. "I'm coming after South America next," she said.

"*El pueblo unido jamás será vencido*," I chanted, fist in the air. Who knew that an unassuming electrician, seamstress, and grandmother of six would be so into world domination? Her performance at the firing range should have been my first clue.

But none of us went down without a fight, and it was midnight before Lafitte zipped the empty pizza boxes back into the carrying cases and moseyed off down the hall.

On Wednesday morning while we were having a room-service breakfast in our breakfast nook overlooking the water park, I announced that I was removing the walking boot.

Theo, who looked marginally more hung over than I did, swallowed her aspirins and made no comment.

"Can you do that?" Ada said, surprised. "Without your doctor's permission?"

"Watch me," I said.

I unstrapped the contraction and kicked it under the table. I held onto the back of my chair and stood up, then took a tentative step. Then I let go of the chair back, took another step, and would have fallen flat if Theo hadn't shot out a hand to brace my hip and steady me.

"Good idea to practice," she said, "with the cane."

So I did. After watching me for half an hour, Theo decided to try it as well, and joined me in my practice, sans cane. Then we went up to the roof and walked the jogging track until we felt pretty confident. I did the last five laps without the cane, but slowly—too slowly.

"You're in great shape for someone who recently had hip replacement surgery," I told her. I'd worried about this. The best second-story man in the world with a bum hip can no longer claim to be the best second-story man in the world. But she'd probably had the same concerns about me and my bum leg.

"That's because I didn't wait as long as most people," she said. "If I'd waited for my doctor to prescribe the surgery, and for the insurance company to approve it, I would have lost half my muscle mass to inertia by the time they got around to it. I knew I needed it, and so when Ada had to go in for the heart valve replacement, I thought, what the hell? Why not join her in the home? We didn't plan on Dottie breaking her hip, of course."

"So you found a surgeon who would do it?" I asked.

"Oh, sure," she said, "as long as I was willing to pay for it. My orthopedist knew that I'd need it eventually, he just wasn't allowed to sign off on it, according to the insurance company, until I'd been given a round of pain shots and become significantly debilitated. Most people can't afford to foot the bill themselves, but I'm fortunate that I can. The insurance company wouldn't have paid for the nursing home, either. They would have expected me to dredge up a spouse or some progeny to take care of me at home."

"I hear you," I said. I'd had plenty of occasion to curse the couples bias that so complicated life as a single person. And like Theo, I was luckier than most, not only because of Fina and Marco Antonio, but because the Levesques took a familial interest in my affairs that was often annoying, sometimes infuriating, mostly touching and occasionally useful.

Ada sat on the sidelines and knitted. "Don't overdo it, you two," she called as we blew past her at a duck's trot. "We still have to go shopping."

Pinky picked us up at noon for lunch and shopping, but we managed to stretch lunch until there wasn't much time left for shopping before our afternoon naps. Anyway, I was having a hard time paying upscale prices for clothing I'd never wear on my own.

"But Marge," Ada objected, "you may have to play the part of a wealthy widow again someday."

"Yeah," Theo put in. "It could become her specialty."

"You mean, she's not a wealthy widow?" Pinky said.

Theo grinned at me. "See?" she said. "You're a natural."

26

We didn't have any trouble finding Rouhani's place, thanks to the built-in GPS in our rental car. Ada was looking around from the front seat, enjoying the view.

"It's like we were kidnap victims the last time we came out here," she said. "Like we were blindfolded so we wouldn't see where we were going."

"It's greener than I expected," I said.

"They're supposed to be recovering from the drought," Ada said. "The rainfall around here is about normal this year—that's what I read. It's got its own kind of beauty, doesn't it?"

"Except for the drilling rigs," Theo said. "Plenty of those to obscure the view."

"I looked at a map online," Ada said. "They put a green dot for every active drilling site, and you could hardly see Fort Worth for all the green dots."

"You'd think Rouhani would be raking it in," I mused. "I know oil prices have fallen, but even so. It's heresy to suggest that Bernie might have missed something so obvious as another offshore bank account, but I wonder."

"Just because they're drilling doesn't mean they're pumping," Theo said. "He could be spending a fortune drilling in all the wrong places."

But if Rouhani was in financial distress, it wasn't obvious from the house or the broad smile on his face as he greeted us. His eyes went to my empty arms.

"The painting's in the back seat," I said, nodding toward the car. "Would you mind?"

The painting, which was almost four feet high and three across, could not be managed easily by someone using a cane, but as I suspected, he was delighted to help. We had all brought our canes tonight, the better to encourage him to underestimate us, as well as to rest our tired legs and hip.

He could tell by the feel of the parcel that the painting wasn't framed. "Now, Marge," he said. "I hope you didn't check this with the luggage and let the baggage handlers push it around."

"Oh, no!" I said. "I wouldn't do that. I mailed it to Pinky, UPS."

He smiled politely but I could tell he was worried.

In the spacious living room, a young man in a white guayabera shirt and tan chinos turned toward our commotion as we entered. He had rather unruly blond hair the color of champagne, an easy smile, and owlish round Harry Potter glasses. If I had to guess his profession, I would have put him down as an accountant.

"I'd like you to meet my friend, Olivier Da Silva," Rouhani said.

I assumed that this young man was the male backup—someone to offer solidarity and support in case the four women ganged up on Rouhani.

As I extended my hand to him, Rouhani added, "He's a professor of art history at U.T. Dallas. I've asked him to come along and look at your painting, Marge."

"Oh, how exciting!" I said, and grasped his hand with warmth. "Do you know Chagall's work, Mr. Da Silva?" I now had the pleasure of seeing two men flinch when I pronounced the artist's name.

"Call me Olivier, please," he said with a friendly smile only slightly askew from the mispronunciation. His own pronunciation sounded Portuguese—I guessed Brazilian. "I do, yes, know Chagall's work." He pronounced the name carefully, carefully enough so that I'd hear it but not with sufficient emphasis to suggest that he was correcting me. "My specialty is modern art." He raised a finger. "But I'm not an appraiser or authenticator. I can give an opinion on whether the work is genuine, based on my familiarity with Chagall's other work, but it would not be definitive, you understand."

We moved on to admiring the living room, where a decorator given a blank check had apparently been hard at work. The room appeared to have been decorated around a vibrant abstract over the fireplace that could have been a Kandinsky, its curves and lines echoed in the shapes of the tables and the arrangement and lines of chairs and couches. The fireplace itself showed enough soot to suggest that it was a working fireplace, though I couldn't imagine when someone would feel cold enough in this climate to light it. Perhaps in the winter Texans cranked up the air conditioning to simulate the cold in other parts of the country, and then huddled around their blazing hearths.

Pinky arrived then, so we had to admire the room—and the view—all over again. All I saw was a landscape of flat scrub relieved by a couple of spindly, drought-dwarfed mesquite trees, but if that was your definition of beauty, this landscape measured up.

Sami served us drinks and we sat and chatted idly. Sami himself proved to be an adept and engaging conversationalist, and we quite liked him. Of course, none of us harbored any particular prejudices against thieves, whatever their motives. But Sami wasn't really a thief, just a man with the money to hire a thief—and, I reminded myself, possibly a killer.

Theo asked him where he was from originally, and when he described himself as an Iranian in exile, she pursued it.

"How old were you when you left Iran? You must have been quite young," she said.

"I was six," he said. "My parents shielded my sisters and me from much of what was going on. All I knew was that we didn't get out as much or go to the places we used to go. I suppose I knew that my parents were upset about something, but I didn't know what—some grown-up thing, I supposed. And then one day my father asked me, 'How would you like to go see some cowboys?' 'Real cowboys?' I said. I was so excited. I didn't know why my mother or my older sisters were crying when we left, or why everything had to be put away in boxes, or even why the samovar had to be packed in my suitcase. I thought I would put my cowboy hat there when we packed to come home."

"And you came to Texas?" Ada asked.

"No," he said, "we moved to Oklahoma. Texas came later. It was many years before I understood what had really happened when we left."

Ada asked if he resented the radical Islamists who had overthrown the shah.

"How can I not?" he said, spreading his arms. "We Iranians had a cultured, modern society—great art, great literature, great universities. We were a secular state, part of the global economy, not just of goods but of ideas. Middle-class Iranians were well educated. We honored our traditions and embraced the West."

"Like you," I said, and he looked gratified.

"And now?" he said. "Artists, writers, and journalists are persecuted, women are covered and monitored and their education is neglected. Everybody must bow to *sharia* as interpreted by whatever imam is in power. My god, we're a country that loves to go to the movies, but the only movies allowed are movies about children. All of those great Iranian films shown at Cannes and other film festivals? Iranians living inside Iran can't see them. Those filmmakers have been arrested and brutally tortured. That's the kind of country it is now."

None of us looked at each other. None of us asked about arrests and torture under the shah. But Ada's "That's terrible!" came a beat too late, and the unspoken comment must have hung in the air so palpably that Sami shifted in his chair and continued in a somewhat conciliatory tone, "Of course, it wasn't perfect, I'm not saying that. God knows, my cousin the shah had his own crimes to answer for."

"You're related to the shah?" I asked, now risking an astonished look at the other two.

"He's my cousin by marriage," Sami said. He touched his lapel pin. "This is the Pahlavi family crest. I wear it in solidarity with the family, with their suffering. It's terrible, what's been done to them." He shook his head in sorrow.

Okay. Before I went to Tehran in 1979, I read a lot of intelligence on the place. This is standard operating procedure at Quixote. No matter how little time the mission is intended to take, we do extensive research in order to minimize risk of the unexpected and maximize the chance for success. I'd seen photographs of people tortured and executed by the SAVAK, the shah's brutal secret police. I knew that by the time of the revolution, the shah was making life hell for more than two thousand political prisoners. I knew that in collusion with family members and his pals among the elite, he had amassed a fortune estimated at up to a billion dollars when the revolution came, though whether that did or didn't count the two thousand villages he owned—how can anybody own a village?—I didn't remember. I did remember that he'd once thrown a birthday party for the monarchy that cost the equivalent of more than one hundred million dollars. Without this kind of wealth, of course, his wife would not have been able to assemble one of the world's most spectacular collections of modern art. In any case, when some ten percent of the Iranian population took to the streets to denounce him, he and his family had flown off into the sunset, most of their wealth secure in foreign banks. Sure, he'd been bounced around a bit because no country had really wanted to shelter a deposed dictator, especially when his presence sparked outrage among its natives, and because the Iranian government was demanding his extradition to face trial for his many crimes. Seven months after I went to Tehran, the shah would manage to pressure Jimmy Carter into letting him into the U.S. for gallstone surgery, a spark that likely ignited long resentment of American collusion with the Pahlavi regime and resulted in the takeover of the American embassy. Still, nobody sent him back, and if he died the next year from cancer, well, my view was that it couldn't have happened to a nastier guy. The price he'd paid for his life of crime had been minimal. He'd gotten off easy.

I noticed that Olivier Da Silva made no comment on this recitation of the revolutionaries' crimes against the middle class. I saw him in profile, backlit against the window, but I thought that if he was Brazilian, he might know a thing or two about totalitarian regimes, though like Sami, he might be too young to remember what it was like to live through the darkest days of a military junta.

If I'd had the kind of face in which my thoughts could be easily read, I wouldn't have survived my first mission for Quixote. So I assumed a sympathetic expression and asked Sami if he was still in contact with his family.

Dinner was served in a well-appointed dining room with a view of the north Texas landscape on one side and a view of the courtyard, with its burbling fountain and greenery, on the other. Though the Devereauxs had served chicken, Rouhani seemed to subscribe to the opinion that tourists came to Texas to eat beef, and served thick slabs of it, branded by the grill. Or rather, the previously invisible Ahmad Rashidi, whom Sami introduced as a former valet in the royal household, served it. The man had the impervious exterior of a concrete block, with the exception of steely dark-gray eyes that looked as deep as the Marianas Trench and as deadly.

Theo took advantage of laughter at the other end of the room to lean toward me and whisper, "If that guy's a former royal valet, I'm Tinkerbelle."

I nodded. "He's got SAVAK written all over him."

She looked down at her plate uneasily. "Think he strangled the poor steer with his bare hands?"

Sami seemed to know a lot about the history of his adopted city, but I took it with a grain of salt, given his heavily biased version of Iranian history. I was willing to stipulate that cowboys and cattle had played an important role in Fort Worth's past, but I imagined that the cattle had a different story to tell than the cowboys, and I wouldn't get their story from a human enthusiast. Still, Pinky offered only minor corrections and demurrals, so much of what he said was probably true. Da Silva deferred to them both because he was a more recent arrival.

Ada pursued that. Da Silva was indeed Brazilian, from Salvador in the Northeast.

"That's on the coast, isn't it?" I said. "How did you come to be in such a landlocked place as Fort Worth?"

He said that art history Ph.D.s had to go where the jobs were, but that he still had hopes that he would end up in a coastal city. Ada encouraged him to talk about his hometown, and he did, with more vivacity than we'd yet seen from him.

Sami waited until dessert to broach the subject of the painting.

Now he leaned toward me and said, "You know, Marge, I was serious about buying the painting myself—if it's genuine. I am something of a collector."

"Oh!" Ada said excitedly. "A collector! Could we see your collection?"

"Of course," he said. He made a gesture that took in the room. "But you've seen some of it already."

On one sideboard was a small bronze figural sculpture that might have been a Miró, or I thought so because the framed drawing behind it was almost certainly Miró. On the adjacent wall were two Picasso drawings of women's heads. On the other sideboard, too far away to see clearly, was a rangy bronze dog that was probably a Giacometti. I'd seen other paintings and small sculptures in the living room, but I hadn't had a chance to investigate them.

"Are any of these by Chagall?" I said, looking around. I made a point of exchanging my "ch" for an "sh," but maintained the flat "a." I was educable, but not a quick study.

Sami couldn't hide his amusement, and Olivier suddenly began scrutinizing his steak. "No, no, Marge," Sami said. "Not these. I have a Chagall in the other room I'll show you. But these are by his contemporaries—Miró and Picasso."

We made suitable noises of awe and astonishment. Everybody had heard of Picasso.

"Don't tell me," Theo said. "Let me guess. Those two drawings." She pointed.

"Very good," Sami said, and he seemed genuinely pleased that one of us, at least, could tell a Picasso drawing from a pietà.

I was thinking that either the oil business had been very good to Sami Rouhani, or his father had gotten out of Iran with more than a samovar to show for his close ties to the ruling family. Because of these thoughts, I wasn't paying much attention to the conversation. Ada had said something about assuming that Iranians would collect Persian art, not Western art, and Pinky had asked whether drawings of people's faces didn't violate Islamic religious tenets.

I didn't hear the answer, but I tuned in again when Da Silva said, "You know, ladies, the Tehran art museum has one of the finest collections of modern art in the world."

"Western art?" Theo asked.

"Yes," he said, "but here's the thing: almost nobody has ever seen it."

Almost, I agreed. Myself included.

27

U rged by his listeners, he went on to tell the story of how Queen Farah had supervised the design and construction of the museum and the assembly of its collection.

"You mean to tell us that nobody's seen these paintings since the revolution?" Pinky asked.

"Well, nobody's seen all of them," Da Silva said. "There was an exhibition in 2005 that lasted for fifty days. It was billed as 'highlights of the permanent collection,' so it didn't include everything."

"Did you see it?" I asked.

He shook his head. "Unfortunately, I was just a poor student in those days. I heard it was marvelous. There was the usual grumbling about what they chose to show and what they held back, but most enthusiasts were just glad to get a glimpse."

"But how could they do that?" Ada asked. "Did the government allow it?"

"Yes and no," Da Silva said. "The government was in transition. The exhibition opened under the presidency of Mohammad Khatami, who favored reform. But then he lost the election to the extremely conservative Mahmoud Ahmadinejad. The exhibition was in its final days when Ahmadinejad took office, so he didn't shut it down, but the museum director was forced into retirement afterward, and all of the paintings were moved back into storage. They haven't been seen since."

"Politics!" Pinky said in disgust.

"Wow!" Ada said. "It's kind of like a mystery, isn't it? How does anybody know they're still there? I mean, that Ahmadinejad could have sold them all on the black market, couldn't he?"

"Unlikely," Da Silva said. "If that many paintings had been sold, even illicitly, we would have heard something, and we haven't heard anything, not even a whisper." He raised his glass to her. "But I salute your imagination, Mrs. Baker. It would make a good mystery if the paintings all disappeared, wouldn't it?"

We all laughed, Sami Rouhani loudest of all.

"But getting back to my painting," I said to him when his laughter had simmered to a chuckle. "Why would you buy the painting from me if I don't have the right paperwork?" I asked. Rashidi set in front of me some kind of decadent concoction of chocolate and meringue sprinkled with cinnamon. Fortunately, I was a well-trained professional not easily sidetracked by decadence, but as soon as my eyes fell on it, I could feel my leg starting to swell.

"Well, you have some paperwork, from this appraiser, right?" he said.

I nodded.

"It's a start," he said. "You understand, I can't pay what you could get if you had the paperwork to establish provenance and sold the painting at auction. But without it—." He raised his hands expressively. "You can't expect anyone to pay top dollar for it. The auctioneers won't touch it." He turned to Da Silva. "Isn't that right, Olivier?"

"I'm afraid it's true," Da Silva admitted. "No legitimate dealer would handle the sale. You might find a less scrupulous one to auction the painting on the black market."

"But she wouldn't want to get mixed up in that," Sami said quickly. "She'd be running a risk, not just from the police but from the unsavory characters she'd have to deal with."

"No, no, probably not," Da Silva said. "You're right."

Sami turned to me. "If someone came to look at the painting and snatched it from you," he said, "what could you do? You have some proof that the painting belongs to you, of course, or rather that you had the painting in your possession, which isn't the same thing. But if the police asked what the guy was doing in your hotel room to begin with, what would you tell them? That you were arranging to sell something on the black market?"

Pinky asked, "But why would it be illegal to sell the painting on the black market? It's her painting. She could sell it on e-Bay if she wanted."

"Of course she could," Sami said. "And she should expect to sell for a fraction of its worth."

"At which point she might as well give the painting to a museum and take the tax write-off," Da Silva pointed out.

Sami frowned at him. Clearly, he was rethinking his strategy to introduce some expertise into the discussion. "Yes," he said, "though it wouldn't amount to much. But if the government finds out that you're selling a valuable painting, they'll expect their cut, which would be substantial. First, of course, they'll want sales tax. But they'll also expect you to report your income on the sale on your income tax form, so that they can tax that." He held up a palm. "I'm a law-abiding citizen, you understand, but don't get me started on taxes."

"Oh, I know!" Pinky said. "Darn those taxes!" And when he looked away she winked at me.

He pushed away from the table. "Let's relax in the living room and look at this painting of yours," he said. "There's no point in discussing anything further until we've seen it."

He exchanged a glance with Da Silva that acknowledged that he was prepared for anything, including a paint-by-numbers version of one of Chagall's most famous paintings. Theo slipped away and I was certain nobody would miss her for the next ten minutes. If she was lucky, Rashidi would be busy in the kitchen, but I doubted it. He didn't look the type to dry dishes.

I suppressed my smile as I unwrapped the painting and, with Theo's help, propped it awkwardly on the coffee table for them to see. Da Silva's mouth formed an involuntary O, while Sami's froze mid-sentence.

"Do I have it right side up?" I asked nervously.

"My god!" Sami said. "Look at that! Olivier, look at that!"

The evening sun coming through the windows was still bright, but after they sat and admired it for a few minutes, they had me lay it down on a large table to one side and turned on a lamp.

"What kind of bird is that?" Ada said, and I pinched her. "Oh! Is it a chicken?"

"It's not a rooster or a dove," Da Silva said. "Or a chicken, I think? A goldfinch?"

I was watching Sami, but he gave no visible reaction to the name, and I thought he might be tuned out. You could tell that he really loved the painting for its own sake, and not just because he might soon have the opportunity to impress a few intimate friends by showing his most recent acquisition. That was there, too, in his expression, but it didn't dominate.

Da Silva scowled at the window. "We need better light," he said.

"All right," Sami said, "let's take it to my office."

Better and better. As we headed down the hall, I said in a loud voice intended for Theo's ears, "Well, at least you didn't declare it a fake right away. Thank goodness for that! I would've felt so stupid!"

Sami cleared off a credenza next to his desk, laid the painting on top, and turned on an architect's lamp. When Theo slipped into the room, I was ready to make my own trip to the ladies' room, but knew that it wasn't a good time. When Sami brought out a magnifying glass, though, I said, "Is this going to take a while? Because if so—."

"Go on, Marge," Pinky took it upon herself to say. Theo's eyes followed me out.

In the hall, I could hear the faint sounds of music and a clatter of dishes coming from the kitchen. I hadn't noticed any security cameras, and I didn't see any in the hall. We had a floor plan of the house, a combination of its floor plan when it was last listed for sale and additions based on a cursory drone surveillance. I was most interested in the additions as likely places to stash a fortune in stolen paintings, and one addition in particular that stood out because it had no windows. I'd already spotted a guest bathroom off the entry hall, but I needed to see the rest of the house. I followed the hall in the opposite direction to a sharp left turn that followed the outline of the rectangular courtyard. Down the intersecting hallway I saw a light coming from a doorway that I knew from the floor plan belonged to another bathroom, but I turned right down a short hall that ended in a door—the door to the windowless room, a door that featured a keypad. The silver closet? A sanctuary for illegal Iranian immigrants? A strong room?

The sweep of my gaze took in a bullet camera above the door. I looked around in feigned confusion and tried the door. Locked. I rattled the handle in frustration and turned to look down the hall, allowing myself to discover the lit doorway and start toward it.

It was instinct that turned me toward the drawing on the wall; I wasn't aware that I'd heard any sound. But out of the corner of my eye I now saw the shadow of a man. I leaned forward on my cane and squinted at a seated nude woman suggested by fewer than twenty decisive lines. It was signed "H Matisse."

I allowed myself to become aware of the watcher. "Oh!" I said, "You startled me. He really *does* own a lot of art, doesn't he?"

"Yes," the man said. "If you will come this way, I'll show you the bathroom."

I followed, but I didn't let him hurry me. I stopped in front of a drawing of a woman with her chin in her hand. "This one isn't signed," I said. "Is it by the same artist as that one back there?" I asked.

"I don't know," he said, standing his ground in an effort to move me on.

I was going to say more, but then I reasoned that he might not take his boss's liberal attitude toward the nude female form, and decided against provoking him. I wanted him to see me as a nonentity, a minor inconvenience, not a threat.

I didn't see any cameras inside the bathroom, but there were more places to hide them, so without searching I couldn't be sure. I pictured Rashidi on guard duty on the other side of the door. But when I opened it a few minutes later, he was nowhere in sight. I turned first one way, then the other, an expression of uncertainty on my face, then headed in the wrong direction.

Since the whole house was laid out around the central courtyard, I figured that eventually I'd end up where I started. I studied the artwork on the walls, as if I were touring a gallery, but I was also looking for additional cameras and more sophisticated locks on doors, like the keypad down the hall.

I was gratified to see that the door to the master bedroom was open. It was off the hall that ran parallel to the hall I'd started out in, at right angles to the hall with the bathroom and two other doors that probably led to bedrooms. That made sense, because the windows faced west, not east, like half of the windows in the living room, so the occupants would not be awakened by morning light. It was a room kept tidy, but clearly occupied, with a pair of slippers sitting on the floor next to the bed and the faint scent of soap and aftershave wafting into the hallway. I kept going until I reached the living room, where Rashidi was setting out coffee.

"Oh!" I said. "I think I'm lost. Do I go that way?" I pointed.

Rashidi, expressionless, nodded and gestured in the same direction.

"Can I stop in the kitchen and compliment your wife on the meal? I asked.

"No English," he said.

"Oh, I bet I can make her understand," I said.

He shrugged, then returned his attention to his work. But I felt his glance like a dagger in the back as I left the room. I paused in the front hall, admired the painting there—a colorful Roualt landscape—and snapped some photos of the security panel and door lock with the camera disguised as a pendant that I wore around my neck.

I stopped in the kitchen, where an attractive middle-aged woman wearing a pantsuit and head scarf was loading the dishwasher.

"Mrs. Rashidi?" I said.

"Yes?" she said, looking up. "What want?"

"I just wanted to tell you how much I enjoyed the dinner," I said. "It was all delicious." I patted my stomach to give her a visual cue and smiled ruefully. "I know I ate too much."

But she understood that I was paying her a compliment. "Thank you," she said, smiling a little shyly. "I like cooking."

"Well, you're very good at it," I said. "I see you have a nice big kitchen to work in. That's nice."

Her eyes followed my gesture and she looked around the room, then back at me, eyebrows raised. "Sorry, I don't—."

I gestured again, and gave her a thumbs-up. "Your kitchen," I said. "Very nice!"

She smiled again. "Yes, very nice kitchen, very big. Sami is very nice boss." Her eyes went to my cane and she gestured toward it, brow creasing. "Hurt?"

I shook my head. "Not so much now, no. Before—." I waved over my shoulder and made an exaggerated grimace that made her smile before she covered the smile with her hand. "Now?" I again gave her a thumbs-up.

She repeated the gesture, and said, "Good."

"Well, I'll let you get back to work," I said, and waved at her as I turned, and found Rashidi blocking the doorway, his expression unreadable. But as I moved forward, smiling at him, he moved out of my way.

"Good news, Marge," Theo said when I appeared in the doorway. She was smiling and there was a glint in her eye. "Olivier thinks your painting is probably the real McCoy."

"Really?" I said. I clasped my hands to my bosom, my cane awkward in one fist. "How exciting!"

Truthfully, this news gave me pause. Was the damn thing real after all? My source for its inauthenticity was hardly reliable.

Da Silva made calming gestures, palms down. "Well, to be more precise, I said that I couldn't detect any signs that it was a forgery. The brushwork looks authentic, and so does the canvas. You would probably need to run several tests, such as a materials analysis, to be sure."

"Materials analysis?" I said. "You mean, they'd scrape off paint? Won't that damage the painting?"

"They can work with minute samples scraped from the part of the canvas that doesn't show," Da Silva said, adjusting his glasses and looking more professorial. "But the carbon-14 dating is only accurate to within about forty years, so it needs to be combined with other methods, such as Morellian analysis or multispectral camera analysis. The first of these has to do with matching the techniques of the painting under analysis to a formula derived from the artist's known technique, using characteristics like the length of brush strokes and so on. A multispectral camera analysis has been known to detect fingerprints, which can then be matched to the artist's."

This guy was a teacher, all right. You could tell he was hoping for more questions from the audience. But I just said, frowning, "Sounds expensive."

"Yes, it can be," Da Silva said. "But in any case, I wouldn't advise you to undertake the testing until you'd shown the painting to other experts. You need a Chagall expert, which I'm not, or ideally, several Chagall experts. If they agree that authentication is worth pursuing, then you should consider a more technologically sophisticated analysis."

Sami patted me on the arm. "Don't look so discouraged, Marge! We'll find another expert or two. But Olivier's opinion is very encouraging—the best we could hope for."

"The certificate looks genuine as well," Da Silva said.

"The name of your painting is 'La Petite Famille,'" Sami said. "The Little Family."

"Oh," I said. "Do you suppose the cow and the goldfinch are part of the family?"

We trooped back to the living room while I entertained myself with thoughts of Dottie's fingerprints on dozens of forgeries over the years, and on my Scottie dogs.

28

I managed to restrain Theo one more day until we had
confirmation from the surveillance team that Rouhani had left
town. On Thursday night, J.K. picked us up in a van with the name
of a heating and cooling company on the side and took us to our
base of operations. This time, there were piles of pillows in the
back to sit on and straps to hang on to.

"He'll be back on Sunday," J.K. told us.

That gave us three nights, counting tonight. Tonight was reconnaissance.

We knew that the Rashidis lived in a separate house behind the
main house. Without Sami around, we thought that they might
whoop it up in the big house, but no; they stayed in their house
until Rashidi left at nine, presumably on an inspection tour of the
main house and grounds. The other outbuildings, apart from the
garage, were a stable with a small corral and an equipment storage
shed. The tour took him about twenty minutes, and then he
returned to the small house. All the lights were out by eleven.
While we waited, Ada and Theo practiced with the night vision
binoculars.

"My night vision's always been good," Theo said, "so I've never used these."

At two, we blacked our faces, strapped on the binoculars, and went to the stables for horses, Sneezy bounding ahead. She loved the smell of camo paint; it told her that the game was afoot. Again, we were a larger group than I would have preferred—practically a Bedouin band riding across the plain. Theo and I were joined by Shorty, who knew the Rouhani dogs, and Ada, who would assess the electrical situation. I gave Theo and Ada mini-transmitters for their ears, and slipped my own in.

I hadn't ridden a horse since I'd broken my leg, but once I got my leg over, everything seemed to work properly, if a bit awkwardly. If my mare was dismayed by my klutziness, she was polite enough not to say so. Shorty stood in front of her and stroked her nose.

"I'm telling her that you're weak on that one side, and she'll have to do her best to figure out where you want to go," she said.

I turned to survey the hip and heart patients, Ada and Theo. I wasn't sure that this was a good idea for either of them. Ada gave me an unsteady smile and Theo raised her thumb.

"Don't worry," she said. "I'll look after Addy. I'll carry her back if I need to."

We walked the horses out the barn doors, waited for our eyes to adjust, and lowered the binoculars. Shorty went first, and we followed.

Shorty had told us to orient ourselves to the drilling rig, which provided us light to see by but also to be seen by and disrupted our vision through the binoculars, so we stayed well to one side of it. The rig was located between the two houses, about a quarter-mile from Rouhani's house on the other side of the barn, so by approaching from that direction we were hidden by the barn. The lowest floodlights were mostly blocked by the acoustic wall that surrounded it on three sides, but the tower of steel girders, which was taller than a ten-story building, was well lit—presumably, to

warn small aircraft. Inadvertently, I looked up at the sky overhead; if the stars were "big and bright," as the song said, you
couldn't tell it because they were washed out by the light from the
rig. And in spite of the acoustic wall, we could hear a low
mechanical roar that drowned out all the usual night noises—
crickets and night birds, the breeze in the mesquite trees, coyotes.
Maybe Rouhani had the house soundproofed. Or maybe he
turned the rig off when he was home—was that possible? I didn't
know. I hadn't been aware of the noise when we'd visited the
other night.

But between the rig and the barn, another shape loomed up in
the dark, and Shorty signaled us to dismount. This was an old well,
what Shorty called a "pumpjack," though Lafitte had entertained us
with an account of its many other names—nodding donkey,
donkey pumper, oil horse, rocking horse, grasshopper pump, and
my favorite, thirsty bird. It stood still and silent in the dark, a relic
of a past age. Since Sami's house was perhaps no more than twenty
or thirty years old, the original house on the property might have
been located elsewhere on the property, farther away from the old
pumper. We tied our horses to a railing and proceeded on foot.

As we approached, Shorty gave a low whistle and two dogs
came running, wagging their tales. The dogs were mutts, but probably shared some Labrador forebear. That was good; Labradors
were silent, hounds were noisy, present company excepted.
Wearing an oversized pair of lineman's gloves, she reached through
the fence to pet them. The dogs were apparently accustomed to this
routine because they came as close to the fence as they dared to
nose at her gloved hand. Sneezy sat on her haunches and watched.
Then Shorty withdrew her hand. Also wearing gloves, I reached
through the fence, patted the dogs, and then scattered peanut
butter treats for them. Then it was Ada's turn; she offered them
liver treats. Now we'd each established our unique bouquet—the
Shorty smell, which sometimes included raw meat; the M.J. smell,

which included peanut butter; and the Ada smell, which included liver.

Ada extracted a voltmeter from her pocket and took a reading. Then we backed off and began walking the perimeter, Ada's eyes following the wires. On the far end of the barn, we spotted a utility pole and mounted on it, a control box. While Ada studied the control box, Theo stood with her arms crossed and gazed off in the direction from which we'd come.

I continued around the perimeter, which meant stepping out from the shelter of the barn where I could be seen from the Rashidis' windows. I thought invisible thoughts and set my feet down carefully, more carefully because I'd left the cane in the hotel room. I'd memorized the floor plan of the main house, as well as Lafitte's map of the property based on aerial photographs, and now I was comparing it with what I was seeing. Like most ranch-style houses, this one wasn't very tall, and its roof, which didn't see much snow to contend with, featured a gentle slope rather than a steep pitch. On the other hand, the roof was adobe, which would register more noise if you walked on it than asphalt shingles or even slate—and more noise still if you limped on it, of course, or toppled over onto your kiester. I'd noticed during my tour of the inside that the central courtyard was outfitted with a retractable sunroof, which had been open at the time. The room I had come to think of as the strong room and the likeliest place to store several million dollars' worth of paintings, was now behind me, since the extension was between the house and the barn. But I saw no means of entry—no doors, no windows. That meant that either we cut our way in with a diamond-bladed saw that would make almost as much racket as a drilling rig or we had to get in through the house. The closest exterior door was adjacent to the strong room, at one end of a walkway that led to the Rashidis' house, and I photographed it, using a telephoto lens. There was another door, a side door, off the kitchen that looked more promising.

A light flashed on in one of the Rashidi windows and I flattened myself on the ground. A shadow showed against the light, but it was ill-defined, so probably some distance from the window. I waited a full ten minutes after the light went out before I stood up and moved on, leading a silent parade of prowlers.

I noted with disapproval that the only exterior camera was mounted above the front door, where it was accessible to any burglar who wanted to disable it. In combination with the camera at the gate, it seemed to suggest that any intruders would announce themselves at the gate, drive their van up the driveway and go in through the front door. Theo caught me looking at the camera and shaking my head and gave me an okay sign with her thumb and forefinger.

I used the telephoto lens to photograph the side door to the kitchen. I couldn't tell whether it was wired into the security system, but it should have been. We completed the circuit and returned to the horses. Theo gave Ada a boost, and we were off. We hadn't spoken a word.

29

"The problem," I said, when we had all squeezed into the command center, "is not getting ourselves in, it's getting the paintings out. If we deactivate the fence, we can hand them to someone on the other side, but parking a truck that close to the house is too risky. It might be heard. Even a tank truck might be noticeable in the middle of the night."

"At least the drilling rig provides enough noise coming from that direction to disguise any other noise," Shorty pointed out.

Theo was leaning, arms crossed, against a file cabinet, which was supposed to be where all of the transcripts, photographs, and sound recordings were stored, neatly labeled. But these days, there wasn't much need for hard copies of anything, which was just as well, since none of the Quixote agents had been hired for their filing skills. If I had to guess, I'd guess that the cabinet contained a pair of Lafitte's sneakers and J.K.'s bocce ball, and not much else.

"I've got a better idea," Theo said. "We run a zip line from the pumpjack to the barn."

"To get over the fence?" Ada said, looking concerned.

But I was smiling. "Not to get us in," I said, admiringly, "but to get the paintings out. I like it."

"We go in, attach a cable and pulley to the barn wall, near the loft doors on the side facing away from the two houses, shoot the other end in the direction of the pump," she said.

"One of us picks it up and attaches the other end to a support post, then pulls the paintings off as they come," Lafitte said, grinning. "I like it, too."

"We have the measurements of the paintings," Theo said. "Addy, your job will be to run up fifteen slings for the paintings, preferably by tomorrow night. Can you do it?"

"If I have help, I can," Ada said. "I'd just be making pockets, and they wouldn't be haute couture."

"What kind of help?" J.K. said. "I'm not much good with a needle and thread."

"Measuring and cutting," Ada said. "You can do that, can't you?"

"How do we disable the fence, Ada?" I asked. "Do we go to the box?"

She shook her head. "Faster and easier to short it out. I'll show you how. But some of the wiring for the floodlights might go to the box."

Because we hadn't approached close enough, we hadn't triggered the motion detectors for the floodlights.

"There aren't any motion detectors in front of the barn, where the dogs hang out," I said. "If there were, they'd be blinking on and off like a strobe light all night long. There's a gate to keep the dogs in the back. Unfortunately, both the side door to the kitchen and the front door are on the other side of the gate, which means within range of the motion sensors."

"So we'll have to shoot them out," Theo said. "Agreed?"

I nodded. I was beginning to appreciate Theo's insistence on a trip to the gun range.

"I photographed the exterior locks and the security system," I said, "but on second thought, I don't know why we'd bother. We can probably climb the ornamental porch columns to the roof and go in through the courtyard. Agreed?"

"Well, I can," Theo said, looking down at my cast. "Can you?"

"You bet," I said, and hoped I meant it.

"The sliding glass doors weren't wired into the security system —I checked on Wednesday night," Theo said.

"Well, all I can say is—." Pilar began.

The four agents in the room chimed in. "— Better them than us," we said. This was another Levesque-Quixote mantra, an acknowledgment that our lives were made considerably easier by less competent security companies, not to mention cheapskate customers who cut crucial corners to save money. The truth was, Sami's security might have been perfectly adequate until he moved one of the world's greatest art collections onto his property, then compounded his vulnerability by a failure of imagination: he just didn't imagine that anyone would come after it. Not really.

On Friday night, Theo and I returned to the ranch house with backpacks full of gear. We'd insisted that Ada remain with Pilar and J.K. next door in the command center, and I think she was relieved. Her horseback ride the night before had taken its toll. If Theo's hip had been daunted by last night's excursion, I couldn't tell. My leg had been grumbling all day but now that the adrenaline had kicked in, I was anaesthetized. We'd left Lafitte and Shorty at the drilling rig, where they'd retrieve the paintings and load them into a panel truck disguised as a tanker. Theo carried a long metal stake and an air gun and I carried a mallet and an ultralightweight folding ladder to use if we needed it. We each carried coils of cable over one shoulder. Neither of us carried canes. The two dogs came running and watched us with interest, but we put our fingers to our lips, the way Shorty had showed us, and they didn't make a sound. I extended a gloved hand through the fence so they could sniff me, patted them, and fed them peanut butter treats.

I waited behind the barn while Theo walked past it to the opening between the barn and garage, shouldered the air gun, took aim through the night scope, and shot out two floodlights with soft pops. She continued to the front of the house and I heard two more pops. Then she returned.

The barn blocked us from view of the Rashidi house as Theo positioned the stake and I tapped it with the mallet. The dogs sat on the other side of the fence, furrowed their brows, tilted their heads, and watched. One gave a very soft whimper that seemed to say, "Are you sure you know what you're doing?" Since the answer to that was no, I made no comment. The mallet was also metal, and we worried about the noise, even with a towel draped over the stake to deaden the sound, but Theo restrained me after two taps, held up five fingers, and we waited and listened for five minutes. The dogs rotated their ears, stared off into space, and appeared to be listening as well. When nothing happened, Theo tested the stake and gave me the okay sign. She retrieved a bottle of water from an outside pocket of her pack and poured it on the ground around the stake. The next part was tricky because we didn't know how the dogs would react. We would be testing Shorty's training. I raised my palms and pushed them forward. The dogs backed up. I changed directions and lowered my palms to the ground. The dogs sat. I put my finger to my lips. The dogs watched intently.

Theo pulled on her lineman's gloves and clipped a copper wire connected to the stake to the fence. Her movements were assured, without hesitation.

I exhaled as a firestorm of sparks erupted from the clip, sizzling in the hot, humid air. One dog retreated, one dog sat up. But they didn't make a sound, and their eyes shone in the light from the sparks. After the initial surprise, they wagged their tales—this was fun! When the sparks died down, Theo extracted a voltmeter from her pocket and tested the fence wires, one by one, before giving me the thumbs-up. I left the ladder where it was and went to work with wire cutters until I'd created an opening that we could walk through, and later run through, if we had to. I worried a little about the dogs, but figured they could hold their own against coyotes if they left the yard and went for a stroll. For now, they seemed too interested in what we were up to. I gave them more treats before we scaled the gate to the front yard, so they were too preoccupied to be disappointed.

Climbing the ornamental columns to the porch roof proved challenging, the challenge having to do with one leg that didn't function the same way it had the last time I'd scaled a building. It was stiff and clumsy, and one of the Velcro straps caught in the lattice work. Once up, I lay down on the roof, hung over the side, and fastened one end of my rope to the column. I felt a pair of strong hands gripping my good ankle. I rose to a crouch and played the rope out as I walked to the edge of the courtyard opening and threw the rope over the edge, taking care to avoid the bougainvillea. No call to make a mess.

Theo went down first and I followed. Theo cut a neat circle in the glass door, attached a handle, and pulled out the glass disk, then reached through to unlock the door, and we were in. In front of the strong room door, we looked at each other. I removed from my pack a small container of phosphorescent dust, and used a brush to dust the keypad. Theo shone the small blacklight on the result. Four numbers lit up—the ones most often pressed by oily human fingertips. Sometimes the old ways are the best. Theo hit the right order on her second try, but I could tell she was disappointed that she hadn't got it on the first, and I patted her on the shoulder.

Inside the room, our roaming flashlights revealed that Sami had indeed uncrated and hung all of the paintings. I allowed myself a small sigh, but at least he'd left us the crates, stacked neatly in a corner. Since Ada's pouches were made to accommodate crates if we had them, we saw no reason not to use them. We each took a crate and began comparing them with paintings for size. When we found a match, we crated the painting, labeled the outside with the artist's name, and left it leaning against the wall. When we'd crated all eleven of them, I went to the kitchen, unbolted the side door, and opened it, knowing that no alarm would be triggered if the door was opened from inside the house. Theo joined me and we walked to the barn, accompanied by the dogs, who had concluded that we were more interesting than anything they would find outside the fence. Thankfully, we didn't have barn horses to contend with; our surveillance team hadn't seen any sign of them. We'd seen enough of the barn from outside to suspect that it might have a hayloft, or the remains of a hayloft, and we weren't disappointed. We climbed a ladder to a bare wooden platform and crossed to a window, through which the drilling rig lit up the night sky and the dark outline of the pumpjack.

Theo set down her backpack and withdrew from it a crossbow with a collapsible stock. In the light of the kitchen earlier, I'd noticed how familiarly she'd handled it, like an old friend—more comfortably even than she'd handled any of the weapons she'd fired at the range. I sprayed hinges with lubricant and opened the loft doors slowly, to minimize the creak of wood on wood. Then I helped Theo unwind and lay out the doubled cable on the floor. She fastened one end to the arrow with a clamp and tightened everything down, the sinews of her hands bulging. This was the part I had been most skeptical about. The arrow would carry not just a single cable but a double, so that the loop would be closed on both ends. What we had to work with had been sent by Didi, a coated line developed by NASA to be lightweight, thin, and strong. When we had practiced with it that afternoon, it had performed admirably.

"That you, M.J.?" Lafitte said into the tiny receiver in my ear. It had the effect of a thought spoken out loud, a voice from inside your head.

"Comin' at ya, Lafitte," I said, as Theo took aim.

Theo let fly, the arrow weighed down by the line attached to it. The motion caused it to light up like a kid's sneaker and we watched it arc over the fence and into the bright light of the tower. While we waited to hear Lafitte's confirmation, I set up our end of the pulley with an eye hook fixed to the wood above the window.

"Got it," he said in my ear, and I felt the line slacken.

Lafitte had performed the calculations, and I knew from experience to trust them. Over the next several minutes I watched the line tense and release. I heard him call Shorty.

"Ready," she said. She would stand below the line with a pole in case any of our packages got stuck.

Meanwhile, Theo was lubricating the pulley one final time.

"Okay, M.J.," Lafitte said. "I'm sending your first hook."

I was hazy on the physics, but Lafitte was an avid skier, so I presumed he'd had plenty of time to study ski lifts to see how they got those T-bars up the side of the mountain without piling them all up at the first support post. The line began to move, whisper-quiet, and within five minutes, the first hook arrived. I retrieved the pouches from my backpack—these also made of some kind of incredibly strong but lightweight fabric developed by NASA—and threw them down to the barn floor. By that time, Theo had carried out two crates and rigged up another rope to haul them up from the barn floor. She was matching each painting to a pouch, fitting them into the pouches, and hauling the pouches up to the hayloft. I clipped the first one to the first hook, and away it sailed. After the first two, we paused while I helped Theo get the rest of the paintings into the hayloft, thinking to myself that I should have spent more time on upper body strength after the cast came off. Some of these paintings were quite large.

It made me smile to watch them, this parade of modern art,

suspended over the Texas brush and backlit by the light from the drilling rig, swinging silently along. Shorty stood halfway with her pole; by now she would have retrieved the ladder from where we'd left it outside the fence. On his end, Lafitte had a pulley with a crank attached. We worked in tandem, he and I, connected by the length of cable and by his voice in my ear, though he rarely spoke.

We had two small pouches to go when J.K.'s voice broke in. "Car coming, M.J. Loud and fast. Maybe it'll pass by."

"Cruiser?" I asked.

"No, shit, it's slowing down," he said. "Not a cruiser unless Texas cops play loud rap. Probably the Rashidis' son, the college student."

The line stopped moving.

I put down the painting I was holding and looked at Theo. I mimed pulling on a rope. She rolled her eyes at me—a reaction I deserved. She'd been the last one up from the barn floor, and like any trained professional, she had pulled the rope up after her. It's a fundamental principle of breaking and entering: when you're finished with a tool, put it away; don't leave it out where it can call attention to itself. The movie burglars who leave drills hanging from doors wouldn't last long in the real world.

We had left the barn door the way we found it, slightly ajar. Passing through with the paintings had been awkward, but we hadn't wanted to risk the noise of opening it farther.

The car screeched to a halt in the driveway outside the barn in a cacophony of rap, barking, and pebbles that crackled like pistol shots and, I hoped, covered any noise from the moving cable as Lafitte retrieved the last of the paintings in transit. I felt the percussion through the soles of my sneakers. Then the rap was cut off, and we heard that voice humans reserve for dogs, fond and happy. I pictured the dogs giving him dog kisses and worried that he'd mention the peanut butter on their breaths to his parents. The next moment, he said, in English, "What have y'all been eating?" I

269

pictured him grasping their muzzles playfully or chucking them under their chins.

A new light shone through the gap in the barn door, and a voice spoke Farsi. This one was easy to translate, even if you didn't know the language. It was raised in anger, and it began with, "Do you have any idea what time it is?" The tirade continued, with a counterpoint of unruffled self-justification, and then a third voice, female, alternating between loving exclamations of delight and soothing demurral aimed, presumably, at son and husband, respectively. Eventually, the furor abated, and I heard the son say that he would put his car away, so I tugged on Theo's arm to pull her back from the edge of the loft where we'd been crouched, listening. Into my microphone, I whispered, "I'm cutting the line, Lafitte. We'll carry the rest. Time to go, everybody."

The barn door groaned as it was opened wider. Then as the engine roared to life and the music blared, I cut the line with bolt cutters and Theo unscrewed the eye bolt. Lafitte would retract the line when I gave him the word. The empty hooks left on the line might make some noise, but it couldn't be helped. If the son took the dogs into the house with him and the Rashidis got a whiff of them, we could be in serious trouble.

We waited until we heard the fading voice cut off by the closed door of the house, wedged the paintings under our arms, clambered down the ladder, made our way to the fence with minimal noise, slipped through the gap, and ran—or rather, given the bulk of our burdens and our general gimpiness, loped. The dogs were nowhere in sight. I would have preferred the leisure to jerry rig a fence repair to keep the dogs in the yard, but there was no time. For that matter, I would have preferred the leisure to cover our footprints, but no dice. It was awkward going, since Theo was again shouldering a coil of rope and carrying the metal stake and air gun, in addition to her pack. I didn't have the ladder this time, but I did have the larger of the two paintings and the mallet, along with my pack. At one point, Theo faltered, but she recovered and stumbled on.

We'd left our horses near the pumpjack, but Pilar had already taken them back to the surveillance site, loaded them onto a horse trailer, and seen them off. Pilar and J.K. would be breaking down the remainder of the equipment and loading it inside a panel truck. This could be accomplished in under fifteen minutes. Everything else, from trash to the Yamaha, had already been loaded, and by the time we reached the pump, Pilar and J.K. should be making a final inspection of the house to make sure they hadn't missed anything. Ada would go with them. Our own retreating footprints would lead to the pumpjack, but not beyond.

As we neared the pump, Shorty, Sneezy, and Lafitte came running toward us. I felt Lafitte's assessing eyes on us and he passed me by. Shorty took the paintings from me, and I began to follow her toward the truck, but Lafitte called me back.

He slipped the rope coil over my arm and handed me the air gun and stake. "Take her stuff," he said.

That was when I noticed what I should have noticed before— that Theo's face was drained of all color, unnaturally bleached in the lights from the rig. He wedged her crate under his arm and turned his back to Theo. "Hop on," he said.

She grimaced, more from embarrassment than pain, but she didn't protest. She wrapped her arms around his neck, and he carried her the rest of the way to the truck.

The truck was disguised as a tanker, with a lightweight metal shell that said "Nortex Oil" and showed a drilling rig silhouetted against a lone star. Shorty had opened the back so that we could climb in with the paintings. Someone—probably Pilar—had thoughtfully provided two cushioned folding loungers, which had been secured to the wall with straps. Shorty helped Theo get situated, and Lafitte handed her some pills along with the bottle of water from her pack. From an ice chest he extracted a fistful of ice, which he dumped in a plastic bag and handed to her. She bent her left leg at the knee and applied the ice pack to her ankle.

"Okay for now?" he asked.

Theo gave him a thumbs-up.

Then we were gone.

30

D idi raised his glass to us. "Well done!" he said.

Normally, I enjoyed these little rituals of congratulation in Didi's office. I didn't even mind the champagne. And I was gratified by the pleasure on Ada's and Theo's faces. But I looked around the room at the other agents. As was customary, everyone who'd had direct involvement with the case was present, including Jerome Childers and Jasmine Zidane. Rafael Sanchez was out of town on assignment. Sneezy was working on a new rawhide chew while Emile fed Doc biscuits dipped in milk to soften them for his few remaining teeth.

We'd been back for a week. Didi had been called out of town for a few days, and Theo had been told to stay off her ankle, so our celebration had been delayed. A week was plenty of time.

My eyes met Lafitte's over the rim of his glass and he raised his eyebrows. So he'd heard it, too. Something was wrong. It had to be the paintings.

"But they're not real, are they?" I said. "The paintings—they're not real."

Didi set down his glass, but I could tell by Bernie's expression what he was going to say.

"No," he said. "I'm sorry, M.J., but they're not real. They're forgeries."

"All of them?" Theo asked.

"We think so, yes," he said. "I'm sorry."

"You mean," Ada said, leaning forward, "we went to all that trouble to steal Dottie's forgeries?"

I thought she'd be disappointed, demoralized, sad. Instead, she raised her eyes and said, "Well, wherever she is, I hope she's enjoying the show."

Emile raised his glass. "To Mrs. Rivers," he said.

There was a chorus of "here, here," and Theo clinked her glass against Ada's.

"Let's hear it," I said when the noise had died down.

"None of them was painted before the mid-50s," Didi said.

"Carbon-14 dating," I said.

"But why the mid-50s?" Ada asked.

"It's when the above-ground nuclear tests began," Didi explained. "The amount of radioactive carbon in the atmosphere doubled between 1955 and 1965. That increased the concentration of Carbon-14 atoms in all Earthly materials." To me, he said, "We didn't have to go as far as the Morellian analysis on most of them. If the forgeries had dated to the 40s or earlier, we would have, but as it is—." He shrugged.

"Some of the materials were older," Emile said. "Mrs. Rivers obviously bought up older canvases and even oil paints when she could, and sometimes painted over the canvases. In two or three cases, where we can't detect an underpainting on these older materials, a Morellian analysis is in order, but we're not optimistic."

"So they weren't easy to detect, the forgeries?" Ada asked.

"Certainly not," Didi said. "You saw for yourselves that Rouhani's art historian friend couldn't detect the forgery. Our experts say that Mrs. Rivers was one of the best they've seen. Two of them believe that they've encountered her work before, although of course, there is no way to know about that, unless you find records somewhere in the house."

"So Dottie not only painted the original forgeries, she painted a second set," I said. "But why? If she had the paintings and kept them in the house, and if she painted the second set as a blind in case thieves came looking for them, she was thorough and much more security-conscious than we gave her credit for. But that's a lot of ifs."

Theo sighed. "She stopped, you know," she said. "She still painted, but she stopped painting the forgeries. She said that her eyesight wasn't good enough. I'm sure it was good enough to fool most viewers, but her standards were high. It's not as if the moderns were known for their fine lines and delicacy, but—." She shrugged. "She said it was the signatures. She couldn't see well enough to do the signatures anymore."

"So where does that leave us?" I said, shifting uncomfortably in my chair. "Are we assuming that Dottie had the paintings stored in the house? Or that she had them long enough to copy, and then sold them, and left the forgeries to the Iranians as some kind of message of—what? Defiance? Warning? Anger? I refuse to believe at this point that she wasn't involved in the Tehran business because all of the forgeries we found, all the ones Rouhani stole, were from that collection."

"Perhaps George Finch has them," Emile said.

"If so, we might never see them again," I said. "He probably doesn't remember he has them, much less what he did with them. They could be in his storeroom. But if not? We'll never find them."

"They could be locked away in a Swiss bank vault," Bernie said.

"I wonder who his heirs will be," Lafitte said.

"Ah, well," Didi said, "maybe Ms. Underwood and Mrs. Baker will find the originals hidden inside the house. In the meantime, there's no reason to cast a pall over this celebration. We located the thief and recovered the paintings. Everyone deserves to be congratulated."

He raised his glass again, and we all drank, but without enthusiasm.

I stayed behind when everybody else cleared out. "What about Dottie's murder?" I asked Didi. "Has anybody talked to Medlock, the detective in charge?"

"I haven't, no," Didi said.

"I have," Theo said from the doorway. She was leaning on her crutch. She stepped inside and pulled the door shut behind her. "He hasn't made much progress," she said. "But he does know that the cause of death was atropine poisoning administered in her cold capsules. Whoever it was used roots and leaves from a plant—."

"Deadly nightshade," I said. "*Atropa belladonna.*"

"That's the one. He thinks Steve or Monica did it, or they did it together, or Calloway / Callahan did it, on his own or with Monica. But he can't tie any of them to the atropine that killed her." She looked from me to Didi. "Can't we do anything about that?"

"What do we know about atropine?" I asked, turning to Didi. "It's derived from belladonna, I know that, and it's used in cold medicines. But I'm sure it accounts for a minute portion of those tiny time pills inside a cold capsule, so she surely didn't overdose on those."

Didi went to his computer, leaned over, and began typing. "Let's see." His eyes moved over the screen. "Used to dilate pupils and treat bradycardia, counteract some poisons, decrease salivation during surgery, and treat intestinal ulcers, irritable bowel, diarrhea, Parkinson's, and joint and nerve pain, among other things. Hmm— hemorrhoid suppositories. Seems to be rather an all-purpose drug."

"Steve has irritable bowel," Theo said. "That's supposedly why he didn't eat lunch with us that day."

Didi wagged his head. "Yes, but—. Any medication would contain a minute amount of the stuff. Unless you were a chemist, I don't see how you could formulate a capsule to contain mostly atropine."

"So we're back to the plant," I said. "Where does it grow?"

Didi typed again, read the screen. "Native to the Mediterranean and North Africa, naturalized in parts of the U.S.—doesn't say which parts. Hang on, here we are: hardy in zones 5 through 9, moist woodlands, mostly in the Northeast and Pacific Northwest."

"Right climate zone, wrong location," Theo said.

"That could work to our advantage if someone went out of their way to acquire a specimen," I said.

"How would we find that out?" Theo said.

I was looking at Didi. He saw me looking at him, and said, "It's a total shot in the dark, M.J. You know that."

I crossed my arms. "I know it."

"It's a one-in-a-million chance we'd find anything," he said.

"I know it."

"Hell," Theo said, "if you want me to hire you to do it, I will."

"Not the point," he said.

"Okay," I said. "How about this? Theo and I will pay a visit to our two principal suspects. And we'll take Bashful." Bashful was our best sniffer dog—a bloodhound mix.

Didi nodded. "Okay," he said. "You find anything, we'll pursue it."

"Deal," I said.

"But remember, M.J.," he said. "This could have nothing to do with the family. Mrs. Rivers was a forger. That means she was involved in some high-level swindling. She had enemies."

"I'll bear it in mind," I said. "But unless someone paid off Macbeth to switch her eye of newt for belladonna berries, I don't see how it could have been done by an outsider."

The next evening I picked up Bashful at the office and then Theo at a townhouse in Georgetown.

"He's adorable," she said, caressing the creases in his face that gave him a look of perpetual worry. "Did you find a sample of belladonna?"

"In the Bishop's Garden at the National Cathedral, if you can believe it," I said. "And get this—the gardens are maintained by the All Hallows Guild."

"That's bad for us, isn't it?" Theo said. "Anybody could help themselves."

"How many people do you know who have toured the Bishop's Garden in the past two months?" I said. "If you were bent on killing somebody, you'd have to know it was there. Unless, of course, you were inspired to kill somebody when you found it there on a tour."

Steve Jeffries lived in a contemporary white brick apartment building in Rockville, where, according to our file on him, he worked for the Montgomery County transportation department. A tired-looking woman with frizzy blond hair opened the door to us, balancing a baby on her hip. The baby had slightly crossed bright blue eyes and a cherry ring like the mark of a medieval plague around her mouth, and she was chewing on a board book. I was about to concede her cuteness when she flung the book at me, scored a direct hit on my good knee, and giggled. Two children—a boy of around eight or nine and a girl who looked slightly younger—were parked in front of the television on a well-worn couch, their eyes on hand-held devices instead of the car chase on the television screen. The kids looked like younger versions of their parents. The woman, whom Theo introduced as Debby, retreated a few steps into the room and called her husband. The apartment smelled like dinner—that familiar scent of fried meat and something slightly sour that might have been cabbage or broccoli, with undercurrents of stale coffee.

The baby, now hanging from her mother's hip, was reaching for

Bashful when the other kids noticed the dog and abandoned their video games. I let go of his leash, and he began his perambulations, his new fan club trailing him around the room.

"What kind is he?" the boy asked, patting him gently on the top of the head.

"Some kind of hound mix," I said. "We don't really know." It was true that we didn't know what breeds were in his family tree besides bloodhound.

"Why does he look so sad?" the girl said, cupping his chin in both her hands. Annoying as this must have been for a dog on a mission, Bashful was a professional and bore the interruption with grace. Then he faked a sneeze—one of his best tricks—and when she backed off, he headed for the kitchen.

I shrugged. "It's just the way they look," I said. "They don't think they look sad."

Steve appeared in the doorway in socks, tee shirt, and jeans. "Oh, hey, Theo," he said casually, as if he were too bored or preoccupied to concentrate on the money he was about to inherit. He sat down with Theo at the dining table and I joined the parade led by Bashful, now limping slightly on my good leg.

"How old is he?" the boy asked.

"Eight," I said.

"Hey! Same as me!" the boy said. "What's his name?"

"Bashful," I said. "Like the dwarf."

"What's he *doing*?" the girl asked, as Bashful swept the lower cabinets with his nose.

"He's sniffing," I said. "Hounds do that. They get most of their information through their noses. He's just curious."

The girl tried sniffing where Bashful had just sniffed.

"I don't smell anything," she said.

"You're not a hound," I pointed out. "Humans don't have a very good sense of smell."

"Or hearing, either, right?" the boy said. "I think I hear real good, but dogs hear a lot more."

"That's right," I said. M. J. Smith, didact for America's youth.

"What does he like to sniff?" the girl asked, as Bashful toured the laundry room off the kitchen.

Right now, I thought, he'd be thrilled to catch a whiff of *atropa belladonna*, but I was rather touched by this question, which seemed to exceed mere politeness in its consideration for Bashful's tastes, as if whatever it was he most enjoyed smelling she would do her best to provide. I was quite warming to these kids, and hoped that their father didn't turn out to be a cold-blooded killer. But if he did, I reasoned, they'd be better off without him.

"Dogs like to sniff poop and dead things and anything that's gross," the boy said to his sister, before looking to me for confirmation. "Isn't that right? My friend Avi has a golden retriever that likes to roll around in dead things and get the smell all over him till he stinks!"

Having cleared the laundry room and kitchen, Bashful was heading purposefully for the hallway to the bedrooms. I heard Theo's voice in an explanatory tone but I didn't pay attention to what they were saying.

"I don't know if hounds are the same way," I admitted. "I think maybe they just like to smell a variety of things. It's like the scents they smell add up to a story, so the more they smell, the more interesting the story."

"Why are you limping?" the girl said.

"Which leg?" I wanted to say. I hadn't brought my cane because I thought it would impede my work with Bashful, but now I missed the support. "I hurt my knee," I said, but her attention had already returned to Bashful.

"He's going in my room," the girl said happily. She followed and threw herself on the bed. She picked up a teddy bear half her size, and held him up for me to admire. "Look!" she said.

"What's his name?" I said.

"Bear," she said.

M. J. Smith, straight man to the stars.

She planted the bear in Bashful's path, and Bashful obligingly sniffed at it.

"He *likes* him!" she squealed. "They like each other."

I heard a snort of disgust from the doorway, where the boy stood, hands on hips and a good imitation of his father's sour look on his puss. Bashful's head disappeared under the bed.

"What's your name?" the girl asked.

"Marge," I said.

"I'm Felicia and that's Tommy," she said. Not relying on my powers of deduction, she added, "He's my brother. I have a Barbie Saddle 'n Ride. Want to see?"

Tommy now stepped out of Bashful's way as he headed for the next room.

"Maybe later," I told Felicia.

This room was clearly Tommy's—more blue than pink. There were two *Star Wars* posters on the wall and on a low shelf a couple of objects that were clearly some kind of flying fighters surrounded by action figures in orange fatigues. Tommy crawled onto his bed and picked up a blue-and-white plastic controller. Bashful and I both jumped when a blue-and-white robot as tall as Bashful surged out of a corner, beeping and whirring and flashing blue and red lights, and crashed into my bad knee. It spun its top and whistled at me. Unsophisticated humor appeared to be the comic specialty of the house.

Tommy giggled but Bashful showed his loyalty by growling at it.

I wish I could say that we got our revenge when Bashful located a stash of belladonna leaves hidden inside the droid, but after a brief sniff, he lost interest.

"You're supposed to be careful and not hurt anybody," Tommy's sister scolded him.

"I didn't hurt anybody," Tommy objected.

I limped down the hall in Bashful's wake. I had high hopes for the master bedroom, but Bashful didn't find anything there, either, while Felicia regaled me with random facts about her life that did not include a murder plot against her great aunt. He also cleared both bathrooms—the one in the master bedroom and the one off the hall. I found a small plastic container of cold capsules that were the same brand as the ones Dottie had been taking. I mentally filed the information, but it was a pretty common brand, probably stocked in half the medicine cabinets in the D.C. metropolitan area. So that was that.

"Why are you looking in the medicine cabinet?" Felicia asked.

"My knee hurts," which was true enough. "I was looking for aspirin."

"We have Tylenol," Tommy said helpfully.

"I'll get some aspirin later," I said.

Theo looked up and smiled at me as we re-entered the living room but I gave her a slight shake of the head.

"Shoot!" she said when we left the building. "I wanted it to be him."

Monica lived in a house that probably passed for "colonial revival" in Leesburg—a one-story brick ranch house to which the builders had added an incongruous portico and a bay window that overlooked the narrow concrete slab of the porch. On the other hand, the front flowerbed and the beds that flanked the driveway in front of the attached garage were a riot of color. I'm not a gardener, but there seemed to be a heavy concentration of flowers even I could identify—zinnias, marigolds, petunias, and geraniums. We parked on the street, and it took us ten minutes to walk Bashful to the front door, he had so much to sniff.

We rang the bell, but Monica appeared around the side of the house. She wore bright green gardening gloves and gardening clogs and carried a pair of clippers. In spite of her sleeveless tee shirt and shorts, she looked hot, and her lank dark blond hair was plastered to her face and neck. We expressed our condolences.

Her lower lip quivered and her eyes went wet, but she just nodded. I couldn't see whether she was still wearing her engagement ring under her gardening gloves.

"I'm out back, gardening," she said. "You'll have to come around back."

Theo lifted an eyebrow at me and I knew what she was thinking. If we didn't get invited in, we'd have to make an excuse. Luckily, at our age, a request to use the bathroom was perfectly plausible.

Monica gave Bashful the fish eye. "I hope he's not a digger," she said.

"Not usually," I said. Only when his target has been buried, I thought.

The backyard was a larger version of the front yard, kaleidoscopic in its profusion of color. I dropped the leash and Bashful trotted off. Monica picked up a hose and continued watering a flowerbed while Theo extracted some papers from a leather portfolio she was carrying and began explaining them to Monica. I watched Bashful from a distance, not wanting to call attention to what he was doing. At Steve's, he could not have escaped his audience, but Monica took no interest in him, and that was fine with me. I was distracted by Monica's questions about when she would receive her first check from the estate, and when I turned back saw that Bashful was indeed digging. In one corner of the yard there was a circular chicken wire enclosure, open on one side, surrounding a compost pile. Bashful was digging in the compost. I snapped my fingers, and he trotted back to me. He sat at my feet and lifted a paw to pat me on the knee.

"Good dog," I said, to let him know I understood.

I interrupted the conversation to ask if I could use the bathroom, and was waved in the direction of the patio doors. I made sure that Monica's back was turned when I slid open the doors and let Bashful pass through in front of me. I found a bathroom off the main hall and checked the medicine cabinet. Then I checked the bathroom in Monica's bedroom, where I found a container of cold capsules, a popular brand. I wondered whether a forensics lab could make anything of them. Whoever had doctored Dottie's capsules had worn gloves, but it seemed to me just possible that someone handling belladonna and removing capsules from this container could have transferred trace amounts of the herb onto the remaining capsules.

Bashful appeared, sat at my feet, and patted my knee. "Show me," I said softly.

As we approached the kitchen, I could see Theo and Monica through the patio door, not four yards away. Theo was talking, leaning on her crutch, and as I caught her eye, I made a circular motion with my index finger. Without pausing for breath, Theo shook her head, gestured at her crutch, and began moving toward a picnic table, signaling for Monica to follow. Bashful stood patiently by a small glass-shelved étagère by the window, where several potted plants were on display. On the bottom shelf were a bag of potting soil, a trowel, and a stack of empty pots. Bashful laid a paw gently on the stack of pots.

I glanced back at Monica and Theo. Monica was bent over a paper Theo was showing her. I bent and extracted the top pot from the pile, a small round black plastic pot with a label from an herb store in Bethesda. Bashful gave it the paw.

I straightened—awkwardly, given my newly dented kneecap— but Bashful wasn't finished. He sniffed around the base of the kitchen counter adjacent to the étagère and then gave it the paw.

"Good boy," I whispered, and we rejoined the others.

As we were leaving, Monica frowned at Bashful. "What kind of dog is that, anyway?" she said, disapproval in her voice.

I turned to regard Bashful. "We're not sure," I said. "We think he has some Basset in him."

31

I called Didi the next day and gave him a report, along with the name of the herb shop.

"Okay, M. J.," he said. "If it checks out, we can give it to Medlock. It ought to be enough for a search warrant, at least."

"You might mention the cold capsules in the master bath," I said.

"M.J., please," he said. "I'm not going to tell the man his job."

"Okay," I said. "You might give Bashful an extra special treat today for performing so well."

He laughed. "Now you're telling me my job," he said. "I think he already got a new chew toy from Bernie."

All morning I was restless. At noon I was meeting Theo and Ada at Dottie's to go over the house. I wasn't willing to give up on the idea that somewhere in it Dottie had stashed eleven of the world's modern masterpieces. Or fifteen, if we counted all the titles on Dottie's inventory rather than the blank spaces on the wall. Of course, they could be inside a Swiss bank vault, as Didi had speculated. But then why would Dottie try to hire Levesque Security before she died? To safeguard eleven forgeries? That didn't make sense.

When I arrived at Dottie's, Jerome Childers was out on the front lawn, showing off his prized possession to Theo and Ada: a drone equipped with a camera.

"Is it armed?" Ada asked.

"Only with a camera," he replied with a smile.

"Isn't it dangerous anyway?" she said. "Can't you get it tangled in a low-flying plane or helicopter and cause a crash?"

"Could," he admitted, "but won't. I'm careful."

He set up his laptop on the hood of Theo's car. "Come over here and watch, M.J., while I take it up," he said.

Theo laid out a floor plan of the house next to the laptop. We'd both studied it before, and now we'd compare it to the aerial video. If we didn't spot anything, we could always measure every wall, inside and outside, and compare measurements, but that was the hard way and we'd avoid it if we could. We watched the screen.

"There's the skylight to her second floor studio," Theo said, pointing.

Childers came to stand behind us. "See anything?" he asked.

I shook my head. "Nothing that shouldn't be there."

"What are we missing?" Theo said. We were all leaning in, as if proximity to the image would yield up its secrets.

"It has to be underground," I said, with a sudden thought. "Remember what Judy said? Dottie had basement problems—a leak, she said. But that could have been a cover for something else."

"Construction of a strong room?" Ada said.

"If so," Theo said, "how do you get into the damn thing?"

We scanned the image for anything that might betray an entrance, but didn't see anything.

"It's no good, Childers," I said. "You might as well bring it down."

The only one of us who was happy was Childers, who'd gotten to play with his toy.

"Let's go through the house again," Theo said with a sigh.

So we did. I hadn't seen the whole house before, so was hopeful that my fresh eyes might spot something. We started in the basement, which was fitted out as a workshop and where Dottie had apparently worked on her framing; she had an extensive collection of antique frames lined up on one wall and stacked in a bin. We paid particular attention to the ductwork, hoping that we might follow it to a concealed room, but couldn't detect any anomalies. We went through the whole house, looking for structural oddities or thermostats with no apparent purpose. We weren't ready yet to examine all Dottie's papers. We ended in the attic, which wasn't much more than a crawl space with dusty trunks and boxes filled with old clothes and photo albums. The photo albums were worth looking into, but I hadn't seen anything else promising. Then, as we replaced the attic stairs and stood in the second-floor hallway, I spotted another pair of paint-by-number Scottie dogs on the wall outside of Dottie's bedroom on the second floor. These had not captured my attention the last time I visited the house because I had seen Dottie as a painter of Scottie dogs. Now I knew better.

"She actually hung them?" I said, incredulous.

And then the house shifted around me. I felt an electric jolt that flashed up through my feet and along the length of my spine to my brain, which vibrated like a tuning fork.

"It's the dogs," I whispered.

Theo leaned in to study them. "What about them?" she said.

"Not these dogs," I said. "*My* dogs."

"What about your dogs?" Ada said.

"They turn into something else," I said. "That's what she said. 'I love the way it looks like one thing, and then turns into something else altogether.' What if—?"

"Well, it's worth a try," Ada said cheerfully, though Theo looked dubious.

I fumbled for my phone and called Marco Antonio to see where he was and whether he could run by my house and pick up the painting. As we waited for him, we took its twin into Dottie's bedroom and laid it on the bed to examine. It was painted on canvas board, so there were no stretchers to conceal anything under, and there was nothing written on the back that we could see. We took it down to the basement and carefully removed the frame, but again, found nothing.

"Maybe it's like clouds, or Ghaznavi's tattoo," I said. "Maybe we need to turn it in different directions."

We had taken it outside to study the Scotties upside down and sideways when Marco Antonio arrived. He wasn't going to take payment, but when I pointed out that I was using the company card, he agreed.

We set my Scotties next to the others on the easel we'd brought out from Dottie's studio and gazed at them.

"Maybe it's like one of those 3-D optical paintings the optometrists use for eye tests," I said. "Maybe you have to—." Then I saw it, and gasped. "Oh, my god," I said. "It's a map."

"I don't see anything," Theo said. "Where?"

"Focus on the dark colors, and filter out the light ones," I said.

"I see it!" Ada said.

"I still don't see anything," Theo complained, clearly frustrated.

I was afraid to look away for fear I'd lose the image, but Ada reached up and steadied Theo's head with her hands. "Soften your eyes," she said. "Don't try so hard. Let the dark colors pop out at you."

"But I—," she began, and stopped. "Oh," she sighed.

"It must be some place in the house, right?" I said.

"It's the basement," Ada said. "There aren't any interior walls. This rectangle here—." She pointed. "That's Dottie's workbench."

"And here she's put a door," Theo said, pointing, "where there is no door."

"Not one that we've found, anyway," I said.

"Let's go," Theo said, reaching for the painting.

I put a hand on her arm to restrain her. "Just a minute," I said. "Let's look at the other painting, now that we know how."

Three gazes shifted to the other painting. Ada spoke first. "It's numbers, isn't it?" she said.

"It's a combination," Theo said.

Something in her voice made me look at her. I smiled and patted her on the arm. "Don't take it so hard," I said. "I'm sure you could have opened it without the combination, and Dottie probably thought so, too. But she couldn't be sure you'd outlive her. Who knows how long ago she painted this? She probably painted it as a reminder to herself."

Theo grinned at me, but she had tears in her eyes. "God, she was—." And then raised her arms in defeat. She couldn't find the words.

I picked up the painting. "Want me to hide it?"

When Theo held out her hand for it, I gave it to her.

According to the map, the door was behind the wood panel studded with hooks and hung with finished frames—some plain, some elaborately carved and gilt, all old.

"She was always looking for frames she liked," Theo said. "Garage sales, flea markets, estate auctions—she picked them up everywhere."

"Do you think there's a secret release button hidden somewhere?" Ada said.

I was studying the edge of the panel. The actual basement wall was limestone block, so this panel had been mounted in front.

"No," I said. "I bet we just remove these two bolts, top and bottom. Let's try it and see where it gets us." Theo handed me a set of socket wrenches, and I went to work.

With the bolts off, the panel swung away from the wall on hinges that were concealed by a set of shelves. Behind it was another door with a vintage combination lock similar to the one on Finch's strong room.

I rapped my knuckles on the door. "Solid steel," I observed, "and thicker, from the feel of it, than the one upstairs." I made way so Theo could work the lock, and for a time there was no sound except the ticking of the dial under Theo's fingers. Then, with a loud click, the door moved. Theo looked back at us, and then pushed the door open.

Lights flickered on to reveal a small gallery whose walls were crowded with paintings. Some were painfully familiar to me because they haunted my dreams— Picasso's *Painter and Model* and *Fenêtre ouverte sur le rue de Penthièvre*, Monet's *Environ de Giverny*, Gaughin's *Nature morte á estampe Japonaise*, a Braque still life, a Degas ballet dancer, a controversial Renoir semi-nude portrait. And yes, there was a Chagall, just like the one I'd recently shipped back to Tuscany, except that this one had a red cock instead of a yellow bird.

They were all beautifully framed—though not in the original frames. I had reason to know that those were sitting in a climate-controlled Quixote storage facility.

For some time, we just walked around and stared.

"The other room was a blind," Theo said. "Rouhani stole the paintings he was supposed to steal—the ones that were easy to find."

"But she was afraid it wasn't enough," I said. "So she wanted to hire Levesque to insure that nobody made it past the front door."

There was a small metallic sound and then a humming noise began.

"Climate control," Theo said, looking up at the ceiling.

"Here's the thermostat and humidistat," Ada said, "right by the door."

"And we missed it," I said.

"The ductwork has to be well concealed," Theo said. "We would have found it eventually."

Ada was counting. "There are fifteen paintings here," she said. "That matches the inventory. But there were only eleven in the other room. How come?"

Theo shrugged. "Probably because she hadn't finished copying them when she decided that her eyesight wasn't up to it anymore," she said. "She probably just ran out of time."

"It could happen to any of us," I said.

"Probably will," Theo agreed.

32

A little over a week later, we met again at Ada's house to begin the arduous task of sifting through Dottie's papers. I had offered to help, and Theo and Ada had accepted with gratitude. Now I stood in Ada's living room, staring at a large painting over the couch. It was a view of a town in the golden light of late afternoon, looking down from a hillside, showing the sun and shadow playing across white stucco walls and red tile roofs. Tuscany.

Ada came and stood next to me. "We had to take it down, you know, before you came," she said. "We didn't know how much you knew."

"Turned out you knew more than we did," Theo said. She was caneless once more, and carrying a large cardboard box. "But we didn't know that at the time."

I approached the painting, but could read the bold signature clearly from two feet away: Rivers.

I handed Ada an envelope. "We made a copy," I said, "but you should keep the original in case you get any legal challenges."

We had found the sealed envelope on a small stand just inside the strong room. It was a handwritten account of how Dottie and an unnamed partner had stolen fifteen paintings from the Tehran Museum of Contemporary Art in the spring of 1979 to keep them safe during the revolution. She explained that when a second team arrived one night and stole paintings from the collection, some of them her forgeries and some originals, she and her partner had been forced to suspend operations. She didn't say how many paintings they had been prepared to replace with forgeries, or how she came to have fifteen forgeries on hand to use in the operation, or how long it had taken her to paint them. From her passport, I thought that she must have begun painting the forgeries as soon as the museum opened. On each subsequent visit, she must have not only studied the paintings she intended to copy but photographed them so that she could go home and paint the forgeries. Had she detected signs of the impending revolution—signs missed by most of the experts? Or just painted the forgeries initially to practice her skills and test her abilities? Or for another purpose—to prepare for the most lucrative art theft ever conceived? We'd never know.

She did say that she had posed as a cleaning woman and confessed to drugging the guard's thermos of tea every night—a kind gesture, however belated, intended to clear him of involvement in the theft. She ended by reiterating the wish, expressed in her will, that the paintings be returned to the Iranian people. The document was signed and the signature notarized.

"I don't know about legal challenges," Theo said. "Monica's going to be too busy defending herself on the murder charge. But Steve might do it."

Monica hadn't yet been arrested, but Didi had reported that the container of cold capsules seized in a search of her house had indeed contained small amounts of dried belladonna leaf, no doubt transferred there by the gloves she had worn when preparing the capsules for Dottie. The evidence was all circumstantial, but it was solid.

"I feel kind of sorry for her, though," Ada admitted. She was using her foot to slide a large box across the floor from the living room to the dining room, where papers were already piled on the table. "She seems to lead a pretty dull life, and then along comes Calloway to offer her romance and excitement."

Theo snorted. "Dottie bought her a house, don't forget," she said.

"Yes, but she doesn't seem very fulfilled, you know?" Ada said, refusing to back down. "I mean, I have my family and my work, and you and Marge have exciting careers and friends, and Dottie had that, too. But what has Monica got?"

"Well, if she goes to prison," Theo said, unrelenting, "she'll have a whole new set of friends to hang out with."

Ada shook her head, and we each took a seat in front of a pile. I looked at mine and wished for the distraction of a toddler or two in the next room.

"Speaking of friends," Ada said, probably as reluctant to start as I was, "what do you hear from Texas?"

"I think Pinky's enjoying it," I said, then hastened to add, "though she's being well compensated, believe me."

"I'll believe it when I see our bill," Theo said.

"She's told Sami that she doesn't have an e-mail address for me, but she'll keep looking for that paper she wrote my new street address on," I said. "She doesn't know why I'm not answering my phone, but she does remember that we were planning to go on a cruise when we got back to Florida. She tells him that she thinks I kind of lost interest in selling the Chagall when she did an online search for me and showed me what Chagalls were selling for at auction. And she says—and I think this was an especially nice touch—that she suggested I hire a detective to try to establish the provenance of the painting."

"He'll never speak to her again!" Theo said.

"But, wait," Ada said. "Is he trying to contact you about the

Chagall or about the stolen paintings? Doesn't he know that we were the ones who stole them?"

"We don't know," I said. "He hasn't mentioned them to Pinky, and he certainly hasn't filed a police report. Even if he followed our footprints to the gas rig, why would he connect them to two old biddies with canes?"

"And speaking of things we don't know," Theo said, "do we suspect the Pahlavis of being in collusion with Sami? Did they finance his escapade? Or do they even know about it?"

I shrugged. "Hard to say, but from what I've read about them, I doubt it. I'm guessing that Sami was flying solo. Whether he ever would have sprung it on them to impress them is anybody's guess."

"He must be furious," Ada said. "And what about Rashidi? I wouldn't want to meet him in a back alley some time. Do you think he can trace us?"

"The only clue he has is your website," I said. "And it's been taken down. That's what really ought to make him suspect us. The phone number listed there has been disconnected, and the street address, if he tries to find it, will take him to a Louis Vuitton warehouse in the Design District of Miami."

"Maybe we should let him steal the paintings back so he'll quit trying," Theo said with a wicked smile.

"And maybe we should just toast Dottie before we get started," Ada said, jumping up.

"Isn't it a little early for you, Addy?" Theo said, as Ada left the room.

We heard the clink of glasses, and then Ada returned, holding three glasses by their stems in one hand and a wine bottle in the other.

"Well, like you said, Theo, we none of us know when we'll run out of time," she said, and she poured three glasses and passed them out.

We toasted Dottie.

"You think she knew what an adventure she was setting us on?" Ada said.

"Maybe she does now," Theo said.

I looked at Theo over my glass. "You know, Theo, if it's adventure you're after, maybe you should leave the dark side and join the good guys. Quixote could put your talents to good use."

She just smiled at me.

"Well?" Ada said. "What do you say, Theo?"

"Anything's possible," she said.

ABOUT THE AUTHOR

A native Texan, Borton became an ardent admirer of Nancy Drew at a young age. By the time she was fourteen, she had acquired her own blue roadster, trained on the freeways of Houston, and begun her travels. She left Texas around the time that everyone else arrived.

In graduate school, Borton converted a lifetime of passionate reading and late-night movie-watching into a doctorate in English. She discovered that people would pay her to discuss literature and writing, although not much. Finding young people entertaining and challenging, she became a college teacher, and survived many generations of students. Later, during a career crisis, she learned that people would pay her to tell stories, although even less than they would pay her to discuss stories written by someone else.

Borton has lived in the Southwest, Midwest, and on the West Coast, where she planted roses and collected three degrees in English without relinquishing her affection for and reliance on nonstan-dard dialects. In her spare time, she gardens, practices aikido, studies languages other than English, and, of course, watches movies and reads.

www.dbborton.com

www.ingramcontent.com/pod-product-compliance
Lightning Source LLC
Chambersburg PA
CBHW031220120726
47905CB00002B/408